EROS & DUST

by Trebor Healey

ReQueered Tales
Los Angeles • Toronto
2024

EROS & DUST

by Trebor Healey

First American edition: 2016
This edition: ReQueered Tales, June 2024

ReQueered Tales version 1.20

Epub edition ISBN-13: 978-1-959902-17-1
Print edition ISBN-13: 978-1-959902-18-8

*For more information about current and future releases,
please contact us:*
E-mail: *requeeredtales@gmail.com*
Facebook (Like us!): www.facebook.com/ReQueeredTales
Twitter: @ReQueered
Instagram: www.instagram.com/requeered
Web: www.ReQueeredTales.com
Blog: www.ReQueeredTales.com/blog
Mailing list (Subscribe for latest news): https://bit.ly/RQTJoin

Praise for
Trebor Healey

"I picture three Trebor Healeys: one poetic, one crazed with lust, and one shaggy with heat and dust. When all of them work in concert as they do in Healey's novels their combined power is formidable. But the shorter pieces, such as those in *Eros & Dust*, reveal the strength of those beasts on a more individual level ... Each voice is as distinctive in solo as it is an essential component of the blend. Truly a marvelous trick to pull off, and Trebor Healey does it with skill and grace."
— Jerry L. Wheeler

"I read *Eros & Dust* over the course of weeks, a story here and there, and walked away well contented. Healey's short fiction themes – here very much a tangle of desire, aging, Mexico and South America, queerness – play lightly at one glance even as they settle into the reader's skin."
— Nathan Burgoine

"Trebor Healey's writing is suffused with the purest emotion, the bravest, funniest tone, and the perfect balance of poetics, daring and charm."
— Joy Nicholson, *The Tribes of Palos Verdes*

"Trebor Healey is all soul ... The way he stacks sentences vibrates on the page. There's an impressive, experimental range in this short story collection *A Perfect Scar*. Trebor Healey uses multiple narrators to bring voice to a variety of human experiences."
— Kirk Read, *How I Learned to Snap*

Also by Trebor Healey

SHORT STORIES

A Perfect Scar (2007)

Eros & Dust (2016)

Falling (2019)

NOVELS

Through It Came Bright Colors (2003)

Faun (2012)

A Horse Named Sorrow (2012)

EROS & DUST

by Trebor Healey

Table of Contents

Previously Published

"Imp" in *Raising Hell*, ed. Todd Gregory (2012).

"Junkyard" in *Van Gogh's Ear*, ed. Felice Picano (Vol 7, 2009).

"Lolito" in *Jonathan*, ed. Raymond Luczak (No 5, 2014).

"The Pancake Circus" in *The Best American Erotica 2007*, ed. Susie Bright (2007) and *Out of Control*, ed. Greg Wharton (2005).

"Pilgrim Soul" in *Jonathan*, ed. Raymond Luczak (No 11, 2016).

"Queer Theory" in *Wilma Loves Betty and Other Hilarious Gay & Lesbian Parodies*, ed. by Scott Brassart and Julie K. Trevelyan (2000)

"Three Things I Pray" in *Foolish Hearts: New Gay Fiction*, ed. Timothy J. Lambert and R.D. Cochrane (2013).

"Trunk" in *Fool for Love: New Gay Fiction*, ed. R.D. Cochrane (2009) and *Best Gay Romance 2010*, ed. Richard Labonté (2010).

Acknowledgements

First and foremost I want to thank those who have championed my work and kept me from the discouragement that is often the writer's lot: Felice Picano, Mar Preston, Bill Cohen, Jim Eigo, Hank Henderson and Mark Lofstrom – you've given me more than you can ever know. And for those who have published some of the work in this collection, a shout out to editors Susie Bright, Richard LaBonté, Raymond Luczak, Greg Herren, R.D. Cochrane, Timothy Lambert, Greg Wharton, Scott Brassart and Julie Trevelyan.

For time and space in which to write, I'm grateful for the generosity of Tin Minh Do, the late Jim Duggins, Mar Preston, Stella Maloyan and Sera Sacks. Many people helped these stories emerge – whether by their foibles, brilliance or dignity – and I thank them accordingly: Daniel Kopyc, Horehound Stillpoint, the late Ernest Posey, Russell Tuazon, Larry-Bob Roberts, Alex Sanchez Correa, Sejal Patel, Fernando Martin Huerga, Gerardo Perez, Ezequiel Yedro, Becky Cochrane and Timothy Lambert.

For their forbearance and friendship, I hugely thank Rafael Lopez-Barrantes, Christian Morales, Isaac Cruz, Karl Soehnlein, Stuart Timmons, Stella Maloyan and Sera Sacks. Thank you Steve Berman and Lethe Press for your patience and belief in my work and for giving my stories a home. And finally, thank you to all the readers who have read and will read these stories and pass them along.

*"The truth does not change according
to our ability to stomach it."*

— Flannery O'Connor

Chile

Jorge preferred not to talk about it, but if Jason insisted, well, then he would.

"I was arrested, yes. And held in the national stadium. About two months."

Jason responded with "Wow" and "intense," in the way of an American.

"I had it better than most. One day they just released me." Jason looked at Jorge as if to say 'go on', but Jorge didn't want to go on. He didn't want to unleash all that – what he could say, would say, should say, wanted to say, needed to say, felt ashamed to say. How he was thrown out, but not like Victor Jarra, who was tossed into the street after his body was riddled with bullets. That's what Pinochet's secret police, the DINA, would do to the ones they truly hated. They'd kill them in the bowels of the stadium and then throw them in the street for everyone to see. To let people know they weren't fucking around. And because they despised communists. Communists were like fags to those fascists. They felt physical disgust for them.

The DINA told Jorge, who actually was a fag, to go. He'd wanted to leave and suddenly he was told to. A soldier pulled him by the arm and pushed him toward the stairs, and then he was alone going up them, emerging into the light of day.

He blinked; it felt strange, like a cruel setup. But once he was up top, he saw a lot of people standing around on the track and knew immediately they were releasing prisoners. They herded the whole group toward one of the stadium entrances and pushed them out into the street. An odd feeling overcame him. Not really relief, more like strangeness or vulnerability. The streets surrounding the stadium were deserted. There weren't even soldiers walking around, and the public didn't dare come near. They'd long since sent away the women who used to sing at the stadium entrance.

A military truck went by at one point as the freed prisoners walked along together. It didn't slow down or acknowledge them in any way. The soldiers in back noticed them but were nonplussed. The released men acted the same. None of them were talking. Jorge thought someone should say something. But what could anyone say? *Glad that's over? Thank God?* Not everyone had been released. They'd all seen people beaten, tortured and killed. Right in front of them. It had felt wrong to celebrate or express gratitude.

Jorge had said, "Pinochet's a bastard." Everyone looked at him, or a lot of the guys anyway. He had the feeling he shouldn't have said it, shouldn't have said anything. But they all agreed. They looked at him in the affirmative, yet said nothing.

Pinochet *was* a bastard. A very cruel bastard. It was a palace coup. A lot of foreigners didn't know that. Allende had appointed him commander in chief of the armed forces just weeks before. They'd shaken hands, expressed friendship even – and then he pulled that stunt. He was a Macbeth, and only the morally compromised of the upper class will attempt to tell you otherwise.

Of course, there are lots of apolitical people who appreciate what Pinochet did. He brought order, turned around the economy – for those at the top. He was a neoliberal whore, offering up his country as a guinea pig for Milton Friedman and his University of Chicago sycophants. Jorge was sickened when he'd hear people talk positively about Pinochet. He consoled himself by thinking that no one respected Pinochet as a human being, even if his presidency was somehow beneficial to them. He'd betrayed his country, whether you liked Allende or not. You don't kill your boss.

It's a macho country, and Jorge thought machismo was just a prettied-up word for cowardice. Because resorting to violence was a failure not only of imagination, but more importantly, it was a failure of one's duty as a human being to deal with the hard truths that life presents. A shirking of responsibility and a failure of courage. Jorge was a doctor. A doctor accepts responsibility for what happens to a person, face to face, touching them.

But Jorge said none of that. He told Jason he'd rather not talk about it. "They let me go. I wasn't tortured much. I was lucky."

Jason was relentless. "How did you get arrested?"

Jorge hesitated but thought he could at least tell that part.

"I was a medical student. Lots of students were politically active at that time. Allende had opened the floodgates. We were looking toward a bright future. There were communist student groups, socialist groups, liberation theology priests and seminarians. A burgeoning feminist movement. It was exciting. Then the curtain came down. When the soldiers came to the university, they came right into the classrooms with their guns and asked us who was a communist or a socialist. No one said anything, of course. Then they started asking us individually. 'Tell me which ones are communists, socialists.' Poking and prodding us with their rifles. Many, like me, said nothing, but others were frightened and began to answer them and point at their peers. Espinosa pointed at me: 'He's a socialist.' He was my friend. I looked at him. What could I say or do? The soldiers grabbed me and yanked me toward the door."

"You must have been pissed."

"No, I wasn't angry, actually. Betrayed, yes. I just kept my eyes on him. It felt very serious to me, something final that couldn't be taken back, and I felt he needed to be very clear about what he had just done.

"Well, here we are," Jorge announced, pulling up to the curb to park at the central market where they were going to have seafood.

Sometimes Jason was just interested in the food, and the *cuenca* dancing and Pablo Neruda, and so together they ate a lot of good seafood and visited Neruda's houses – all of them whimsical and charming. One was in Santiago, another in Valparaiso, and a third at Isla Negra by the sea. It was hard not to envy Neruda his charmed life, though it ended badly at the hands of Pinochet and his goons. An avowed communist, Neruda was dismissed by some for staying too long at the fair, a supporter of the Soviet Union well after there was substantial proof of Stalin's tyranny and brutality. There are mean people in Chile, and some of them thought it served Neruda right to be brought to heel by a tyrant. Any tyrant would do, apparently. These were generally the same people who thought Pinochet was good for the economy. Catholics mostly.

Jason wanted to go to the peace park at Villa Grimaldi as well as the Museum of Memory, of course; he was making a study of Chile's dark history. It was only natural, Jorge told himself: this is what intelligent tourists do, apparently.

* * *

The Museum of Memory was professionally curated – what they called a world-class museum. Jorge found it cold and antiseptic with its Bauhaus modern glass architecture, its escalators and spacious salons with hardwood floors. It was the official left's response to the official right's, and it felt like a mausoleum. Outside, the food stands crowding the street and the nearby metro station teemed with life. We're alive, Jorge thought, going about our business. That's a better memorial than a behemoth of a museum, with all its space, which just felt like emptiness and death to him. Well, maybe that was the point. Who knew who the architect had been?

Probably not even a Chilean. World-class.

Jorge went to the Villa Grimaldi with Jason a week later, which *was* something of a mausoleum and yet didn't feel like one. Its exhibits were mostly outdoors, situated in the gardens of an estate that had been used as a torture center. There were slogans painted on its brick walls, and Victor Jarra songs playing, gardens with roses planted for each one of the disappeared. Thousands of flowers. As if the dead had come back and reclaimed the place where they'd been killed. Many of the exhibits – crude sculpted dioramas, mosaics and painted tiles – were childlike and clearly rendered by non-artists. The effect was uncannily devastating and suggested something larger in human nature: the inability to express something, or to pull something off.

Jorge became upset and told Jason that he wanted to leave. But an animated Jason started talking about how he felt as well. He said it felt to him like a country raped and unhealed, that in Argentina, the dictatorship and the disappearances were talked about openly and so there was less shame. Everyone despised the generals there. No one ever expressed any sort of silver lining to the mass murder, as he would hear in Chile on the street every day. The Argentines were "out" and Chile was a traumatized closet case.

Jorge stiffened with offense at this on top of everything else he was feeling. "Well, this is my country and you're visiting it," was all he could think to say. A vexed Jason looked at him but understood that he'd transgressed, even if he was unsure how or to what degree he'd done so.

Jorge became further upset now that he had scolded Jason. He did not want to chase away the young man's company. But this *was* his country. What was he supposed to do? Agree with him? Was he supposed to admire Argentines who act like fools half the time? They hadn't even been capable of doing a dictatorship correctly. Argentina was a mess; how dare he put it above Chile? Chile had the longest history of democracy in all of Latin America. Was it Chile's fault that Kissinger and Nixon meddled in their affairs? Did he have to listen to some tourist from that very same country insult his own? How could Jason insult his people at the same time he seemed so confident of his compassion for them?

It was the first time Jorge thought seriously of ending things with Jason. But he told himself he had to try to understand that Jason was naïve. He needed to be educated – and not in the way he thought or was going about it, thrilled by the darkness. Jason knew plenty about the coup and the Pinochet era, more than any American Jorge had ever met, but it was all romanticized facts, reinterpreted as if for some movie. Jorge perceived that Jason seemed to think that by knowing him – someone who'd experienced the darkness – he was gaining empirical credits or something.

"Are you as hard on your own country?" Jorge challenged him.

"Yes."

"And so, if Argentina is 'out' and Chile is a closet case, what is America?"

Jason looked out the window as they drove along the road past squat cement houses with barred windows, thinking of a good analogy. "America is like the privileged white guy who goes to the gym a lot and takes gay cruises. Maybe he has two houses. One in San Francisco and one in Palm Springs." He looked directly at Jorge then. "My country is a lie. It's built on slaves and cheap immigrant labor. It's not closeted, just in denial. Everyone actually believes its lies. It's like the Chileans who think Pinochet was good for the country. They think Reagan was good for the country." He reconsidered. "Well, it's just like here actually. There're those who do and those who don't. Black people and Native Americans know the score. They are the disappeared there."

"The world is a mess," was all that Jorge could think to respond.

Jason smiled. "I'll drink to that."

Jorge said nothing and kept driving but soon pulled over at a metro stop. Jason looked at him.

"Why don't you take the subway home?" Jorge suggested.

"But why? Where are you going?"

"I'm fine. I just need some time."

"Have I upset you?"

Poor Jason, Jorge thought. It actually made him smile. Is this why people liked Americans? Was their ingenuousness charming? Child-like?

"I'll call you tomorrow," Jorge offered and looked into his rearview mirror, preparing to pull back into traffic.

Jason shrugged. "Okay. Thanks for taking me to the Peace Park."

"You're welcome."

Jason had his *Bip* card and liked the subway system in Santiago and lived just blocks from a stop, so he didn't feel inconvenienced or abandoned, but he was concerned about Jorge's kicking him out of the car. Jorge had a lot of problems, that was obvious – coming out late, the way he deferred to his family and kept his personal life to himself, even though his children were all now adults and they went on and on about their boyfriends and girlfriends. And all those stories Jorge'd told Jason about the young men he'd picked up. Some had robbed him, most never called again. "Thank God I have a big dick," Jorge had shrugged, "or I'd never hook up with anyone."

Jason had repressed his urge to chuckle. He was so much more jaded than Jorge, and being the younger of the two by twenty years, he found it awkward, this role reversal. Life was sad and yet it threw you consolations. Like Pinochet that way, he thought cynically. What had that woman said of the dictatorship: "You've got to break a few eggs to make an omelet." They weren't her eggs, that was for sure.

He stood on the platform, waiting for the train, scouting the crowd for cute Chileans. There were always a few. A lanky one with a scruffy chin captured his attention, but as soon as their eyes met Jason knew he was straight. Which didn't make him any less nice to look at. Jason had discussed with Jorge his preference for non-monogamy and Jorge had been amenable. But Jason could tell he was only being agreeable because he was used to not getting what he wanted and even took some masochistic comfort in it. Which made Jason not want to meet other guys. He didn't want to feed Jorge's neurosis. He thought better of that whenever he'd see someone like the scruff-chinned boy, of course. If that boy had been gay and interested, wouldn't he have followed him home? And wasn't not doing so being as neurotic as Jorge? Because Jason believed the very idea of monogamy was in itself a neurosis.

The train arrived. He forgot the lanky scruff-chinned guy as he stepped through the doors and plopped down in a window seat, looking out into the distance at the Andean foothills rising all along the eastern side of the city. Hopping off at Bellas Artes, he made his away along the wooded hillside of the Cerro Santa Lucia to the shiny new high-rise where he was renting an apartment. He'd chosen the neighborhood for its central location, but as it turned out, it was also a very gay neighborhood and his building was clearly a gay address. In the elevator, an attractive young man with a dignified manner, dark eyes and a unibrow stood next to him. Jason made small talk, and there was a moment of hesitation when the man got off on the twelfth floor, smiling shyly as he said, "See you around." The doors closed and Jason traveled the additional six floors up to his apartment, but he found himself thinking of the young man as he stepped out of the elevator and proceeded to the door of his own apartment. He could go back down to the twelfth floor, he considered. Well, he'd passed up his chance – or had he? Was he reacting to the perceived rejection by Jorge? He'd think about that later. He turned around and went back to the elevator and took it down six floors. He walked the length of the hall on the twelfth floor, and bingo, he saw a door cracked open an inch or two. If it turned out not to be the young man's apartment, he would apologize and say he'd gotten the wrong door. But that wasn't necessary. He knocked and it was the right door and he closed it behind him.

Jorge called the next day just like he said he would. "Would you like to take a ride down the coast?" Far from and more or less devoid of the memorials that dotted the capital.

"Of course, I'd love that."

They met down on the street at a nearby café where they had coffee and a pastry and Jorge spread out a map, showing the route he had in mind and the various things to see there.

They worked their way out of the traffic-clogged city and were soon enough among vineyards and fruit orchards before reaching the coastal fog belt that enshrouded Valparaiso. Jason loved Valparaiso with its winding streets that snaked up the hillside, the whole city shaped like a giant amphitheater, with all the spectators being tiny little houses, many with tin roofs. "It looks like a Claymation world, or something," Jason offered, unable to find the right words to describe the enchanted, otherworldly fairy-tale character of the place.

"Let's come back here tonight," Jorge offered, "I don't want to lose any daylight with all that coast to cover."

And as they traveled on the winding highway south of Valparaiso, Jason kept saying how "it looked a lot like California." And it did. The road skirted the sea, and there were huge wind-bent cypresses, the coast rocky and varied as it spilled into the crashing surf. It looked like the Monterey Peninsula, and when they got to Neruda's house at Isla Negra Jason remembered Robinson Jeffers's house in Carmel, and he thought as well of Steinbeck, who like Neruda found a way to work his political beliefs seamlessly into his art.

The house was as whimsical as the other two they'd visited, with scrimshaw, art, porthole windows, lots of books and photos of course, and delightful spaces for entertaining. This house was unique in that it was the largest of Neruda's three houses and right on the beach. It was also the last place Neruda had lived and where the soldiers came for him. They'd apparently trashed the place and it had remained boarded up all during the Pinochet era.

There was a restaurant built next to it, and they stayed for lunch. Jason asked Jorge what he'd done during the afternoon yesterday after dropping him off at the subway, and Jorge answered that he'd just taken care of chores – laundry, bills, shopping, things like that. Jason asked him if he were upset with him.

"Those places are difficult, that's all. I get emotional. It's not important. What did you do yesterday?"

"Not much. I met a hot boy on the elevator and played with him for awhile. Then I just went for coffee and read some Bolaño."

Jorge wished Jason hadn't bothered to mention the elevator liaison. Was that really necessary? And yet it was typical of Jason's American transparency that he kept no secrets. He looked at Jason, but Jason was stirring his iced tea and looking for a waiter, hoping to commandeer another lemon.

"Did you read the Bolaño in Spanish?"

"Oh no, he's too hard in Spanish. I'm reading it in English. It's called *By Night in Chile* and it's about –"

"Yes, I know, the dictatorship." Of course.

"Bolaño was arrested as well, you know. But only for a couple days."

Jorge was nodding, thinking how did it end up back here on the same subject as always. Was Jason just answering the question or was he being insensitive? Or was he, in fact, cruel? And was there a difference?

They paid their bill and left the enormous restaurant with its numerous empty tables. In that way, Jason thought, it's very similar to Argentina. Very big restaurants with no one in them.

They headed further south. El Tabo. Cartagena. They pulled off at a beach, parked and walked out onto the sand. Something big was dead in the sand and Jason ran over to it: a squid, about three feet long. "Wow. Intense."

"The sea here is full of life." Jorge smiled. There was a pelican walking along the edge of the water and when they passed it, it walked right up to them. How strange, Jason thought. Jorge shrugged.

They got back on the road and came around a curve, the sea next to them disappearing into infinity as the sun dipped toward sunset. Jason watched a far-off tanker and a closer fishing boat. And when he turned to look ahead, he saw the enormous hotel casino that dwarfed the little town of San Antonio.

"Do you gamble?" Jorge asked him.

"Not really. Do you?"

"Sometimes."

They pulled into the parking lot that separated the hotel from the highway.

Jorge wanted to play blackjack and sat down at a table after obtaining some chips from the cash cage. Jason drifted off to play a few slots. Jorge proceeded to play a few hands, lost, and got up. And then he saw him, sitting at another blackjack table. He didn't know what to do. He couldn't very well go up to him and tap him on the shoulder. But he wanted to look him in the eye again. So he waited against the wall. Finally, Espinosa got up and Jorge stared at him. Espinosa stared back. They stood stock still for maybe thirty seconds, ten or twelve feet apart. Espinosa nodded and walked away.

Jorge went to the bar and ordered a beer. He drank it slowly and ate some peanuts. There was a soccer game on the television behind the bar. Chile vs. Ecuador. Chile scored and several patrons cheered. He wanted to ask them: Are you proud to be Chilean? Is it best to forget? Forgive and forget – that's how to get through life, his mother had always said.

Jason came up to the bar then. "How'd you do?"

"Nothing. Yourself?"

"I lost some pesos. No big deal."

"Would you like a beer?" Jorge asked.

"Sure."

Jason looked around, and turned back to Jorge when his beer arrived.

"Do you think you'll you see this boy again, Jason?"

Jason looked at him with a perplexed expression. "Oh. Carlos. His name is Carlos. Yeah, we had fun."

"Where does that leave me?"

Jason reached out his hand, but Jorge pulled his away, offering a disarming smile. "Not here."

Jason had to remind himself that Chile was not particularly hip to demonstrative homosexuality. "Jorge, you're my special one. I'm not going down the coast with Carlos."

Going down the coast, sounds like a good term for it, Jorge thought, and laughed to himself.

"What's so funny? You don't believe me?"

Jorge thought about how Jason's honesty – which he clearly considered to be among his virtues – was almost a vice and increasingly annoying to Jorge. Jason seemed to think his honesty was a kind of integrity, but Jorge saw it as narcissism, almost a boastfulness. Jason was the kind of person who would have been tortured and killed, Jorge thought. In South America, there is a time and a place for the truth, and it's something you figure out quickly as a kid. You respect it. Jorge was shocked at the thought and upset with himself for thinking it. Was it some kind of vengeful urge that had put that thought in his head?

Again he thought of the Pinochet years. The right killed their leftist victims because they thought them proud and that they needed to be humbled, even humiliated for it. Victor Jarra's songs of freedom. The story was that the soldiers made Jarra sing before they shot him. "Sing!" they demanded. He sang "We Shall Overcome," which obviously infuriated them, and it quickly led to his death.

But what was Jorge doing comparing Victor Jarra to this spoiled American kid? Or was he doubting the integrity of the left and how they'd played their hand? Yet is revolution any place for humility? Well, Jorge had been humbled. Once he was released from detention, he had abandoned activism. Granted, it was far more dangerous, and few but the most dedicated continued with the struggle. But had he just gone along then? Was his humility of the 'tyranny needs only for good people to do nothing' kind? Had his arrest, his torture been in vain?

Had Doctor Espinosa just played him for a fool? And was he really learning this from an American ingénue with a dark interest in his country's tragedy and an insatiable lust for young men? Or was Jason just singing? Is that what he was doing? In the way of Whitman?

He shrugged. "When are you leaving?"

Jason looked surprised. "Uh, not until April. My lease goes till then, and I'm signed up for classes. Are you getting sick of me?" Jason looked at him intently. "Do we need to take some time off?"

"No, no," Jorge said. "I'm sorry, I don't want you to leave. I ..."

Jason reached out his hand, and Jorge did not pull his away this time. "You what?"

Why is he asking me that? Why can't he leave anything alone? *I need to go to the bathroom."*

"Okay. I'll wait here."

Jorge's eyes filled as he crossed the wide carpeted expanse of the casino. He stepped into the restroom and looked in the mirror, shaking his head. And then, seemingly out of nowhere, he saw Espinosa in the mirror next to him. With that same blank stare. He turned toward him, and before he knew what was happening, he had his hands around Espinosa's neck and was slamming his head against the metal stall door opposite the sink. Espinosa was resisting, holding Jorge's outstretched arms, his face expressionless, but his eyes full of terror. Then Jorge turned him around and got behind him, holding his neck in a headlock with his right arm while he pushed open the stall door and dragged Espinosa into it, forcing him to his knees and then shoving his head down into the bowl repeatedly and holding it down longer and longer with each dunk. And then there were hands on him and he was being pulled back, and he heard Espinosa gasping for breath and saw him fall backward onto the floor. Two young men had Jorge pinned against the wall now, assailing him with questions: "What the fuck are you doing? Are you fucking crazy? You nearly killed him!"

He shouted, "That man worked for Pinochet!" He knew his accusation was absurd. Espinosa had just been another student, but how else to explain his rage?

The young men stepped back then and let go of him, looking back and forth between Espinosa and Jorge. They said nothing more and stood aside as Jorge tucked in his shirt and proceeded past them back out into the casino.

Jason could see Jorge looked upset and flushed as he marched back toward the bar.

"Are you okay?"

"We're leaving." And Jorge proceeded to walk right past him.

Flustered, Jason motioned for the check, watching as Jorge left through the front glass door. Jason paid the bill and hurried to the door and out into the parking lot toward Jorge's car.

Jason hopped into the passenger seat. "What's the matter? I'm sorry, I'm always saying the wrong thing."

But Jorge grabbed hold of him then and embraced him and began to weep in earnest. "It's not you. It's not you."

Jason held him as he sobbed. After a few minutes, Jorge sat back in his seat, collected himself and put on some music. They pulled out.

"Jorge?"

He stared straight ahead. "It's not you."

They drove back to Santiago, not saying a word. Jason watched the sun approaching the horizon, and as they reached Valparaiso, the tin roofs shimmering in the last light.

Jorge dropped Jason off and told him he would call him tomorrow, imagining Jason would likely run off to see Carlos. Jason in fact did. Jorge went home and turned on his computer and began searching for songs by Victor Jarra, Violeta and Angel Parra. He sang along. Eventually he began writing a letter to Jason. He wanted to thank him and profess his love and ask Jason to stay. Forever.

Across town, Jason was lying spent with Carlos, comforted by the seeming lack of complication between them, and wondering if Carlos had been to the Atacama Desert where Jason planned to go in April when his lease was up and classes completed. Jason remembered how Jorge had told him about the trip he'd taken there with his mother. His mother was difficult of course, but he was a devoted son.

"It's full of volcanoes and light," he'd said.

"I heard Pinochet used it for secret mass graves of the disappeared."

They hadn't talked anymore about the Atacama. Jorge was complicated; there were too many difficult and prolonged silences. They'd met on the Internet, and Jason hadn't expected it to be more than a casual thing anyway. But Jorge had offered to take him everywhere. He was the ideal guy for a traveler, Jason had thought. What a generous, kind person. Jason was grateful for the time they'd spent together. He wished him the best and hoped he would find the partner he seemed so intent upon finding. He thought of how he wanted to give him something, a token of thanks. Perhaps a nice dinner somewhere – one of those Peruvian places he likes – on his last night in Santiago.

He leaned over and kissed Carlos. "I like Chile," he said. "I want to see more of it. Have you ever been to the Atacama Desert?"

Elmer Rosewater

ELMER ROSEWATER
42101 HIGHWAY 162
COVELO, CA 95428

Hey Elmer,

I went to an amazing show today at the Pasadena Art Museum and thought of you. It was called "**An Opening of the Field: Jess, Robert Duncan, and Their Circle**" and was all about the painters and artists who were grouped around Robert Duncan and his painter/lover, Jess. I didn't know Duncan was such a hub. But he's always lived in my mind from that one line of poetry of his I adore: *Sometimes I am permitted to return to a meadow*. Yes, sometimes. Not often enough. And if you'll forgive my being overly literal, I remember that line whenever I go up to the High Sierra with my backpack summers. Man, am I permitted when I'm up there :). Not a bigger, wider meadow anywhere than what you find up there, with all that high mule's ear grass and surrounded by big pines and far-off peaks and ridges. Damn. Poetry.

Oh yeah, then there's the meadow of *your* world. Your cabin, the river. I guess it's more of a canyon ... well a slanted meadow then, all those oaks and golden grass and the rail-road tracks and the creek. Damn I miss it. And you! You are a meadow of the mind, my friend :).

Anyway, this exhibit was so, so inspiring. You've got to see it and I so wish you were here to see it with me because you're my Art Daddy :). It started in Sacramento because the collection belongs to the Crocker Museum of California Art, which is an awesome, unsung museum, as you well know. Did you know that along with the Oakland Museum and this Pasadena Museum where I was today, these are the only ones that focus specifically or maybe even exclusively on California art, as far as I know? Which is underappreciated to say the least! I know you have work at the Oakland Museum. We need to get your stuff into these other two as well and I'm gonna pitch them :).

So, the reason I got there (even though I had it on my list of shit to do since it opened) was cuz my friend Larry sent me a Facebook note telling me and a bunch of other people in SoCal that we had to NOT MISS IT and it was leaving town Sunday. This was on Saturday. So I dropped what I was doing and hopped on the train – I'm totally into the train now, as you know how I hate driving. The stop is like five blocks from the museum, so even though it was raining, it was totally do-able.

I didn't know what to expect, and it's a small museum, so I didn't expect much. But the minute I walked in, I was just sort of bowled over by the poetry of it. I didn't know who any of the artists were and yet the stuff was beautiful. I could have felt all tragic or angry (as I often do) that so much good art goes unrecognized and unrewarded, but I didn't feel that way. Because I loved this art SO MUCH, I just felt really happy that people make such stuff, and the fact that it's unrecognized made me kind of love it more, and made me feel like I was let in on some special secret. Not to diminish the horrible pain being an unrecognized artist entails. Don't I know it? Don't we both? So I have permission to feel happy about it too :). That friggin' meadow! Actually, lately I've been kind of feeling happy that I don't get much attention. There's a purity to it, there really is. I have a screenwriter friend who makes tons of money and he told me once he envied me. I was like, what? But he longs for anonymity, for being able to create exactly what he wants instead of having to please other people, which is what his success entails. He wasn't complaining, just I think reminding me of the good part of being unknown. Fame and wealth are hell for a lot of people. We don't have to endure that. Aren't we lucky ... har, har, har.

But back to the work. Man, so many little modernist gems of painting. Rooms and gardens, flowers and oak-studded hillsides, intense Modigliani-like faces, café scenes and street corners. Like the Paris of the mind that is painting. This whole exhibit expressed the greatness of San Francisco that won't be appreciated for another hundred years. And then they'll get it, and these guys, and you and me too, are part of that. I'm Baudelaire and you're Cezanne :) Oh yeah, I'm still an arrogant, romantic fuck. But that's why you love me, right? :).

So, there was also lots of collage that Jess did (he called them "paste-ups") which I still love so much even though technology and photoshop and all that has fucked it up as a form. Nothing like juxtaposing magazine ads with hard news stories or photos from archaeology or anthropology books. *National Geographic*! I probably like them cuz even I can do them :P. Well, I'm gonna do some more. Basically, this exhibit made me want to do everything (write, collage, paint, draw) shadowbox! Shadowbox? Put 'em up, put 'em up :). Ah, what is art, Elmer, but shadowboxing with the angel instead of wrestling with him? :)

That's why I go to museums. Down with foodies and all these damn restaurants. It's museums that feed me. So, I wonder if you know of any of these artists. I bet you do, even though they are a little before your time. There was R. B. Kitaj, Edward Corbett, Wallace Berman, Lawrence Jordan, George Herms, and of course, work by poets! – Jack Spicer, Robin Blaser, Michael McClure. There was a lot of 'word' in this show, maybe that's why it spoke to me so much ... like in the collages, there were these tidbits of wisdom, lost in but plucked out of the media barrage we live in, making me think of William Carlos Williams' poem: "It is difficult to get the news from poems/yet men die miserably every day/for lack of what is found there."

Now contemplate these lines:

One exchanges the empire of one's desires for the anarchy of pleasures (I keep thinking about this – it separates desire and pleasure. That is so very revelatory)

Tolerance is the mask of prejudice (to embrace, not to put up with, is what art calls us to do ... you know Father Boyle who created Homeboys? He's all about this – loving those who no one will love. Goes the same for things ... makes you think art can save the world, if they'd only listen. Ah, maybe it already has :) Wherever would we be without it?

He who augments knowledge, augments sorrow (oh no, am I depressing myself and you by sharing this experience :P – Sorry! But truly, for a knowledge-seeker, this is caution-ary, or is it just an eloquent way of saying ignorance is bliss? Embrace the sorrow then. The truth has to be the ultimate reward, come what may. Life is school.)

The joy that exceeds pleasure (back to the above one about empire of desires – So true! Shit, am I becoming religious?)

Apparently Duncan and Jess's house, which was a big Victorian in the Mission, was a meeting place – back when even poets could afford mortgages – or at least poets like Duncan who in one of the videos said he got left a little trust when his parents passed away which allowed him to cover the $250! mortgage. The videos were great – Duncan talking about his interest in mythology, his outsider status as a poet and artist when New York was even more annoying and proprietary than it still is. One video was like a tour of the house, showing his bookshelves (all of Frank Baum's books :)) and a lot of the art in this show, which he had all over his walls. He'd say all these great things as he led the camera/videographer around: "We read and write the world." Yes! He talked about when he was a young fag and said he tried to be "alluring" which was socially disastrous. I'm not totally sure what he meant, but I think as a literary artist one can't play the cute young thing and be taken seriously or connect to people the way one wants to connect. Probably more true back then in the 50s or 40s. But then, there is more than one way to be alluring. Someone said something about all attraction, friendship, connection is erotic (was it Ned Rorem? I don't know, maybe) – I think there's something to that. So perhaps it's in the subtlety of how one allures, or totally out of our control – some kind of pheromone thing you just have to roll with. I also think to just be an artist is alluring. But maybe ole Bob Duncan was showing up in tight jeans and purring in the corner. He doesn't strike me as someone who would necessarily know how to be seductive, and he doesn't have the type of body for it. Though he was young once, as were we all, and might have been a hot young thing. Of course, he's an intellectual, and they generally don't know how to be sexy in the usual manner. They allure in a different way. Maybe he learned that. Because his body looks comfortable like his house. Cozy more than sexy. Does that make him a Bear? :) Anyway, he just kept saying interesting things and he's been in my head talking ever since the show. A meadow named Bob :).

Anyway, their house served as like a salon and gallery space for their artist friends. He filled the place with flowers. He said he was drawn to being a householder, so that's what he became. He had an acceptance of himself and what he liked and he struck me as someone who really KNEW himself. I found that calming and encouraging. Yet I've never been like that! Aspiration. I kind of envied him, but not completely. Of course, I don't know his whole life and all he suffered. But I just mean I like to run from and chase after myself, I guess. Though, sometimes I long for the kind of partnership guys like Robert and Jess have, and I think it comes from self-knowledge and self-acceptance. Jess's collages were used in Duncan's books. You could tell they inspired each other to create. Now that is the ideal lover thing, isn't it?

And Duncan was not just a poet, Elmer! The guy did crayon art! Something even I could do. So, guess what? On my way home, I stopped at the 99 cent store and bought crayons, paper and even a little kids watercolor set. Three bucks, Elmer, and my visual art career is launched! Or re-launched! I'm still doing the shadowboxes you inspired me to do with your own, but am now venturing out onto the page, which I've always been totally afraid to do. And don't give me shit for my abstracts. I can't draw, alright, I have no choice but to be an abstract expressionist :). Anyway, I also realized that the shadowboxes really are collage in a 3-D way. Duh. I'm sure you're well aware of that, but it just occurred to me during this show.

I have like a dozen of yours up on my wall now because my studio is too small to hang your paintings ;/ I love the horse one so much – why'd you make it so big?! :P

Oh, how I wish I could come up and see you this summer. Man, those times at your cabin are the best memories I have. I can't believe I sold it and that lady's living there now. It would be too weird to send this letter to her! If I could find a way, I'd send this letter to you, of course, but I think in just writing it, it gets to you somehow.

I love you Elmer, I miss you. I think seeing art reconnects me to you. Maybe that's why I'm happy even though all these artists struggled and suffered and never were loved as hugely as they loved the world through their work. Ah, you know all this. Maybe you know a lot more than that. Be well and happy and all that shit, whatever that might mean in whatever reality or nonreality you're in. Your meadow! I'm sure there's a meadow on the other side. The empire of my desire! Ah, fuckin' life ... death, whatever. This show brought you back to me. I felt you there. Like you went outside to have a cigarette even. In the rain! And then you didn't fucking come back. I thought living men were elusive – ah, you dead guys, you take the cake!

I am always and across the universe, and time, and big bang bliss bullshit your buddy, your student, your son ... ah,

I go on and on. Please tell me somehow that I will see you again. There's a fucking hole in my world where a meadow should be. And it's your fault! :). Permit me, Elmer :P

Love, art and poetry,
Willie

El Santo

I don't know when I first started calling him that, but it wasn't because he was a do-gooder. He was a dark saint, a St. Anthony, undergoing trials and the patron of diseases of the skin – or a St. Roch, invoked against plagues. I met him as one of a gaggle of poets in San Francisco back in the 80s. He'd survived into the twenty-first century, I could say that much. Many of the others in that group had since been lost to heroin, crystal meth, alcohol or simply the chance vicissitudes of physical being – car accidents, cancer, AIDS. A tiny number had gone on to success, or what counts as success for serious writers. They were good enough to have a small following. None were bad enough, mercenary enough (though a few tried and were generally disdained for it) or important enough to have a large following. I don't think any of those who remained ever stopped writing. They were true, and they were difficult, and I was proud to have known them and to have been counted among them for a few years.

El Santo, like the rest, was someone I lost touch with for long periods of time. I'd left San Francisco after all, and none of the others ever did, nor did they engage often with those outside the walls of that oddly mysterious and Byzantine city (a place unto itself and capable of old world curses and horrific, often labyrinthine fates). I was eventually unable to continue to tempt its fairy-tale soul – San Francisco often destroyed the sensitive (it seemed especially interested in sadistically toying with them) in its duplicitous garden of earthly delights, and I feared it would one day destroy me.

El Santo, while unable to evade San Francisco's curse – or perhaps, in his case, there was some deep subconscious will all along to tempt it – *did* have an odd ability to remain apart from the poetry scene and its particular or specific curses, and yet continue to partake of it. This was not so easily done in a city of scenes where you were *in* or you were *out*. I think it was because he did not believe in such binaries, and generally he knew that no one can make you feel excluded, or even exclude you successfully, if you don't believe exclusion is in fact a reality – or not one that others can project anyway. Ultimately, he just didn't care about such things. But nor were the poets unkind. They were simply cloistered, and he was generally welcomed when he appeared again.

And that scene was, sadly and for all intents and purposes, unraveling by 1992, co-opted by poetry slams and the rapid deterioration of the city's sustainability as a bohemian enclave under the assault of the tech revolution. This was America after all – and California as well – so there were those who had even found ways to *monetize* poetry. Gap and HBO came calling, and many flat broke poets stepped up to audition for such projects, though with a sense of irony which was only matched by how ironically – or not – said corporations almost always chose those who "looked" like poets over those who were *in fact* poets, and so the marginalization of the true proceeded apace.

In time, those who could procured MFAs at the local affordable college, San Francisco State, eventually fleeing toward academia and the creative writing programs that offered jobs which paid a pittance (though such low salaries were generally enough for a bohemian poet, even in a place like San Francisco). Those who could not accept such a surrender pursued SSI, or failing that, went to Oakland where they sometimes drifted into more drugs and often untimely deaths. But none of them left.

Save myself. I'd had the good fortune to find paying work for an economic justice nonprofit in Los Angeles through a friend, after years of temp jobs that made me feel increasingly desperate. Now at least I could work toward chipping away at Mammon and handing the scrapings to the working poor, the majority of whom were Central American and generally innocent of the excesses we poets railed against onstage in the beer, ammonia and urine-scented clubs that would still host us in the increasingly glass and steel terrarium that was San Francisco as the twentieth century came to a close.

Due to a strange possession – an enchantment really of progressive politics, the celebration of eccentricity and a belief that any place outside of San Francisco was in some way dangerous to the best part of themselves – the poets and many like them were unable to leave. I was perhaps blessed – or was it grace? – in being permitted an exit from the high psychic walls that surrounded that citadel. Perhaps because I was actually from San Francisco. The rest were from places like Buffalo, Minnesota, Ohio (El Santo for instance), West Virginia, Los Angeles, Massachusetts. San Francisco lets its natives leave, but its true believers (who are all outsiders) never. It feeds on their love and enthusiasm, their religious devotion. What can one compare it to? A kind of piety, or a taking of refuge? Here in Mexico, where I've further fled, one sees a parallel with the terrifying god, Tezcatlipoca, called also – and tellingly – the smoking mirror, who demands that those who assume his likeness are celebrated and feted, and then ultimately sacrificed.

As it happened, El Santo and I shared more commonalities than the others. We were both gay, for example, and we studied Buddhism and Eastern practices as serious students, keeping in touch via long meandering letters full of poetry and news, which were often the same (letters because El Santo shunned technology generally, including even landline telephones). And like myself, El Santo found work outside the poetry, alternative or art scene, bussing and waiting tables at various hotels and restaurants far from Bohemia, in places like Fisherman's Wharf and Union Square, treasuring his anonymity among what was left of the city's working class who increasingly commuted into the city to perform their low-paying jobs. The city, like most cities in America at the turn of the new century, had demographically reversed itself, as if it had belched the wealthy white middle class out during the 70s and then inhaled them back in by the 90s. The working class, for their part, were digested by the economy as always, going where fate directed them, down through the intestines of time, powerlessness and injustice to be farted or shit out into the east or south bay. But they were still necessary, of course, to fertilize the new tech wealth – the start-ups sprouting up in the city like great ripe cabbages. I'd been fortunate to leave before this vast and foul gastrointestinal analogy had expressed itself fully.

El Santo, of course, had never left. Which made him what? A form of constipation? Or perhaps a particularly resilient form of E. coli that had established permanent residence in the long psychic tubules of our fair enchanted city. He and the city as one? For it's true that El Santo suffered terrible assaults upon his physical body.

In the late 90s, I'd learned through others that he was ill. He'd always struggled with his health, and was plagued by a plethora of autoimmune and other annoying disorders – chronic fatigue and fibromyalgia, irritable bowel syndrome and diverticulosis, food allergies, chronic prostatitis, outbreaks of hives, kidney and gallstones, hemorrhoids and endless colds and flus. But he was also a meditator and a vegetarian – never one of the meat-eating drunks of the poetry scene, or the odd San Francisco hybrids who claimed to be vegan but couldn't always afford it and saw no contradiction in using crystal meth and vast quantities of alcohol as part of their "health" regimen – both of which harmed no animals but themselves, of course. The heroin addicts, on the other hand, tended not to eat much of anything, and often had interesting dietary viewpoints, from macrobiotics to the benefits of fasting, which they sometimes pursued by default.

El Santo's latest setback had been a series of skin rashes, culminating in a six-month battle with what turned out to be undiagnosed scabies, a condition brought on by mites that burrow under your skin and most likely a result of sexual contact. He'd vanished from the scene, and, as it turned out, the city itself, having shunned the drugs that hadn't worked and taken to herbal remedies while holed up in a shack north of the legendary counterculture town of Bolinas.

By the time I was able to reach him by email, he'd achieved a cure with some sort of veterinary concoction used on horses, and was back in the city, reading, writing and pursuing sexual encounters with abandon. El Santo was sexually compulsive, and yet he often fell in love, complicating matters and leading to yet more emotional suffering, setbacks and near breakdowns.

But through it all he wrote. Oddly joyful odes in the mode of Whitman or e.e. cummings that seemed wholly dissonant with his experience. But like I say, he was a dark saint and had a strange ability to tear down through the layers of his agony to a kind of ecstasy that was nothing but the sheer will to live, or to pleasure, or perhaps even joy. A gratefulness that only those who've experienced severe suffering know. This had of course initially led him to his interest in and embracing of Eastern religion, which in many ways, like Christianity, celebrated suffering, or if not that, believed in its redemptive potential. And El Santo was an example of such, and so the name.

Because there was definitely a purity to his agony. And being pure as a mendicant medieval saint, El Santo could not be found on Facebook (whatever banalities would he report or post?) and he rarely used email. But as I mentioned, he did write letters – long hand-written meandering monologues crammed into large envelopes covered in stickers and stuffed with handbills he picked up around San Francisco, announcing underground art happenings, raves and the like. El Santo sometimes attended such events, but more often not.

El Santo was world-weary in the way of an El Greco saint. Peaked and tired of this mortal coil. He said he had seen and done everything and was waiting to die. He had miraculously evaded HIV and most forms of venereal disease, putting the lie to the belief that promiscuity was a health hazard. Statistics, as any gambler knows, were not cumulative. A smart slut was a healthy slut, as simple as that. What the church fathers and the NIH don't want you to know. Stupidity, complacency, bad habits, denial and drug abuse are the real culprits: products of the highly touted 'freedoms' that Americans inevitably either abuse or botch terribly. Thus the rules.

El Santo only smoked marijuana. He'd had a medical card for years and was somewhat expert at determining the virtues of one kush versus another. He was an authority others would go to, what with his resume of illnesses. And so he had a place in the social fabric, like many of the city's eccentric denizens.

El Santo not only never left San Francisco, he never left the first apartment he'd procured there back in the mid-1980s. He'd lived in the same little studio on 3rd Street since the years when it was still the lower end of skid row, before transforming itself into the hub of the dotcom revolution and finally the barrio of Twitter, et al. He stayed put through it all, benefitting from rent control (that charming holdover from when capitalism was still only tipsy and not a raging drunk) as the building was never sold or upgraded, right up until the place filled up with bedbugs and El Santo nearly lost his mind. He'd struggled to rid himself of the pests, but was unsuccessful, and ended up once again losing his job when his paranoia had increased to a level bordering on agoraphobia and he called in sick one too many times, wholly unaware that he'd been on thin ice at that particular hotel for months with his frequent emotional meltdowns in the kitchen and odd, though arguably friendly, remarks to customers.

Now unemployed, he deserted the apartment altogether at one point to go live in the Zen Center where there was a residency program for students who wanted a monastic setting. It did calm him in time, and he was able to return to the apartment where all his belongings were now packed in plastic cartons.

I wondered sometimes if El Santo was in some kind of negative spiral. I wondered the same about myself. But it was cruel to think of El Santo that way. He was open and he was true and he, above all, embraced life. One can't blame a saint. If there is any blame to extend to such a person, it must be aimed directly at the deity involved. Which would be who? He was an atheistic Buddhist; his God could only be his own consciousness, his personality, his contract with this life, whatever it might be. A life that often repulsed and horrified me. The letter that arrived while he was battling bedbugs was read and burned in the garden for fear of a tiny traveler or one of its eggs. And so then, why did I find myself so intrigued by El Santo's continuing adversities? Why did I keep writing back? Was it pity? Never. And I wasn't gloating, though I was often grateful I'd been spared his misfortunes. I think it was that I had an immense admiration for El Santo's fortitude, the openness of his heart and mind in the midst of what could only be called a hell, a trial by one fire after another. The Temptation of St. Anthony indeed. He made me curious. How can a man live like this? Perhaps he was simply not the suicidal type? Is there a type, and if so, what is its relation to circumstance?

As I said, El Santo wrote poems of love, inspiration and metaphysical beauty while his life collapsed around him. And that's why I called him El Santo. Like St. John of God or Saint Theresa – or as mentioned previously, Saint Anthony or San Lorenzo – he found moments of an almost ecstatic joy in his miserable existence that could be called nothing other than saintly. He was, in fact, progressing somewhere. Like the God and Satan of *Paradise Lost* or the cities of America in the late twentieth century, a universe turned inside out was the picture El Santo showed the world. For one as bored as myself, it was intriguing, compelling.

He was my teacher, but not within any kind of faith,

unless it was our common interest in Eastern religion. As I've said, he frightened me at times. My own physical body was often assaulted as well by chronic conditions. What could happen to people terrified me. It could happen to me! And it did happen to El Santo. The terrifying specter of physical disintegration without death. Living in pain with no possibility of relief. El Santo never considered suicide. As did I. I say *considered*. I knew I was incapable of it, thus my terrors about what the body could undergo while alive. I was incapable of enduring what El Santo endured, and yet if he were my teacher in the Eastern sense, roles would eventually be reversed. Perhaps he was not then, as I really didn't have any interest in or certainly not the courage to live what he was teaching. Or did I? Regardless, I didn't want to know there were such eventualities, such horrors in the world. Like not wanting to study medicine or civil engineering – I didn't want to know what lay underneath the clear solutions I preferred to see in those recovered from illnesses, in bridges standing, beautiful and seemingly indestructible. I didn't want to see. El Santo showed me anyway. *Look*. Every letter said *look*. And I felt oddly, dissonantly grateful. He appealed to my better self, the one interested in the truth. The one that reached. The one I often evaded.

And yet all through that period (what they call an epoch here), El Santo possessed a healthy sense of the dramatic and the epicality of one's own life – to be clear, it was not a self-indulgence so much as paying close attention to a conundrum. There are those who wrestle with the angel. Such was El Santo.

All those months between letters, El Santo went about his business, often in pain, and when there was a reprieve – or even if there were not – he'd often decide to smoke a joint and visit the backrooms south of Market, taking untold numbers of penises down his throat, lying completely nude in urinals while a dozen men emptied their bladders onto his flesh. This is where sexuality goes if one pursues it as a passion and with real curiosity. And many do in San Francisco. As for myself, like suicide, I only considered the idea, terrified of what my life was becoming without such excess – even if such excess were the path to truth. I preferred pleasure to truth? Believed they were different? I'm not a saint, I told myself. And what church would have El Santo, patron one day of all the gloriously perverse, their protector and intercessor with the pigs of heaven? Any church worth its salt, actually, because El Santo cared for and was touched deeply by all of the men he encountered and served. Perhaps God was not who everyone thought. Perhaps he did not make love to Mary to bring forth a son because he was far beyond such vanilla activity as missionary-style heterosexual intercourse all those eons into his creation. After all that time – even if his creation was only four thousand years old – God was likely deep into blood and scat, and so forced to employ an angel to deliver the seed. Who knew, maybe the world was the vicious, violent hellhole it was because our holy father was directing a massive snuff film. No stars, just an infinity of extras.

And who would the devil be in all that? Perhaps it was all other than what it seemed. All turned around. No surprise there. The real evil ones then were those moralizers who in fact – and unknowingly – condemned God's true nature. These fallen filled stadiums praising Jesus and unwittingly insulting God's creation and his perversions. And so, hell then was a small Oklahoma town full of puritanical Republicans. And who was Jesus? God's suicide really. And they worshipped it. America was arguably an asylum, which isn't news.

I'd long since retreated to Mexico – which may not sound like a retreat. But, believe me, to be an expatriate is to be an outsider forever, like a bacteria encased in a cyst. It may be a clear membrane that you can see out of, but it's a membrane nonetheless, a shield. To run away is to run away. Period. El Santo never ran.

And then one day came the news of El Santo's death. I was at first shocked, then almost immediately relieved, as no doubt, was he.

The news had not come in a stickered envelope, of course, though if anyone would have had the ability as well as inclination to write of the news of their own death in such manner, it would be El Santo.

No, the news came from a mutual friend, and if it had not been for email and the Internet, I would never have known, as El Santo and I had ceased writing letters at that time, faced with the unreliability of the Mexican postal service.

In his last letter to me before I crossed the border, El Santo related how he had been, for a time, at relative peace, working aboard a ship that took parties out on to the bay. He wrote in his letter to me, *You've heard of sea legs? Ha, ha, I have sea spirit. I'm completely unbalanced.*

His end was as strange as his life. It seems, prior to his job aboard the ship, he had once again been let go at a restaurant with a view of Alcatraz, the former federal prison, the ruins of which stood like foreboding bunkers on an island far out in the bay:

> *I look out and strangely long for it. I'd love to live there all alone, just watching the wind's doings, meditating, sitting there in the center of the bay. It must, I'm sure, hold all the city's secrets. It must be the heart of this whole mess.*

He'd soon have a chance to draw nearer, though never to reach its shores. His most recent illness had been brought on by a persistent case of migraines coupled with vertigo and tinnitus that he'd been unable to eradicate, and in his growing paranoia, he'd ingested massive amounts of silver or manganese or some metal, I don't recall which. But it had affected his mind and he'd been carted off by the landlord one day after screaming for three solid hours that the bedbugs were back. His employer was at first understanding, until the two-week leave threatened to stretch for months if he applied for medical leave (which he never did), and so he was fired. By mail.

After six weeks, he was ready to once again work but

eying Perdition. Through a waitress he'd befriended at the restaurant, he'd landed a job on the boat that took excursions out onto the Bay. Soon, donning a white shirt with black bow-tie and slacks, he was serving cocktails and hors d'oeuvres to legions of whomever. Tourists, wedding parties, bar mitzvahs. He was still shaking, though, still suffering the vertigo and tinnitus, and he was aware that a ship was a poor locale for recovery from such a condition. *But this is perfect, of course!* he maniacally sang out in his long rambling letters. *We wouldn't want it to be easy now, would we?!* His poetry veered toward Robinson Jeffers and Eugene O'Neill.

Excursions were often cancelled on stormy days, but the bay was by nature windy, and unless there was rain, the boat usually went out. As it did that night, the second of September, 2015. The vessel bobbed like a cork. The passengers, a college graduation party, I think it was, grumbled while not ordering as many drinks as any would expect them to. They sampled less than a healthy amount of the canapés circulating courtesy of El Santo and the catering crew. The graduate himself put on a show of being unperturbed, ostensibly concerned both for the amount of money his parents had put out for the boat as well as to save face before the assembled frowning guests. He and his close friends had just ordered a dozen steins of beer, and El Santo moved through the crowd along the rails toward the stern where the young men were hooting and carrying on above the ship's wake.

All at once, the ship rolled hard – *the smile left his face*, a passenger later recalled – and El Santo fell sideways, then backward, but instead of dropping the heavy tray he carried, he lifted it as if to save it, and hitting the rail, the weight of what he carried and the momentum from his loss of balance carried him over the side of the vessel and into the sea.

A fast-thinking teen threw a life preserver overboard almost immediately in the general direction of his fall. A man called to the bridge to cut the engines. One man looked ready to dive in after him. Two of the boys peeled off their shirts in a show of heroics. All waited to spot him bobbing like a cork, screaming, or otherwise expressing his presence before they took whatever step would be next. But El Santo never surfaced.

The ship's engines were idled and the captain turned the boat to circle back, assuming what everyone else had assumed – El Santo would appear, his head bobbing above the waves, calling, perhaps a hand waving. But nothing. The waters of the bay are cold, but not so cold that one cannot survive for probably up to an hour or more. Wherever had he gone?

The party was clearly over, and after circling three or four times, the boat (it was a corporation after all and couldn't inconvenience or unnecessarily disturb its paying guests) headed back to its pier at Fisherman's Wharf. A somber mood pervaded the passengers, not so much because they'd lost someone they knew, but for the reality that someone's life could be plucked like fruit from a tree and tossed into the infinite, never to return. *That cheerful waiter, that hard-working young man ...* (one always thought of El Santo as boyish and young, even though he was well into his 50s).

The ship's captain, of course, reported the loss to the Coast Guard and local authorities per protocol. And would they dredge the bay for his corpse? Only in the case of a crime in order to obtain evidence. For an accidental death such as El Santo's, they simply waited for the body to appear. As it did three days later, bloated, of a bluish-green hue, with the same vacant eyes as the suicides retrieved from under the Golden Gate Bridge. Whatever El Santo had been had left his body.

The cause of death was blunt force trauma to the head followed by drowning. Because of the head trauma, members of the crew and a few passengers who'd been nearby were interviewed by the maritime police to rule out foul play, and it was eventually assumed that the serving tray or something floating in the water were the likely culprits. Perhaps even something on the floor of the bay if his body descended that far.

The email from an acquaintance had said: *I hate to be the*

bearer of such news, but we've lost him. It was an accident. He fell off a boat and drowned. When I received this news, I rejected the verbs the writer had chosen. El Santo could neither be lost – if anything he was finally found – nor could he "fall," ever. It's the one thing he never did. Perhaps the waters had grabbed him, enveloped him, swallowed him. He could have been thrown, hurled, catapulted. He might have even jumped or dived. I like to think he entered the sea willingly. We were all poets, what can I say? But it struck me that way.

Days later, having dreamt of him and heard his laughter, I'd thought of Pip in *Moby Dick*:

> *The sea had jeeringly kept his finite body up, but drowned the infinite of his soul. Not drowned entirely, though. Rather carried down alive to wondrous depths, where strange shapes of the unwarped primal world glided to and fro before his passive eyes; and the miser-merman, Wisdom, revealed his hoarded heaps; and among the joyous, heartless, ever-juvenile eternities, Pip saw the multitudinous, God-omnipresent, coral insects, that out of the firmament of waters heaved the colossal orbs. He saw God's foot upon the treadle of the loom, and spoke it; and therefore his shipmates called him mad. So man's insanity is heaven's sense; and wandering from all mortal reason, man comes at last to that celestial thought, which, to reason, is absurd and frantic; and weal or woe, feels then uncompromised, indifferent as his God.*

As far as I know, there was no memorial. His work remains unpublished.

Los Angeles

It grew out of a cam habit. Fred would not be the first to fall headlong into that sinkhole of debauchery, but he took it somewhere few others did or would. The boys, on the other hand, were simply there to solve their financial problems: school, crashed cars, drug habits, marriage licenses, offspring – all manner of responsibilities and/or irresponsibilities. It was clearly expensive being a young man, and even more so if he were too busy or too proud to stoop to the humiliating jobs available to him. With education costs rising and wages plummeting, young men today were forced to find additional means of support.

There should be an app! sang the Greek chorus.

Enter Chaturbate.

Camming was tempting. Masturbating for money. Most of them, if not all of them, were masturbating anyway – alone and for free. Why not get paid for it?

You didn't have to show your face, no one could trace you if you were squeamish. Many were straight, and shy at first, but once the money started rolling in, they grew bolder. They got money *and* praise. Power was what they felt, and what they'd actually come looking for, truth be told. Safe behind their digital one-way mirrors, they forgot or ceased to care that they performed almost solely for middle-aged gay men who wanted nothing better than to fuck them like dogs until all their arrogance ran out of them in their paltry little semen shots which they thought were the cat's meow. Well, maybe they were partly correct. Cats do like milk. Here, kitty, kitty.

Fred was part of this community. Fred wasn't masturbating on camera, of course – not least because no one would want to watch a big-bellied fifty-year-old masturbate – but he had more in common with the boys than they ever suspected. Fred was flat broke just like them, and though his body was not going to be a resource as it was for all these twenty-year-old boys with their six-packs and crooked baseball caps, he had a few aces up his sleeve that they didn't – after all, they were buck naked and thus wholly sleeveless. There should be an app indeed. Cunning was an app unto itself and though it was a download that often took years, that's just what Fred had and they didn't. Experience 2.0.

But otherwise, he was no different from them. He too was priming the pump.

In the meantime, he bought and gave his tokens to all those beautiful young men who got off just right or did what he told them to do. He spent hundreds, but Fred was a cheap bastard at heart and he'd done the math. Everything's a pyramid scheme to the cunning. These boys were hungry and like any good restaurateur, Fred fed them what they wanted, and since they were desperate, he figured he could cut the food off eventually and then hire them. And you know what that means. They'd no longer be paid what they were worth. Which was what they were getting used to in neoliberal America. They were becoming slaves, saddled with college loans and no choice but to take whatever job was offered to keep up with the payments. Better to be a slave to one's dick than to the Man, they must have figured, not stopping to think that this very website was the Man – and by extension, so was Fred.

Fred had seen how all the token-paying trolls grew quickly bored after a week or two of whoever was the new meat. The boys didn't get it and were always surprised when their take lessened, their capital deteriorated. They were young enough not to know that even beauty was a quickly depreciating asset. Like addicts, they wondered why three hours of masturbation wasn't getting them as high as it used to. So they dropped the job at Subway and jacked off six hours a day instead of three. And still, masturbation was not going to be their holy grail anymore than a low interest home loan was for the generation previous. No, masturbation was, in fact, yet another loan, as Fred saw it. And when the principal came due and they couldn't pay, Fred, like any good loan shark, would be there to offer them a chance to pay it back in trade.

"I've got a job I need done," he'd quipped one day to a self-involved ornery punk, Ned, who rarely gave a good show, whose token take was way down consequently. Fred knew he was ripe for exploitation.

"I'm your man," Ned joked, brandishing his big uncut trailer-park tool.

"You are *the* man."

Ned stroked it until his low hangers bounced like a pair of stripper's tits.

"It'll be a piece of cake, Neddy."

"It's Ned."

But Fred was already thinking it through. You see, one of Fred's aces, as it turned out, was that he'd been named in the will of an aging spinster in the San Gabriel foothills. She was sitting on a cool half million with that house of hers, but she was also healthy – spry even – and since she was only ten or fifteen years his senior, there was a good chance she'd live a good long time, and maybe even outlive him. Fred had to make sure that that didn't happen and he'd been considering various strategies to move her along, if you will, toward the pearly gates and his own financial prosperity. Unemployed for almost two years now, Fred had few prospects as an auto mechanic specializing in AMC cars, Yugos, DeLoreans and more recently, in an effort at practicality, Saturns after he'd taken yet another certification course, graduating just days before GM listed and nearly sank, resulting in management's decision to abandon the Saturn line altogether.

So he went online like everybody else. But eBay wasn't for him, as he owned nothing of value. Day trading was out as numbers bored him and he was broke. He'd discovered the beat-off chat rooms quite by accident, and for a while simply left them on in the background while he trolled for money-making schemes. What was all this about medical billing anyway? Boring. It must be a scam.

It was more fun to talk to these young men. And Obama kept approving more unemployment. Fuck the job hunt. He'd no sooner cash his unemployment check than he'd be buying tokens to get the boys to do acrobatics and pelvic thrusts while he practiced shooting birds to ostensibly improve his quickly depreciating mental acuity on Lumosity.com. He justified his behavior by reasoning that he was actually stimulating the economy by tipping these boys, who'd then go out and buy all number of hamburgers, electronics and college courses. Why, he was making up for Obama's timidity, providing stimulus and flooding the economy with cold hard cash while the rest of the unemployed scrimped and saved, doing nothing to prime the pump.

The problem was that these macroeconomic exercises, while making the rounds of the young and lean, were in no way circulating back toward Fred. What was this, a new kind of Passover? Was there blood on his door? The mythic always insinuated itself.

Well, the door he had marked was the spinster's. Now more than ever, as he'd spent nearly $1500 on the camboys, and it was high time he cashed in and got a return on his investment. God knows he'd enjoyed the shows, and God bless the lads, but no series of miniscule cumshots was going to pay the rent and fill the tank.

No, he needed that house and the boys were going to help him get it.

There were a million ways to off somebody, of course. But Fred was no cold-blooded killer. No, he needed to set things in motion while keeping his own hands clean. And who better to dirty their hands than these arrogant boys who spent a good deal of their time fingering their assholes anyway, if not splooging all over their palms?

The spinster had mentioned recently, while a fire raged somewhere up the coast near Ojai, that the hills behind her house hadn't burned since the '60s and she worried they might ignite at any moment. He nodded and raised his brows, while in his mind he began to ruthlessly calculate, Grinchlike.

Cindy had invited Fred over for morel and arugula tortellini and red wine. She was a fabulous cook, having worked at restaurants most of her life until she'd contracted a particularly virulent amoebic dysentery while on a ceviche junket along the Oaxacan coast. She'd been so ill that she ended up taking a leave from the high-end Berkeley restaurant, Puer, where she'd finally gained the position she'd longed for. Sadly, her brush with gourmet glory was not to last as her guts began to unravel courtesy of that rare mollusk found only in the tidepools of Puerto Escondido. She eventually lost three feet of her small intestine and a good six inches of her large, ending up on long-term disability and what's more, forced home to care for her ailing parents, who soon passed on and left her the family ranch-style house in suburban Glendora. But she had since recovered after those harrowing ten years and was back at full strength, even if she hadn't let the feds know that. And who could blame her at sixty-one? Was she going to start over? Oh, Fred knew how hard that was even at fifty, let alone crowning toward social security.

He eyed the gas flame as she scattered all number of herbs into the simmering marinara. He'd met her at the health food store when she'd first returned home. She was using a walker, and pale as a ghost. Fred had been frequenting the place to cure a nasty case of chronic prostatitis – saw palmetto, bee pollen, grapefruit extract – that had seriously curbed his boy hunting. She was living solely on lichi fruit, beetle antennae and special herbs from the taiga at that point. They chatted in the way of the chronically ill in such places. When she mentioned she'd lost both parents on top of her own health challenges, but had thankfully inherited their house, he pursued a friendship, ran errands for her, did yard work, the works. Contrary to the plan, she improved and was soon turning down his offers for help around the house. "I feel reborn, Fred. God, I'm indebted to you. You've been such a help, such a good friend." Fred felt betrayed. Sure, he'd been named in the will, but what he wanted was to 'close.'

But she was not going to die anytime soon – from that old mollusk, or any of the other myriad illnesses she'd endured. In fact, she was a walking case study in *what doesn't kill you makes you stronger*, because, as it turned out, she'd not only survived said dysentery, but ovarian cancer, dengue fever and even that flesh-eating virus you hear so much about in the media nowadays. A regular Rasputin, he knew a blunt object was of no use with her, nor would arsenic or ricin or any of those do the trick against such a beast. Only something elemental would suffice. Earth? Air? Water? Fire!

It seemed like the perfect crime, but forensics was getting so good these days, even a fire couldn't eliminate evidence. And he didn't really want her to suffer too much. He imagined her running through the streets engulfed in flames, screaming. That seemed so ungrateful, in that she was leaving him her house, after all. It would be best if he could work it so the fire hit at dawn. She would awaken, have a heart attack, upon seeing the wall of flame climb over the back fence like a prowler.

He poured her another glass of Malbec. She giggled and he smiled back at her like Elliot Rodger. Sleep soundly, sweet princess, for you shall awake to fire. Was that Shakespeare, Blake? No, it wasn't anybody but dear old Fred thinking it, but it sure sounded grave and literary, which somehow made the crime less so.

Everything would have to come together perfectly to pull it off, of course. But even if it didn't provide the desired effect, it couldn't hurt. He'd be doing the community a favor regardless. The hills needed to burn every decade or two. And if they contained it, he would have singlehandedly extended the community's safety for another twenty years before the plant life grew back to burnable level. And even a contained fire might still do the trick for Fred, as a good burn would at least prepare the soil for a devastating flood when the spring storms hit. Timing was everything. A late summer fire followed by a spring flood. If the flames and smoke didn't get her, the grim reaper could please cut to the chase and bury her alive in a wall of mud. It would be more merciful. There'd be no running through the streets. She'd simply disappear into the ooze after a few futile flailing motions. A faint gurgle in place of that horrific, deathly scream.

Whatever the case, it was his job to make sure it was a good blazer of a fire. There'd be zero tolerance for any Rasputin shenanigans, he'd see to that. The last thing he wanted to do was visit her in the burn unit and have to yank out the respirator electrical cord or something else undignified. The old pillow smother? He was certainly not going to sit through another recovery, wasting countless years helping her convalesce. He might as well *earn* the half million. No, no, he wanted to be stage left and simply cash in.

"How about a little camping trip, Ned? I'll provide the equipment and a couple other young studs, and I won't even bother you guys by camping with you! I just want you young ones to have the good experiences I had when I was young."

"I ain't going out there with any gay dudes, man. I'll do a private show here in my room, but why would I hassle with going out in the woods, especially with two other guys, when I'm pretty damn sure an old perv like you is totally conspiring to get us to do shit together? No way, dude, I don't show butt and I don't do butt, so don't even ask."

"You're right, I'm an old perv, Ned, that's why I would never deign to even watch gay boys. I like my boys straight, and you know that. Shame on you for suggesting I'd do such a thing. I love straight boys cuz they're straight, silly! I aim to send three straight boys out to have some fun. And when I say fun, I mean a bottle of tequila, some weed, Pop-Tarts, pizza, whatever. Pick your poison. All you guys gotta do is let me watch you party as you build a big bonfire and chill. That's all – that's what's hot to me. If you guys touch each other, you'll ruin the whole effect. I want straight boys! Razz each other, punch each other, insult each other. I don't care! Just party together. And I've got a thousand for each of you, $500 now, $500 after. Wait, Ned, what the hell, let's give you $800 both sides and cut the other two to $350."

That got a smile. What a joke. Shoveling shit and he's eating it up. Open wide.

"I'm in, Fred. When we gonna do this? And who are the other guys?"

"I haven't picked 'em yet, Ned. Just you. Why don't you help me pick them?"

"I don't really care, as long as they ain't gay."

These boys are so gullible – such dopes – they won't even know they're arsonists, and I'll have deleted my account the minute I see the smoke rising. Well, maybe not dopes really, more like Spanish conquistadors, the way they hunt gold at any cost and how they arrogantly conquer hearts and pocketbooks and disrespect the natives. That would be me. They, like Cortez et al, are confident in their god, and his name is Priapus. Who knew that El Dorado, that legendary city of gold, was in fact a wall of golden flame – or a ginger's crotch. Well then, let's get it done, boys.

All they'd need was a pack of cigarettes and a match. And all Fred would need was to send through the tokens, necessitating a large charge to his nearly maxed credit card. He'd have to get the boys to the proper trailhead, of course, which could be hugely challenging with people who were careless enough in the first place to traipse into the canyons with smokes.

The point was to not, under any circumstances, meet them. Because they'd get caught if they survived. And they'd squawk like all cowardly young men. No honor among masturbators. But who was this Fred they kept talking about? Fred? You mean the account that was deleted the day before the fire? That Fred? You mean the Fred whose name is actually Tom and was using the ISP of a local Starbucks besides? You mean that Fred? *That* untraceable Fred? He'd be backing over his aging laptop and then tossing it into the nearby Puddingstone Reservoir before anyone even yelled "Fire!"

He sent Ned a gob of tokens to motivate his search for co-conspirators – was that what they were? Hardly. They had no idea what they'd be getting into.

"Let's find two right now," Fred said in the chatbox as Ned bucked his hips and moaned, hoarsely groaning, "Bro, I'm close." Fred wondered if it had yet occurred to Ned that tokens – and by extension money – were now not only his preferred, but maybe even his necessary, aphrodisiac.

After a quick cleanup with a sock, Ned laughed and took a few deep breaths. "Yeah, Fred, I need new rims."

"And you'll have them. TTYL."

He'll never drive again once he gets twenty years, Fred thought and laughed to himself. And off Fred went to Bevmo where he'd heard there was a sale on tequila. Why do you think he'd suggested tequila? He'd be getting two bottles for one. One for the boys and one for him to celebrate with in the La Quinta Motor Inn out in Palm Desert while he watched the 'returns' on the fire. He grabbed a few bags of chips and some peanuts. Why not splurge?

Fred was anxious to get home and nearly ran over two school kids in a crosswalk as he ogled a boy on a skateboard racing down the sidewalk. He gathered his concentration: *Don't blow this now, Freddy. This is your big chance. Any legal problems now would bring much unneeded exposure.* Still, he shot the last stop sign and skidded into his parking place in the big ugly stucco apartment house abutting the freeway that was all that was left in his price range as rents skyrocketed throughout the southland.

Fred stepped inside the dark, messy apartment, and knocking some soiled t-shirts off his desk, found the mouse and signed on to Chaturbate. Only to find Ned whining that he needed more tokens if he was going to continue this friggin' needle-in-a-haystack bullshit.

"Your needle, my haystack," Fred said.

"Har, har, har, Fred – got any tokens?"

Fred offered twenty-five. Cheap, but Ned was basically worthless. *Two hours and not one prospect?* "Come on, Ned, let's do this together."

Fred began trolling for cute boys around L.A., but at some point during the search, he realized he could care less if the other boys were cute. He just needed a job done, and certainly there'd be more justice in killing off a few of the more self-involved rude boys than victimizing some cute young harmless thing who couldn't pay his tuition this month. Then again, the rude ones were harder to direct and/or control. Oh well, perhaps a nice one would need to be sacrificed. Again, the mythic. Any number of ancient cultures had preyed on the innocent, and who was Fred to buck the system? Whatever boy got committed to the flames would be dying for a good cause.

By 5 p.m., they'd cornered two more: one in Baldwin Park and one in Azusa – and the outing was on. Ned could pick them up on his way over from Duarte. Fred sent a Google map showing exactly where the trailhead was that he wanted them to use. "You've got to be careful. They don't like people in there after dark, so go far enough in to be out of sight of the houses. There's a nice little meadow about a half mile down the trail – you can't miss it. It's all dry grass that you'll hear crackling under your feet." Fred giggled, thinking of how fast the flames would consume that grass before moving on to the oil-filled branches of the nearby manzanita that would soon make quick work of several dozen homes – hell, maybe the whole town. He hated that town anyway, full as it was with rightwing Christians, cops and Joe-the-plumber types. Then again, he wanted to protect his soon-to-be-inherited property value, and the town's good schools, law-abiding citizens and shopping centers were reasons it had value. Life was such a paradox.

"Oh, and bring one of those tins of barbecue lighter fluid

for the campfire – the wood out there doesn't always light that easy and the wind might blow out your matches. Of course, your cigarettes will stay lit – bring a couple packs. I love to see boys smoking around the campfire!"

A pang of conscience assailed him then and he almost wanted to add a warning to make sure to remind them to run once the fire started. There'd be no way to stop it, and he really had no intention of killing anybody except his friend, Cindy. These boys were doing him a big favor, after all, and had their whole lives in front of them, even if they would be spent behind bars. It would be cruel to kill them.

Well, then again, they were mercenary types – why else were they proffering their sacred seed for all to see? He doubted they were the types who'd risk their hides for any-thing but the most self-serving of motives. He didn't have to worry that they might make an effort to put the fire out – he could count on them making a run for it as soon as the sparks took hold of the grass stalks.

"So, you gonna meet us somewhere to give us the pizza and stuff," Ned asked him as the fateful day approached.

"I didn't think you'd want to meet me, Ned. Can I cop a feel?"

"No fucking way, dude. I ain't gay, I told you that."

"Well, I wouldn't be able to keep my hands off a stud like you, so tell you what, I'll put the stuff somewhere behind some bushes in the park near the river in Duarte, and you can pick it up and no shenanigans. I don't wanna mess this cool party up for you or for me!"

"That's cool, Fred." But could he count on Ned to find the right bush? Well, it was a chance he'd have to take.

"And don't forget the cash," Ned added.

"I won't. There will be tequila, beer, chips and pizza. What kind you like?"

"Pepperoni, and I really like cheese puffs."

"Your wish is my command, Neddie."

"It's Ned."

Whatever. It meant Fred had to go back out for the beer

and cheese puffs or pick them up when he picked up the pizza. The little prick was demanding. Well, it'll make it all the more easy on his conscience, he consoled himself, when he sees the boys go down hard in a court of law.

As it was, they were scheduled to pick up the goods at 6:00 p.m. and be at the trailhead by 6:30 to begin their summer eve party. It was blistering hot and all systems were go. Fred had to be careful when he dropped by the park, which was usually full of kids, mothers and suburban dads. Pulling up in his butt-ugly white Mercury, and looking how he did, he elicited a common response at such places, and it included parents calling out for their children or pulling them close. If there was a stereotype for a pedophile, Fred was it. But he'd thought ahead. He'd gone to the uniform store and bought an outfit that made him look like some kind of Edison employee or park maintenance man. Yes, khaki pants and a matching shirt, work boots and a khaki ball cap. He put the pizza, booze, beer and snacks in a large duffel with a big pair of bush clippers sticking out. And locating the agreed-upon bush, he casually dropped it off and did a little weeding nearby to avoid suspicion.

The boys were likely not as nonchalant when they arrived and marched over to the bush and dragged out the bag, discarding the clippers and digging around for the money before they even considered someone might be watching them.

At 6:35, Fred, sitting at his desk in the dark apartment, signed on to Chaturbate and got a message from Ned in a private party chat box. "Okay, we're here, gathering firewood and about to go live."

"I'm ready, Ned, let her rip!"

"Let what rip?"

"The party, silly. You boys drinking yet?"

"We just got here, but yeah, we each cracked a beer."

The others soon crowded into the frame and showed themselves, and then each signed on so Fred had three screens in which to view the action. There they were, all smiles on their little smart phones, their pockets stuffed with cash, looking like there was no tomorrow. Because there wasn't, Fred laughed. He sighed when he saw young Pablo, who had the cutest scruff along his chin – and those big brown eyes. He was wearing a Batman shirt, and next to Lawrence – a gangly black boy – who just happened to be wearing a Superman t-shirt. They were like the Justice League itself. Fred grinned at the good omen. Finally, justice, and owning that piece of California real estate that was rightfully his.

It was late August, so the sun would be setting around 7:20. Fred had time to double-check his packed bag for the weekend getaway to Palm Desert. His apartment's burning down in the fire, being as it was down near the freeway, was remote at best. Too bad. Anything he had of value he could throw into his overnight bag.

At 7:15 the boys lit the campfire as they put back shots of tequila to commemorate the beginning of the official festivities. Already Ned was showing attitude, and Lawrence had said 'fuck that' to at least two of his suggestions: a game of cards and drinking a whole beer while doing a headstand. Fred sensed the conflict between the two suggested Lawrence was gay, though as Fred recalled, he claimed to be bi on his Chaturbate profile. Well, that would be enough to upset Ned. Pablo just sat there sweetly and watched the other two, saying nothing and nursing a beer.

It took no time at all. By 7:50, all three boys' screens had gone Blair Witch shaky as Lawrence shouted "What the fuck?!" And then, "Not the tequila, you idiot, that won't put it out!" followed by "Fuck you, faggot," courtesy of Ned, and "Where the fuck are *you* going, Pablo?"

"Let's get the fuck out of here," Lawrence shouted, and the game was on. Run, boys. Fred shut down his computer and headed for the car, looking over his shoulder as he hopped in. No smoke yet. Well, it was dusk now besides.

He felt relaxed, knowing the boys had started a forest fire just a half mile from his property. Yes, *his*. He was feeling good. They'd run as he expected and would survive, although they were also driving, and who knew how much they'd imbibed? Well, the quicker the arrest the better. Get this all behind him, and get to work with a contractor building the new house atop the smoking foundation of the last. It occurred to him that he should have found underage boys to do the deed as they'd likely serve less time. Those nasty pangs of conscience. Then again, the youngsters wouldn't be allowed on Chaturbate, would they? Another reason America's draconian sex laws were a disservice to everyone.

Firefighters were yet another problem. They heroically responded within a matter of minutes, and, after only ten homes were burned, had driven the fire back into the hills.

*   *   *

Fred had been glued to the television for the last hour at the motor inn and was able to identify up to five of the houses, which were right up the street from *his* home. There'd been several fatalities.

"It crashed down this street like a wave – we couldn't save everyone. The only consolation is that they most likely didn't know what hit them." But who – *who?!* Fred was exasperated with one pretty television journalist after another melodramatically sympathizing with the dead but always finishing on the same tired note: "The names of the deceased are being withheld until notification of next of kin."

"She had no kin, you idiots! Just put her name out there so I can get moving on my future!"

His cell rang, and he grabbed it. "What?!"

"Tom, it's Cindy. There's been a fire. Haven't you heard?"

He collected himself. "Oh my God, no … yes … of course. Are you okay?"

"I'm fine. And the house is fine. But I've got a problem I need you to help me with." Fred (who we now know is Tom) heard voices in the background.

"Of course, anything. My God, I'm so glad you're okay. Who's there with you?"

"Well, that's just it, Tom. You know my friend, Darlene? Well, her son is here completely freaked out. He apparently accidentally started the fire and you know what they do to people nowadays. I just don't know what to do, but I want to protect him."

Tom's jaw and Fred's figurative one dropped simultaneously. "Darlene has a son?" Tom Rolodexed quickly through his mind – Darlene, Darlene ... shit, that's the lady she goes to swap meets with.

"Yes, she does, and he's in trouble."

"Is it just him?"

"No, there are three of them here. And they don't seem to know each other. It's very strange. Anyway, how soon can you get here?"

* * *

Fred was red as a beet and considered believing in God again. He also considered stopping by the local library and accessing Chaturbate to make contact with the boys and try to get them out of *his* house. Tom, on the other hand, considered suicide. And damage control. "An hour, two, I'll head out now."

"Where are you?"

"Palm Springs ... I've uh, I've been out here the last few days."

On the drive back, he reassured himself that the boys would never suspect he was Fred, and nor would any arson task force. They'd never heard his voice, or seen his picture, and couldn't trace the ISP, but he hadn't lied about his age, and this car – the damn car would make them think of Fred even if they didn't suspect him, and he needed to make sure there was not even a whiff of suspicion. Was he being paranoid? Well, yes. But who wouldn't be, considering what he'd set in motion?

He pulled off at Yucaipa and started looking for a Mexican barrio. You could sell a car literally within minutes in a barrio if the price was right. He got $500 and a ride to the Kia dealership where he made it his down payment, and thanks to Obama's unemployment, passed the credit check and drove off the lot, looking like a legitimate, though badly out of shape, middle-aged citizen with a life of some kind.

He considered his options. Turning the boys in seemed like the best option. Protecting them was insane and made him an accomplice after the fact – and how long before he'd somehow end up implicated *before* the fact? In other words, it all came down to the elemental. Play with fire. He was way too close to the flames for comfort.

In a sense, it was Cindy actually who was stumbling into felonious behavior, and if he just let her continue – the longer it spun out, the better – he could turn them all in, and if she got twenty years, he'd end up with the house pretty much by default. He wouldn't even have to kill her. Though he'd likely have to visit her in the can once a month. A small price to pay, considering. Hopefully they'd place her in a nearby federal penitentiary. He'd be damned if he was going to drive nine hours to Pelican Bay.

Of course, to take her down would necessitate sacrificing the boys to a grim fate as well. The homosexual in him wanted to save the boys, and he thought of how that urge was stronger than any consideration for his friend. Sacrificing his friend, after all, offered wealth. Sacrificing the boys really offered him nothing but sadness and three fewer pretty boys to masturbate to. Of course, such boys were legion. But greed being what it is … he wondered if they allow Chaturbate in federal prisons?

He felt a sudden surge of heroism. He could turn her in and make it look like she'd discouraged the boys from confessing. That it had all been an accident – it had been! – and this evil Lady Macbeth had brainwashed these naïve young men into not doing their duty. The old tramp, she clearly planned to bed them all and keep them as her private sex slaves. She wasn't just aiding and abetting arsonists, she was a child abuser, a pedophile, a sick pervert. Why, she'd probably picked them up on Chaturbate! There were always a few women there – or men who claimed to be to get the straight boys energized. Well, same difference. He could pin the Fred moniker squarely on her. How crafty of her, impersonating a man who resembled her dear selfless friend, Tom. Tom, who was wholly innocent, a knight in shining armor. He'd save the boys, and what's more, they could stay on in the house with him benefitting from his altruism, wise guidance and largesse. A regular role model.

It was a win-win: a house and three beautiful room-mates, one of which would likely eventually put out. And they could all joke about "Fred" endlessly. *Do you think she was really him?* And then a wave of dread invaded Tom's fantasy. He knew he'd probably eventually give himself away by mentioning something in passing that only Fred could have known. And then the whole truth would come out, the vindicated spinster back from prison, the boys looking even more innocent than ever then. They'd all live happily ever after – Cindy and her boy posse – while Tom was raped and killed in some federal penitentiary within weeks of his conviction.

Tom considered faking his death. A car accident? But the Mercury that Cindy thought was his was now in the hands of Israel Ramirez of Yucaipa. Well, perhaps Israel had stolen the vehicle after murdering Tom? Wasn't that possible? That would depend on Israel's record, of course. He'd seemed like a nice guy, but perhaps he'd had a DUI or wasn't legal – something that might make him panic and run, which would assume guilt, and the justice system, being what it is, would make quick work of the innocent man courtesy of some incompetent public defender flailing before a rightwing prosecutor intent on sealing the borders.

But how does one fake one's death? I guess by just disappearing? God knows, no one would miss him, except perhaps Cindy. Maybe she'd end up implicated in his disappearance – a person of interest. If he left a few bloody gloves and knives around her house with his blood and DNA on them, they wouldn't need to find a body. She'd be done for.

But none of that would get him the house. Well, maybe

that ship had sailed with the failed fire. Maybe he needed to cut his losses and make sure he never went anywhere near those boys. Disappearance was key right now. Fred was gone, dead, drowned in the Puddingstone Reservoir. But what if they dredged it for some reason, or because some other poor sap had been murdered? Someone might even claim having seen the Mercury at the reservoir just prior to Tom's disappearance. They would they dredge and find no Tom ... but they'd find the computer, and the case the investigators had been building against Cindy, which by then might have involved a sinister love triangle between Israel, Cindy and Ned. Israel's wife found out her husband was bopping not just another woman, but a young friend of hers, who in his despondency that Israel was losing interest in him, goes out to camp in the hills and either accidentally or on purpose (oh, how the young act out!) sets a terrible fire. Said case would surely collapse with the discovery of this mysterious cyberstalker, Fred. The holy computer would then eventually reveal all, as the mysterious Fred was discovered to be none other than this disappeared Tom who would now be on the FBI's most wanted list. He'd need to find a sanctuary with no extradition treaties with the U.S. Somewhere in Africa perhaps. Or better yet, Russia. That's where Snowden had found refuge. But why would Putin and the Russians protect a pervert? Well, Putin seemed a little like one of those closeted macho gays with a penchant for twinks, didn't he?

It was all too convoluted. Better to just do the right thing. Go to Cindy's, calm her and the boys down and go to the police. Let them go on and on about this "Fred" character. The fact was they were all adults, and they started the fire, not Fred. Fred would never be found. Let it go, pay your dues, boys, and in five years you'll be back on cam making forty dollars a week. Not sure how a probation officer would look at that source of income, but that was really irrelevant for now. First things first.

Tom took a deep breath, pulled into Cindy's driveway, and

knocked on the door. Darlene was there now and Tom could see she'd already stolen his thunder, having more or less convinced everyone that they had to go to the police, get a good lawyer and fight for a reduced sentence, using the sinister "Fred" as the Svengali behind it all. Ned was in tears, bawling like a baby, his ego having taken a drubbing, admitting to his mother he was masturbating for a living. Lawrence and Pablo sat stock still, stage left of the central drama unfolding between Cindy, her friend Darlene, and Darlene's onanist arsonist son gracelessly weathering the throes of becoming a man.

Tom nodded to the assembled group. "Shall we head down to City Hall?"

Ned began to wail.

"Please, honey, for godsakes, we'll get through this," Darlene pleaded, her face puffy and flushed, streaked with tears. Lawrence and Pablo stood up. Darlene gathered herself and did the same, and looked at Ned. Another wail burst out of him as she reached for his arm to get him to stand up. He resisted, burrowing back into the chair.

"Help me," Darlene begged, looking at Tom.

He stepped forward and reached out for Ned's other arm.

"No!" the boy cried out.

Tom gently pushed Darlene aside and grabbed Ned full force to drag him to his feet.

"Let go of me!" He kicked and screamed like a two-year-old in a tantrum. Tom caught a hard kick in the shin.

"For chrissakes, Ned, be a fucking man!" Silence. Ned stopped struggling suddenly, his eyes bugging out.

Tom turned pale and reeled, looking at Darlene.

"His name is Brandon," she muttered through her tears.

Tom blushed and slowly turned back to Ned, but before he could fully turn, Brandon/Ned's fist caught him in the temple and he went down. Pablo and Lawrence quickly joined the fray, kicking and punching him, and Tom, now curled up in a ball, felt a strange peace, thinking 'sex is violence, sex is violence.' His phallus rose to the occasion and he orgasmed just as Ned held him by the collar, screaming into his face: "You useless piece of shit pervert!"

IMP

For Alex Sanchez

I was living in the wheel well of a derelict Volvo off Dwight Way in Berkeley when I met the pooka. Living on cat kibble and nostalgia mostly.

I'd been there in the wheel well for several months, ever since Covington Hall had imploded into its final chaos. I'd stumbled disoriented into the old poet's yard, my eyes stinging from the tear gas – and I'd never planned to stay. But Covington had belied the order of things for humans and mythic creatures alike, so that imps like everyone else lost their bearings, drunk as we all were on the sweet heady nectar of excess.

I'd have never chosen it. But an imp doesn't choose. An imp is compelled to seek mischief – or mischief seeks him – and Covington was mischief's ground zero. The ultimate counterculture student co-op, Covington prided itself on creating a space for the freedom to do whatever you wanted to do. Rules were a necessary evil, and that included basic Newtonian physics. So hiding keys, misplacing textbooks, stealing panties – the basic day's work of an imp – seemed to have little effect on the residents. It was all in a day's wonder. Delighted at first, this irritated me in time, for an imp feeds on the human confusion he sows. I was growing malnour-ished and desperate. Which just made me more determined – not a particularly good thing for an imp. Imps don't have any other cause than mischief, and the more casual their re-lationship to their work the better. Keep them well-fed like a human and they'll generally not cause too much trouble. Starve them, and serious mischief, even mayhem, can ensue.

I'd met my match. For at Covington, an imp's mischief was more or less the norm. Covington had always pushed the envelope, even among co-ops – and now apparently even among mythic creatures – daring to manifest what was only dreamed of by others. While promoting the counter-culture's more idealistic urges – the walls were covered in psychedelic murals, graffiti and Marxist theory, and locks and even door hinges and nobs were discouraged – Covington also embraced its excesses. Sexual freedom and all manner of drugs were rife, and if you were a political refugee, they of-fered sanctuary (but no one took them up on it – who would, considering? El Salvador and Flushing, NY, hardly produce the same kind of freedom-seeker). Each year they hosted an annual insect banquet and the dining room was eventually converted into a punk rock club. They were the child of all that had come before and so one could not judge them so easily. They were in fact the plant that grew from the seeds sown in '68. The kudzu, frankly. Freedom, my friends. The Berkeley dream had grown ripe and heavy on the branch and it was about to fall and likely commence to rot on the ground.

Someone spiked the punch with acid? There was no one who was interested in finding out who'd done it, as there'd be dozens of suspects – and besides, it was just how things went at Covington. If you didn't want to risk spiked punch, don't drink the punch. Yes, everyone at Covington was an imp of sorts. And so, it drew me like a magnet. And then it reversed its polarity when it all came down and spat me back out as if to say: *I'm a bigger imp than you'll ever be.*

Yes, I'd met my match. But how Covington really defeated me, or should I say the City of Berkeley, or the United

Students Association of Cooperatives, or humankind itself –
for it felt like a grand conspiracy of that particular realm and
all its annoying bureaucracies – was by taking from me my
dear Buford.

Covington killed itself in killing him, and though I survived, my soul was full of heartbreak, guilt and regret in place
of mischief. And so I was no longer a true imp. I'd become
nothing more than a sorry little troll or gargoyle at that point.
Imp-otent. I didn't know what the future held for such a one.
I was only grateful for that defunct and motionless old Volvo,
that refuge.

It was a faded yellow '69 model 145 with a nice creak
to its springs when someone sat on its back bumper to tie
their shoes. Parked off to one side of the gravel drive against
a hedge, there was high grass around its wheels which kept
it warm and somewhat secretive, and the sleeping was good,
for the tires were firm but softened by age like a good mattress, and the treads gave a nice massage while I slept. I liked
the concavity of it too, as I preferred to sleep face down,
splayed out arms and legs in opposite directions, like a newt.

I'd avoided detection for the most part during the months
I lived there, but the old poet who lived in the house knew
about me, though I don't think his wife did. He'd just smile
and go about his business whenever he spied me – the kind
of smile you'd give to a harmless child, letting me know he'd
leave me be. I appreciated that. Most people don't like imps,
if they even know what they are. And when they don't, they
scream and freak out and send dogs after us or call animal
control – or worse yet, lie in wait or bring over an exorcist.
Any other neighbor would have likely assumed me some
Beelzebub birthed like a mutant phoenix from the final ho-
locaust of Covington, launched hunching and clawing about
for evil and mischief. They'd have fed me to dogs. But not the
poet.

He'd lived a block south of Covington Hall for two
decades. I'd seen him from time to time, always with that satisfied, half-amused smile on his lean and craggy face. I think

he found Covington an interesting show. He probably wondered how it would play out, or perhaps he knew and was thus never shocked or perturbed by the antics that issued forth from that place. Regardless, I figured nothing could surprise him now, which was why he tolerated me and seemed wholly unfazed by a little mythic beast who kept quietly to himself. Besides, I was cute for an imp, a breed generally not known for their attractiveness. But you see, I didn't have that demonic little wrinkled-up changeling look that most have. Granted my ears were pointed, but my face was smooth and unwrinkled. I looked more mousey with my pronounced nose and big brown eyes. I was anything but impishly repulsive. Which hadn't always served me well. Back in the forests of Rumania where I'd spent the previous four centuries, I'd been commandeered for courts and circuses more than once and it had never turned out well. Imps do not make good pets.

Ah, but imps have a lust – a need – for humans and their machinations, and I felt the draw of the poet. Perhaps the poet thought me a muse. I preferred that. For if I had to relate to those devious human beasts at all anymore, I wanted to keep at least an archetypal distance between us. Sometimes I wondered if the poet ever wrote about me directly, and I checked the local journals from time to time at Cody's Books late at night when I'd sneak in and root about. But I never found anything about an imp. He wrote about horses mostly. Which intrigued me. In such an urban setting – and I never saw him leave, his Volvo defunct after all – whatever acquaintance would he have with a horse? Well, perhaps a childhood out west or a matriculation in Kentucky. But I didn't dare to make his acquaintance. I'd had it with humans after Covington, and regardless of how my need for them played out, I'd simply lost the one thing an imp needs in order to relate – an overarching urge to confound those sad bedeviled creatures. But after Buford – never again. No, I was through with them. I even avoided their trash and fought instead with cats over rats and mice when I wasn't stealing their kibble.

But the life of an imp, when he's sworn off impishness,

is like the dubious junkyard life of any creature in this sad world when it's devoid of a symbiosis with humans (and yes, trickery has its uses, think about it). Because you can't milk an imp, you can't put it in a zoo (it always gets loose and the mischief it engenders is not worth the trouble of risking putting it in a cage), you can't eat one (less meat on it than a chicken's foot), and you certainly can't train it to do your chores or watch your things – and like I say, it makes for a disastrous pet. About the only humans – other than the enchanted (poets, crazy people and the oversensitive) – who ever showed any real interest in us nowadays were the medical establishment and the religious, of course – for obvious reasons I won't go into, but which usually led to abuse and early death.

No, an imp's relationship to humans was in causing them mischief, period, and when that desire waned, what point did an imp have? I was at my imp's end.

Well I'd had a good run. I'd lived a good 456 years (young for an imp), doing impish things, reveling in them, a healthy hearty imp out and about and exuberantly – gleefully even – fucking with people. Before Covington, back in the early 80s, when I'd still been consumed with the lusty drive for humans and the mischief they invited, I'd been lucky enough to find a kindly homeless man named Sam on Telegraph Avenue who'd taken me on as a sort of helper, confessor and advisor. He appreciated my mythic qualities and thought me wise, and in a way, I am – the wisdom born of always being on the run and suspected of malignancy. You inevitably learn a few things in 456 years, besides. Anyway, we helped and protected one another. Sam had been saddled with the catch-all diagnosis of schizophrenia when he was young and his life had been a terrifying labyrinth ever since, meandering as he had from hospitals to group homes, to doorways and ultimately hopeless attempts at reconciliation with his family. Over time, he'd learned to be meek and mild, for it kept him invisible and just out of reach of the authorities. But he had terrible bouts of paranoia and would get paralyzed with it now and again.

And when that happened, he might be arrested by the police who prowled by night watching for the weak whom they'd pounce on and feed to the Moloch of bureaucracy that would then only reluctantly shit its hapless victims back out after burdening them with fines and sentences, and all manner of requirements and contingencies involving shelters, counselors and the like.

I'd chanced upon Sam in People's Park, and as I'd always been drawn to the kindly, I invaded his knapsack and mismatched all his socks before running off. Later when he awoke, I watched the confusion furrow his brow as he handled and looked curiously at the orange sock tangled with the blue, the black with the white.

I hounded him for days after that, untying his boots and stealing his shoelaces, shaving off half his mustache and filling his ears with honey.

Finally, he raved and madness overtook him, and the bright blue flashing lights of the Berkeley PD came from three different directions and cornered him on College Avenue. How he screamed and thrashed, ending his struggle in enormous sobs that rose like bubbles from deep inside the sea of him, bursting with such pathos that even I was shocked by what I'd wrought.

It is, of course, an imp's first and foremost duty to cause a being mischief and to continue to do so until the poor soul is so worn down that compassion is born in the shriveled heart of the imp, after which said imp seeks only to serve that being – by causing mischief to others that ultimately will benefit his master.

And so I fell for him thus, and after he wended his way through the horrors of the bureaucratic intestines he knew and hated so well, I followed him back to People's Park where I revealed myself to him in impish fashion, taking care not to rouse his paranoia. At first, I disguised myself as a squirrel, whom he proceeded to eagerly feed. Once I'd gained his trust, I threw back my furry hood and introduced myself as "Balthazar, Silesian imp of the ancient world," bowing for effect and announcing, "You have captured my imp's heart and I am henceforth at your service, Mr. Samuel Frederick Aldridge."

He didn't miss a beat and held out his hand to shake mine. Like a good paranoiac, he was afraid of all the wrong things and had no terror of inexplicable creatures come to greet him in the night offering their services.

That isn't to say I couldn't still play with him, albeit in a more kindly manner, for imps are neither slavish nor demonic. I'm an imp and I have a predilection for mischief, plain and simple. Sometimes I made him do all sorts of odd and embarrassing things. "Sing, Sam, sing Gloria Gaynor!"

Once I took him to a fraternity party and enchanted him, putting all sorts of words in his mouth which he'd then mimic: How he'd been a member of that very fraternity, had gone into investment banking upon graduation and then had met a beautiful woman who soon enough broke his heart – "... and look at me now!" he cackled. The frat boys, rapt, would then offer him beers, fear furrowing their brows, for all they thought about was money and women, and he was a man who spoke of losing both – "... and it's easier to do than you think," he'd lean into them.

It got him free beer and snacks, and the ears of the young, which he longed for. Sam loved children. Every job program he'd taken part in, he'd opted for day care until the laws surrounded him like a vice and expelled him from that vocation once and for all, like some blackhead grown too big for its paltry pore.

Perhaps then it was my diminutiveness that captured Sam's affections. He was good to me, feeding me and keeping me warm and away from prying eyes, allowing me to sleep in his rucksack most of the day while he scavenged. Then, in the evening, it was my turn. I spent a lot of time over at the university late at night in professors' offices moving their things around, or misplacing keys and notes, and gathering change out of their drawers, or bringing Sam books to read. He liked Victor Hugo, Theodore Dreiser and Emile Zola. And if I didn't get too carried away with my antics among the offices of the faculty, I'd gather up some treats for us in the dorms and university cafeterias, so that between the two of us we ate pretty well as we traveled between the marina and Grizzly Peak, sometimes sleeping in doorways, or up along Fish Ranch Road on the pine duff in the forest where I liked it best. We never stayed anywhere more than one night – a good policy for the homeless – but we still had our favorite spots which we'd return to once a fortnight or so on our circuit as we wandered back and forth from the hills to the sea.

But all was not blissful camaraderie between us. Sam was angered by my preference for sweets. Of course, that's just the impish diet, and I was as stubborn about my preferences as he was about his. He wanted roast beef sandwiches and I'd bring him Ho-Hos and Snowballs. I wanted candy and bacon and he'd bring me Berkeley crap like sprouted wheat veggie sandwiches with cucumbers and sprouts, which I'd then stuff in his socks. So he dropkicked my Snowballs across Durant Avenue and flung my donuts to the wild cats and rats of People's Park like Frisbees. In retaliation, I spiked his sodas and coffee with Windex and Pine Sol.

One winter evening when it got terribly cold, I dispensed with mischief and crawled up a sewer into Dwinelle Hall, eventually snuggling up in a heating duct for a cozy sleep. I headed back to People's Park at dawn and found Sam scrunched up beside a tree under a heap of blankets. Ah, the guilt. It was a truly vicious Bay Area night, cold and damp, and it looked like a miserable day ahead as the light began to emerge somewhere far beyond the overcast skies that frowned above us. I thought briefly of ways I might smuggle such a huge creature as a human through a sewer and into a heating duct, but alas, it was just an imp's neurasthenic empathy surfacing. So I crawled into the rucksack among Sam's clothes, sleeping for nearly three more hours, before waking with a start of my own accord. I'd always waited for Sam's futzing about to wake me, but there'd been none that cold morning. My dear Sam, it turned out, had expired sometime during the night from the cold. I hoped he died peacefully;

he looked like he was only asleep.

There are no rites for the dead for a one such as Sam, and so I grabbed a few bread rolls, the paltry cash and an orange from the rucksack, gave Sam a kiss on the forehead and went off to hide until I could figure out what to do next.

And not half a block down the street was where I came upon dear Buford, my fateful, final human – or so I believed then. Oh, and did he ever look like an ideal mark for an imp's mischief. Sitting on the curb, wearing a battered top hat, a torn up t-shirt with felt pen script scrawled upon it ("Rubber Ducky You're the One – We've Been Waiting for"), and skinny jeans. He was a scraggly character, razor thin and with a dumb look on his face that belied his intelligence. He appeared hung over and at a loss. I hid in a mangled little bush and watched him for a spell. All he did was sit, brooding, letting out a sigh now and again and taking occasional deep breaths before tossing little pebbles into the street. Intrigued, I rolled the orange out across the sidewalk and watched it meander toward him, coming to rest gently against his thigh.

He didn't even startle, but calmly looked to see what had bumped him. Unsurprised, he picked up the orange and began to peel it. He pulled it apart slice by slice, popping each piece into his mouth. Then he took a big breath, stood up, and picking up the orange peels, proceeded to stroll slowly down Dwight Way. But he didn't get far as I'd hexed the orange, and in seconds he lost his balance and was sprawled on the sidewalk in the same manner a flying squirrel sprawls on air.

He slowly lifted himself, and that's when he noticed the orange peels tumbling along down the sidewalk like wind-driven leaves. Only there was no wind and even if there had been, it couldn't have budged an orange peel. He stood and watched, seemingly nonplussed by this odd phenomenon. Then he followed them. And I followed him. Surreptitiously, of course, having hitched a ride on a passing lark who flew to the top of Cody's Books where I could better view Buford and the orange peels from high above as he crossed empty, early morning Telegraph Avenue following the orange peels like the last baby duck in a long series of them. Buford followed them another block down to Dana Street, forcing me to ride my bird over to the belfry of the First Presbyterian Church on the corner. My mark skipped across the street, and reaching the opposite sidewalk, suddenly bolted after the peels, which then took flight, sending our man careening into a parking meter that caught him square in the chest, knocking the wind out of him and laying him out flat on the sidewalk.

That's when my pesky little regret began to emerge. *Poor boy*. But I was beaten to the punch by a pudgy gal in fishnets who came barreling out of the backside of the building that stood towering over Buford's folly – Covington Hall. She screeched and hollered back to the building once she'd reached him, "Quick, come help! Buford's back and he's in trouble."

Out staggered an enormous bouncer of a man in a Black Flag t-shirt and combat boots, along with two long-haired shirtless waifs, one with a Grateful Dead rose-garlanded skull tattooed on his chest and the other with what looked like an infected nipple ring piercing. The motley crew carried Buford inside and right away, I missed him. Because imps grow quickly attached to those they play their mischief on. It's almost like a romantic thing, and strong impish feelings begin to emerge. And so I kept thinking of Buford and the tricks I might play on him: scrawling Nazi slogans on his t-shirt for a stroll through Sather Gate; housing a fat white rabbit in that top hat of his; flinging him off the top of Bowles Hall into a hedge to break his fall. The worse the mischief an imp dreamed of playing on someone, the greater grew the crush.

It had been that way with Sam at first too. He was so innocent in so many ways, he often didn't notice when he was being watched and had no self-consciousness when rifling trash cans on busy street corners and talking about his views on Dwight Eisenhower and other past thoughts that seemed to haunt him from his childhood. I'd first played mischief with his voice, switching out names and circumstances – and confusing him considerably as he began to talk about Karen Carpenter's views on Jell-O molds.

He'd looked around to find the source of his own voice, and charmed, I enthused and soon had him tripping and sprawling and guffawing like a hobo clown in no time flat. By evening he was terrified by his own farts, which were substantial as I'd enchanted his bowels.

And so I dreamed of Buford that night and the next night too, and after that, I knew I'd need to haunt him, and so down the fire escape I went under cover of darkness at 5 a.m. and into the never-locked front door of Covington Hall, on the hunt for Buford. It didn't take long. An imp always senses his quarry, and though Covington had a population of nearly 200 or more legal and/or squats, I found Buford in no time at all on the third floor, buried under a purple velvet duvet, snoring like a small dog, for he was slight and even his lungs were a paltry bellows.

I capped his head with a jockstrap I'd found hanging on a chandelier in the hall and proceeded to braid his pubic hair – and since the place was rife with hair dye, I dyed his head yellow, his armpits green and the hairs of his scrotum magenta.

And my dear Buford, once again, seemed wholly nonplussed by my mischief. He looked at his beautified crotch and shrugged, muttering, "Hmm, that's kinda cool – when did I do that?"

You see, Buford was not easy to play mischief on, for he was so carefree it simply didn't register. I always hated to do it – what I did next – but you have to understand, an imp falls hard and is only satisfied with an equal response from his human quarry. I gotta eat like anyone else! So I doused the poor lad in scabies, which weren't hard to locate in the halls of Covington. Oh, and how the poor boy scratched.

In their wisdom, the student managers at Covington had designated a bug room for those infested with lice or scabies, as epidemics had often spread through the co-op like wildfire, and, once established in the building's human population, were difficult to eradicate. Of course, many inhabitants felt the residents should embrace such bugs, as they'd always be back and were organic naturally-occurring creatures with a right to the pursuit of their own bacchanals besides. Why not be like the Breughelian peasants of the Middle Ages – they looked so happy, so earthy, in those paintings – and simply tolerate the bugs?

Because all beings seek comfort, that's why. And there was such a thing as the Alameda County Public Health Department besides, which had already put Covington on notice. And class – one had to go to class, right?!

Buford recovered in time, and so I hammered him with shingles. I guided him through a patch of nettles in Strawberry Canyon once he'd recovered from that, and then I tossed him into a bank of poison oak up near Grizzly Peak. Being Buford, and being that poison oak, nettles and shingles were not bugs, he'd been unable to seek care in what had passed for a clinic of sorts in Covington's bug room, and so had turned to seducing female caretakers, but with no luck, considering his condition. Sadly, this time he was on his own, and that wasn't Buford's strong point. I sent 'help' of course, and Buford soon found himself shooting heroin when he could no longer stand the caustic itch of the poison oak. After a three-day binge, he discovered his blistered and bleeding forearm dripped pus from broken, purplish skin. Even those at the free clinic bugged out their eyes. Those who'd seen it all.

"Oh sweet pea, you must be from Covington," the black nurse said. They fixed him up and pumped him full of hydrocortisone, warning him to steer clear of narcotics.

Slinking home, tired and hungry, I couldn't resist pummeling him with a little food poisoning care of the falafel cart on Telegraph Avenue. He rained vomit for three days.

I should have known by then that Buford had an odd immunity to mischief. But it's not in an imp's nature to cease or desist. Like I say, it just made me more determined. Still, nothing seemed to faze Buford or, for that matter, his co-habitants at Covington Hall. People had hardly noticed the boy's ordeal, as many of his ailments were common enough among the co-op's denizens. The fact that he'd been assaulted with all of them seemingly at once, or one after another, appeared as just bad luck.

So what did I have to do – kill him?

I'm an imp, not a virus. I don't want to kill my prey, I want to connect to them and keep them alive for my entertainment – I'm like the pharmaceutical industry that way. The difference being that ultimately I want to serve them. But I couldn't seem to break Buford, and I didn't even think killing him would break him. Contrary to what anyone on planet Earth might think, Buford Henry O'Rourke was turning out to be as invincible as a superhero.

For, even amidst all these ordeals, he was still attending class. An environmental science major, Buford had actually been one of the more involved Covingtonians before I began to harass him. In fact, he'd been the recycling coordinator for the co-op, which was why I'd housed myself in the broom closet of the third floor, so I could keep an eye on him and confound him with various unpermitted and unrecyclable chemicals, pesticides and cleaners which I'd place all over the shelves to his perpetual consternation.

Buford was fairly diligent as the RC, though his repeated absences created certain inconveniences, and he might have lost his position even if I'd never entered the picture. And therein lay Buford's weakness – an opening for an imp if there ever was one. Why had it taken me so long to figure it out? Our initial encounter that early morning, wherein I found him on the curb tossing gravel amidst frequent sighs, could have no other source. Buford had girl problems. And the states of melancholy that followed the frequent breakups led him to neglect his duties and sent him away on junkets where no one could find him.

Cute in an elfish sort of way, and carefree as I've noted, Buford was irresistible until he wasn't. He was the kind of socially awkward cute boy girls were drawn to like a puppy. A passive spectator of sorts in his own romantic life, and repeatedly picked up and soon after dumped, Buford's heart was raw as fresh kill and forever baffled by the rollercoaster of it all. As such, he was wholly unnerved by the social life at the bars and dorms near campus and thus had naturally gravitated toward the punk shows of Gilman Street, where one night several months ago he'd met a lass from Covington named Amanda. Blazing on sensimilla proferred by some nerd he'd met on the smoking porch, he'd felt so elated he'd chanced the suggestion that they bed down, and to his surprise, locking her mouth on his, she readily agreed and dragged him home to Covington where'd he'd been ever since.

Buford became an actual legal resident in time, though the relationship with the woman who had snatched his virginity was increasingly tumultuous, the first of a series of tortuous entanglements with the opposite sex, mostly due to Buford's carefree nature, which was of course a brilliant mask for the fissile meltdown going on at his core. Monogamy wasn't the problem, as they lived at Covington, where it was hardly required or promoted, but Amanda complained that he didn't care about her feelings and had a bad habit of sleeping with her roommates. She was, as well, peeved at the way he disappeared for days on end without explanation. Then there was his seeming lack of ambition to make himself the punk star they both knew he would one day become. He had, in fact, pawned his guitar not a month after purchasing it, and when she confronted him with the absurdity of the next Sid Vicious pawning his guitar, he'd responded carelessly, "It's actually way more punk rock to pawn your guitar than to play it."

He was right, of course, and this exasperated her further. An answer for everything. Buford was, in the last analysis, unreachable, which had frustrated Amanda right up until she left for Portland. And now he was frustrating me in like fashion. Amanda, of course, was a mere mortal, but I was an imp. Confound the boy!

Perhaps I was wrong again. His was a heart that could be broken and mended repeatedly. Madness then was all I had left to employ, short of castrating or killing him. I enchanted his tongue, so he could only speak Urdu, a tongue not known for its pickup lines. He failed all his classes and was expelled. And still he seemed unperturbed, avoiding the opposite sex, buying a new guitar and spending hours reinterpreting Urdu folk ballads.

Then I had him dress as a woman: sundresses, miniskirts and the like, along with dizzyingly high heels. He kept breaking the heels, and in the process, sprained both ankles, cracked his femur and strained a tendon. Then, for three weeks, he only walked on his hands with his legs in the air. Yes, dresses and no underwear. This got him arrested for public indecency, of course. They threw him in a cell with the transsexuals, who later showed up at Covington, having learned from Buford how easy it was to squat there, and how accepting it was.

Covington swelled with her newfound friends, as she always did, and notched up the excess. Like a black hole, or American pop culture, there seemed nothing the superlative Berkeley co-op couldn't absorb. Drag shows and cabaret of unspeakable disgust and filth followed. And none of any of this alienated or led to any kind of ostracization for Buford. In fact, the cult of Buford grew. His girl problems suddenly morphed into a sort of Don Juan stage – Urdu pillowtalk and drag became all the rage – where he gravitated to the care-free girls, thus avoiding complications of the emotional variety, while spending his semen like a rich kid with bottomless credit. A super hero or a monster, I didn't know which, but I was subtly aware that I was in effect authoring whatever it/he was becoming, all the while destroying his future and getting nowhere in forging my own relationship with him. For he, like a very select few mortals, seemed to feed on chaos and confusion. Perhaps it explained his interest in environmentalism, sex and nature. Whatever the case, I could not break him. I was making him ever more resistant, like a bacterium that had overcome every antibiotic thrown its way.

I chose to blame it on Covington. I was an imp and I was just doing my job. Covington was a human invention and its hubris offended my otherworldly pride. It and it alone allowed Buford to grow so impenetrable. It was, in a sense, out-imping me. And it wasn't just Buford! I'd added four inches to the dong of every resident during one Thursday night bacchanal and watched the ensuing sexual exploits nearly rupture their hapless victims, and not a one of them flinched or thought it odd. In like fashion, I'd swelled the breasts of co-eds until the women's room resembled a melon patch. I planted ever stranger ideas in the willing perverted minds of the Covingtonistas: candied rats, cockroach marmalade, turd art, talking pears and dancing ginseng root. All of which then came to pass, manifesting overnight like squash in a garden, and not one curious or disturbed look of inquiry into what the hell was going on. I proceeded to provide thunder and lightning for the punk shows, eight-hour orgasms for the orgies, and food of such delectability the dining hall filled with guttural moans of pleasure. They took it all in stride as the "natural" order of things – not even a reflection or question posed, let alone protests of being disturbed by any of it. Such complacency in the face of mischief supreme would cost Covington dearly in the end.

But Covington had always dared to manifest what was only dreamed of by others. I was playing right into its impish hands. What a fool I'd been. And yet I could not extricate myself.

I did love my dear Buford as much as ever, though still in the crush way, not in the way I needed, which required his vulnerability – his surrender for my own. One morning, in a panic, I decided to try to wrest him free of that cursed co-op that embraced whatever mischief I threw at it. It might prove my only chance to reach him. And so I steered him into joining the Hare Krishnas, hoping he'd renounce his former life at Covington once and for all, but his refusal to forego meat sunk that prospect and he was right back at Covington within a fortnight, sprawled out in ecstatic excess on some drug while the maidens attended his every pleasure. And he kept the bald pate and Krishna tail for several more months, which just added to his charms.

And then I chanced upon the sorority girl. That would do it. Blonde and sweatered, studying business administration, the antithesis to Covington and the final assault on his wounded yet impenetrable heart.

He fell for her in short order while sipping a latte at the student union. The Covingtonistas were shocked, to say the least. The unshockable had finally met something that truly horrified them: their dear Buford, the image of all that was holy in their iconoclasm, the Bacchus of Berkeley, gone Junior League. Say it ain't so! He moved out of his own accord, grew out his hair and began to sport a frat-boy haircut, bought Izod shirts and khakis – how I grinned like the Cheshire Cat – and begged the horrified girl for a date. But she flatly refused. Buford rushed the fraternities, trying whatever strategy was available to him to land a date with the blonde beauty of Kappa Kappa Gamma. He was only able to get into a mid-range frat house, however, which didn't of course impress the princess who only dated Betas and Zetes, and finally, beside himself with frustration, Buford drank too much beer with the brothers one night, and chancing upon her in the street, he Romeo-ed her to the best of his ability, falling to one knee, at which she laughed and dumped her beer in his face, running off with her girlfriends. "Oh my God, that was so mean!" the chorus of co-eds echoed as they disappeared around a corner. But this Juliet only giggled with self-satisfaction, knowing she could have the pick of tomorrow's stockbrokers and didn't need some second-string skinny frat boy (Theta Chi? Hello!) from Ohio (where was that anyway?) embarrassing her on the street.

That did it. My heart swelled Grinch-like, and now it was clearly and finally my turn. I hopped off the eave of the sorority house, and alighting on the sidewalk, onto one knee I went, offering my services: "I am Balthazar. You have captured my imp's heart and I am henceforth at your service,

Mr. Buford Henry O'Rourke."

He grimaced. He launched his beer at my face. "Covington trash!" he barked, storming off as I sat back on my haunches near weeping. This had never happened to me or to any imp I'd ever met, and I knew not what to do. I dared not follow him, for my love for him was now complete and I was terrified of what might manifest if it were denied.

Beside myself with despair, I morosely slunk back to Covington dragging my knuckles on the pavement, only to be welcomed by the usual shenanigans. A girl was being mounted on the dining room table for their annual Roman Supper, the attendant diners flinging mashed potatoes, capers and asparagus crowns at her rotund buttocks and voluminous dugs, cheering and guffawing, some of them going so far as to climb up on their chairs, where they dropped their drawers and contributed their own young seed to the spectacle. It was anarchy incarnate, impishness writ large – in a word, mayhem. I cursed that Kali bitch Covington's hubris and set loose several electrical fires, which caused the alarms to ring, the fire trucks to arrive and the party to be ruined.

But no one blamed Covington, and of course no one blamed me in the days that followed. The press and the community continued to blame the students and the negligent university, reporting on the state of student housing that would have such sub-code wiring, the drugs that had been found, the sex witnessed. But what would you expect? The world knew nothing of imps or what could be conjured from misunderstood ideas (albeit ideal and beautiful) set loose upon an ignorant, imperfect, unprepared – and yes, brutal and beastly – world. Think of the guillotine and the beauty of a mushroom cloud. Right up against the sublime we were. I turned my back too. Let it burn, I scowled, dragging myself up the stairs to my broom closet. Yet I did feel a momentary remorse for boldly abandoning the determined and admirable young activists – Buford had been among them once – who kept the place running, displaying in the process some of the best human qualities and ideals I'd witnessed in my 456 years. But they had no sense of folly, these Americans. I'd only arrived from Eastern Europe in that Ukrainian suitcase when the pogrom against creatures such as I had ensued after Chernobyl. Hubris was hubris, and a meltdown was a meltdown, plain and simple, and there would be consequences.

Yes, the jig was up, and the Co-op association soon abandoned them while the Berkeley police began to come around more and more, rabid for drugs during that time in the '80s when the nation lurched downright Mexican in its narcotic pandemonium.

Still, Covington persisted. Despite my best efforts and its own insanity. It had, in fact, managed to enchant enough attorneys and activists to keep itself alive. Which only made me more determined to bring it down utterly, engaged now in a mythic struggle against a human institution that dared to humiliate a being such as I, from the other side, where the true power resided (we too have our pride after all). Ah yes, what strange bedfellows politics make – I was suddenly on the side of the Berkeley P.D. and the United Student Co-op Association, for God's sake.

This was Berkeley and this ballsy Covington had found a fertile ground among those who had called human civilization's bluff. They'd have to be dragged away, she had charmed her children so. Covington would be no Faust. Leave that for the academic wankers. No deals. Paradise Lost and Paradise Regained. Covington was Lucifer's second coming, the rise after the long-ago fall. Covington had grown archetypal, become a manifestation of the underworld risen like a festering boil on the flesh of the world. The Karmic chickens of 1969 come home to roost. All they needed was a Robespierre to roll in a guillotine. Well, the city did them that service – or was it me? Good old Communist Berkeley, in true communist style, killed the messenger. The battle was now on. Police raids and shutdowns grew frequent, legal battles over squatters' rights and the accountability of the USCA filled the university's halls, insurance and public health hassles threatened a final shutdown of the facility, while the sensationalist press continued to focus on the drugs and sex alone – oh, and myths, of course. The myth of Berkeley. One day a few hundred years hence, children will read the American press like kids read *Bulfinch's Mythology* today. A certain kind of truth, I'll leave it at that. I'm an imp after all – I'd much prefer to tell lies.

In the end it was the press's hyperbolic rumors born of Covington's libertinism that roused the rabid forces of order more than the truth ever could – and how much of it I've told you you'll never know, for I was accursed by unrequited love, a conjurer of illusion if there ever was one. But as for Buford – there was no sign of Buford. I kept a wary eye, for fear of what might transpire if I were to come across him.

There were rumors about him, of course. Gilman Street rumors about "Urdu," the latest punk sensation who ate live insects on stage and did Hare Krishna covers at high decibel.

The sheer weight of story, my friends. That's the deadweight in the end. Covington was no different, for Covington had created of itself an antiheroic character, an ego of immense appetite, and it was now facing the tragic consequences of its fatal flaw. *Et tu, Brute?* You're damn right!

They were kids, in the last analysis – nearly two hundred of them – living in an extreme and bacchanalian paradise run amok. Even among the other students at the university, it had a certain mystique of almost ominous excess. "I went to a party at Covington," you might hear a student say. "Really?" would be the response as the one spoken to offered a quick double take, perusing his companion for previously unimagined scars or some subtle mark of the Beast.

Ultimately, the best of them – those who had attempted to manage their beloved Covington – were worn down by the raging battle, the rumors – the imp! – and their own frustrations, or were finally drowned by the drugs, violence, hysteria and anger when the boil finally burst, Shivic in its mystery and intensity, comatose bodies scattered upon the beer-soaked, needle-strewn floor.

The Dead Kennedys indeed.

It happened on a Tuesday. A punk show, a party, lots of outsiders, many carrying drugs. The police had planned their raid for weeks and lay in wait. They'd have maximum justification and lots to back it up. The students streamed in after their classes, their friends arrived in gaggles of three or four, pot smoke wafted out the windows with their tattered drapes. Frat boys came down from up the hill, hip grad students who knew some of the residents from discussion and section. And then there he was – I'll be damned – Buford himself, a bedraggled mess, come home from a long bender or perhaps a tour, the frat clothes long gone, his legs graced by army fatigues, and written in Sharpie across his white t-shirt: *Kill the Imp*.

My heart pounded and I nearly lost my breath. Everyone else laughed and hugged him, but he never smiled at anyone the whole night. Oh, how my crush for him pained my imp's heart. I shadowed him all evening, tripped him, spiked his punch with brake fluid, made him puke, followed him up to the roof where I presented myself to him once again, this time boldly: "You have captured my imp's heart, mortal, and I am henceforth at your service, Mr. Buford Henry O'Rourke – whether you fucking like it or not."

He grimaced, and then in a flash, reached for an old broom to swing at me. I made quick work of that broom, placing it between his legs while he circled the roof midair like a Halloween witch. Suddenly, he turned and aimed himself straight at me, his eyes blazing with hatred. Startled, I backhanded him with my left claw, propelling him backward off the roof. Right as the police were pouring in the gate, tossing the first canisters of tear gas, he flopped dead on the concrete before them. So much for my long ago fantasy of flinging him off Bowles Hall into a hedge. I peered over the roof's edge, horrified at my deed, shocked at how I'd been robbed of my usual composure and control of my emotions.

My hatred for Covington, like a jealous lover's, had killed the very thing I loved. Now my anger, guilt and self-loathing knew no quarter and found its only expression in rage: *Covington dies tonight and all those who love her shall sink with her*. A fitting end for those who had trusted the experiment, embraced chaos and waited to see what might come next out of their hallucinogenic visions, their all-night discussions, the robust group fuck sessions, the deafening punk rock and the scattered detritus of a civilization that they all, for the most part, concurred was on the verge of utter collapse. Why, they even allowed imps – and God knows what else – to lodge among them, the human fools.

Well, here's to your open-mindedness, your sincerity, here's to your fertile ground, humans – and I rolled my eyeballs and sparked every wire in the building until it was a howling, smoking, orange-pink cloud of my fury. Reaching for the sky. Reach, dear Lucifer, you pathetic fallen angel – even your paltry flames slither close to the ground.

I shimmied down a drainpipe and made my escape.

Oh no, I did not sleep well that night. Imps are amoral beings by nature, but they get infected by the souls of those they serve and they never really shake the human thing that grows in them. I dreamed of Sam that night, and the Rumanian clowns and princes of long ago too. And I dreamed of Buford in his top hat. I who'd always been drawn to the kind.

Weeks later, I'd go across the street on those sleepless nights when I was haunted by human conscience. Not even my own. But a dog's bark doesn't have to be from your own dog to stop you from sleeping and wondering: *what does the damn thing want?*

And there before me gaped the dark cavernous black empty windows of the gutted Covington, its cyclone fence, the ghosts of a hundred beautiful young punks and idealists thrown as they'd been upon the sacrificial fire.

They hadn't counted on an imp.

And I hadn't counted on all this coming down just weeks before Halloween, heady times for mythic ones such as I. For on that day the veil between the living and the dead (between the real and the mythic) grows thinnest, and one can as soon dismiss the dead as set an imp loose in a stimulus package and expect full employment.

On the night of All Souls itself, having gleaned a few slabs of neglected pizza off a table at La Val's, I returned late to the Volvo and discovered one of its back doors open. Curious, and assuming a homeless person had likely jimmied the lock and climbed in, I tiptoed forward, hopped up on the running board and peered in across the backseat. No one was snuggled up in an old blanket as would be the norm in such a circumstance. Instead, there was a beautiful wooden box in the middle of the vinyl seat, carved and painted with what appeared to be Celtic designs. Atop the box was one of the poet's many volumes, and so I assumed he'd perhaps resuscitated the Volvo and was planning to take a trip. A reading perhaps at some distant university. Why, he'd likely appear any minute with a suitcase and umbrella. But why the box? What could be in it that he needed? Who could say? I shrugged, losing interest. After all, poets were collectors of such things as feathers, seeds and stones, and I had to assume it was likely full of such things and part of his performance. Mythic accessories, if you will.

Indeed. For it was then that my eyes grew accustomed to the dark and I noticed what was on the cover of the book: a black and white photo displaying the twisted wreckage of Buford's dead body, sprawled on its back, the t-shirt showing, covered in blood, the words in black felt-marker still legible: *Kill the Imp.*

The box lurched then, knocking the book to the floor, and my eyes bugged out, momentarily frightened that what was in it was set on my destruction. But I remembered what happened last time I'd allowed fear to overcome me, and so regained my composure. Curiosity was my strength – what little remained.

What's he got in that box anyway, I wondered – a white rat, a gerbil? Or perhaps one of Covington's cockroaches grown huge from inhaling tear gas for too many months? I huffed, but I was also saddened and disturbed at seeing

Buford's image again – and not only that, but angered by the poet's exploiting it. Disgusted, my curiosity waned and I jumped down from the runner then and reached to shut the door, intent on getting some sleep – and as for the poet and his books and boxes – let him drive away on his book tour and crush me in the process. For I've no reason to go on. Bitter in my anger, I grabbed the door to slam it. That's when I heard the belch. No gerbil's belch that. It was deep, like a beer-swilling frat boy's, and its source was the box, whose lid just then cracked open a notch to release a putrid miasma of orange and yellow gunk, smelling distinctly of vomit.

I let go of the door then and inhaled deeply of the strange scent, and it was otherworldly, no mistaking it. I was an imp still, and my curiosity re-aroused, I stood my ground. I may have been out-imped by a building but I would not be out-imped by a magic box, and to avoid such an eventuality, I sought the upper hand by going on the offensive, leaping in one motion onto the seat, and with my little claws yanking up the lid of the box, releasing a near explosion of vomit, which soaked me and ran across the seat. But I was not to be discouraged, and wiping away the putrid chunks, I drove my fist into the broiling mass, intent on its source. A stone, just as I'd suspected. A stone that pulsed and squirmed in my hand and made me smile. A mythic stone that likely housed a being. I tossed it into the yard, and as I suspected, there was a flash and a crack, and from out of the ensuing smoke appeared a creature.

It was a shining black horse with downturned eyes, and it made a friendly neigh. Its beauty was astounding, breathtaking, and so irresistible that my heart swelled with impishness reborn and I longed to yank its tail, tickle its hooves or feed it a wax apple. If he were here to kill me, well, bring it on. I immediately marched over, and placing my hands upon my little hips, I announced: "You have captured my imp's heart, creature. Who are you? I am Balthazar and I am henceforth at your service. Do what thou wilt."

Coy, it whispered, "Pooka," and turned to present its

backside. I hopped aboard bareback and kicked with all the might my little legs could muster. The horse rode with fury through the yard next door, over a fence and then veering down a gravel drive, it galloped thunderously up Dwight Way past Telegraph Avenue and the dorms, through frat-house row and up past the stadium into the hills, all the way up to Fish Ranch Road and Sam's and my favorite clearing with the pine duff, where it finally ceased its running, secure now in the wood, steam streaming out from its nostrils in the misty night air. It whinnied and then grew calm, dropped its head and began to nibble the grass. Sensing we were out of danger, I hopped down and looked about – a faerie mound was there before me, sure thing: mushrooms and moss all growing circular on a little hummock of dirt. When I turned, the pooka grew blurry and shapeshifted into a sort of man, but one with hooves still and hairy haunches, and pointed, elfin ears. A beautiful perfectly built mangoat – a satyr.

"Imp, I am a pooka, and I am here to process you."

"Process me? Whatever can you mean?"

"Did you not see the book of poetry that rested upon the box?"

"But for a moment – your vomit sent it to the floor before I could have a look. What about it?"

"You and I share something, imp."

"Do we?"

"Indeed we do, and only bards can bring creatures like us together. You see, he thought us each a muse, my dear imp. He's held me hostage for fifty years for just that reason. A poem he wrote about me formed the foundation of his career and he locked me in that box believing me his muse. He wrote about nothing but horses from then on."

"So that's why he was obsessed with horses. But why didn't you try to escape?"

"It was a nice box. Besides, I'm not like you. I don't breed mischief. I like to bless. And the blessing I wanted for him was to find the inspiration he needed to write poems. He'd suffered a spell of terrible writer's block when I'd encountered him. And no wonder that, for he was serving in the military then, it was 1942, and he'd been stationed as a guard at Topaz Internment Camp in Utah, where they'd sequestered nearly ten thousand Japanese citizens. At first he'd written haiku, but he felt it too exploitive, considering the situation. And so, on his days off, he'd not write at all, but simply wander the canyons in that part of Utah. There were wild horses there and it became his obsession to spot them. They were secretive creatures, startling at any approach by a human, wholly untamed. What better place for me to dwell but among them? Though I only came out at night and only chanced upon him as he'd gotten lost up Dead Man's Canyon, which forked back up into the mountains like a great lung in the desert, until he'd completely lost his bearings. I offered him my back and carried him all the way down to the camp where I left him. I assumed that was the end of it, but he came looking for me again, for that night I'd dropped him off he'd filled with the ambrosial spirit of art and had produced a beautiful poem about a horse he'd discovered while lost in the desert. He didn't believe in himself basically and thought he needed me as a muse to continue to write. I pitied him, I did, and so I vanished before his eyes in a puff of smoke and morphed into a glowing crystal stone, which he then picked up and took back with him and has kept by his side all these nearly fifty years."

"Nice story, pooka – I could tell a few like it – but what's this got to do with me?"

"Because you inspired him too! As you can see, he wrote a whole book about you and has published it. At first he thought you his new muse, and so he wanted you to stay and hoped you too would turn into a stone offering. And then all those terrible things happened with Covington and he sensed that what had happened to Covington had also happened to you, and it was pity more than greed that filled his heart. He saw that you felt like he had felt once long ago in the Utah desert. But instead of writer's block, he could see you were in despair and likely had mischief block, just as fatal. And what had saved him? Well, he thought I had, and as he was old and established, why hang on to me any longer? So he resolved to give me to you."

"And if I don't want you?"

"You're hellbound, imp, for killing Buford. It is only I, by the gift of the poet, who stands between you and your being dissolved in the sacred fire. And so you must make your choice: annihilation or atonement?"

And so Buford wasn't my last mark after all. The poet was.

I'd wandered back down the hill after the pooka'd morphed into a crow and flown away. I'd proceeded to sneak right into the poet's house, replacing his dentures with those of a vampire so that all that day he'd walked about with fangs, none the wiser.

He was over seventy, so I couldn't knock him about, but oh, how the poor man suffered with losing things, until he'd been reduced to hypochondria and found himself in a doctor's waiting room, sure that he'd be diagnosed with Alzheimer's and be done for.

I presented myself to him. "You have captured my imp's heart, Thomas Hart Van Cleve. I am Balthazar and I am henceforth at your service."

The poet wept at seeing me, and reached down to me. "Can you take away this terrible illness?"

"I am the illness," I said, and realized with a terrible shock that it was in fact true.

And so I ravaged my poor poet as I'd longed to ravage Buford. I was a changed imp though, saddled with a conscience, for once an imp has killed and agreed to atone, I soon learned, the mischief that is his only skill suddenly pains him instead of delighting him. And no way to stop it, so that even when my heart filled and I longed to do the poet a kindness, it always came out bad. I was hexed, jinxed, condemned.

I'd made a choice, after all. On the roof of Covington, I'd made it. I'd killed the thing I loved.

How many years I must suffer I do not know. I live doubly horrified, not only at my own suffering but at that of the person I love with all my imp's heart. And I know I am not the first to realize hell is right here in this world. But all is not lost. For I am an imp still, and as such, I have figured a way to make mischief with darkness. Hell is my primary relationship, after all, and so I've found a way to play mischief on it and turn its darkness into light. Which is a blessing. And I, like the pooka, bless the dear poet, who has forgotten he's a poet. Which is why I bring him pen and paper now and whisper in his ear the story of the pooka, at which he re-writes his seminal poem in a great fury and is overjoyed at the experience, as he was all those years ago. The greatest moment of his life daily relived because he's forgotten everything and so he can experience it anew, completely fresh each day.

And it is I who gift him with this blessed, blessed lie. A dear lie. Supreme, kind mischief. My penance and both of our salvations. I cross myself and offer it up for the repose of the soul of my dearly beloved, Buford Henry O'Rourke.

Junkyard

My radiator blew, and I called my mechanic ex-lover Ron in Pacoima for advice on how to dodge my autoshop's five hundred dollar bullet. I'd expected him to have some, to me, unimaginable idea – maybe some kind of quick-fix way to plug the hole or a cheap radiator shop he was privy to. Instead, he said: "No way around it, you need a new radiator. We'll go get one at the junkyard and do it ourselves."

"You sure you got the time?" I hesitated.

"What else am I gonna do?" he drolly replied, hinting at the idleness brought on by his recent relationship woes with his current alcoholic boyfriend Jim, whom he just couldn't seem to let go of. I didn't want to get into any of that, nor give him ideas about how best to spend his time – I could think of lots of things better than scrounging around a junkyard. That was before I'd been to U-Pick, of course.

Down among the cement plants and other wrecking yards, U-Pick loomed, identifiable by its totemic trucks, tanks and jeeps poised high above its vast lot on large metal poles, giving it the air of a medieval fortress boasting severed heads from a recent battle.

A broken water main at the intersection in front of the junkyard made things more ominous still. We forded and entered, arriving late – just in time for the guy on the loudspeaker to announce (first in English, then in Spanish): "The jard es closing in tain minits!"

We paid our two bucks anyway and dodged around looking for the Ford Tauruses. Lined up on blocks (which in this case were two wheels piled atop one another) were dozens, row after row of them. We found a clean one that didn't look like it had been in a front-end collision and set to work, Ron opening his briefcase of ratchet wrenches like a safecracker, working fast and efficiently. But ten minutes wasn't enough time, and these guys don't give you a grace period. Ron quipped on the way out as we passed the security guard: "I haven't seen a security guard with an actual gun in a long time."

In the car I asked him: "Jim home?"

"Yeah. Your place?"

We returned next morning at 8 a.m, worried someone might lift our already half-butchered radiator if we dallied. This was definitely a hunting ground. We joined the eager line of mostly Latino men paying their two bucks to get inside and make meat.

Under overcast skies threatening rain – or something worse at the hands of one of those totems – we got our radiator and carried it like a carcass back to Ron's truck. They stamp your hands at the junkyard, just like at a nightclub, so we decided to go back in and just look around. The place was like a massive attic and it had piqued our curiosity. We wandered about, peering in the windows of other trashed cars and opening doors to investigate further. We went through all the Chevys, then the Fords and Lincolns, Cutlasses, Cadillacs, Chryslers – even some decaying limos. Most were full of valueless trash – fast food wrappers, cigarette butts, soda cans, a fifth of Popov vodka. We found spare change, toy soldiers, tampons, several cheese puffs (one of the more indestructible foods), condom wrappers, hypodermic needles, a crucifix, a small wooden skull. In glove compartments, we found insurance policies, parking tickets, credit card bills, pink slips and insurance envelopes with Social Security numbers, addresses and phone numbers (a jackpot for anybody considering identity theft). In backseats: a girl's phone number complete with plump, scripted heart; photographs of children and teenagers, grandmas; *elotes* stripped bare. So many of these cars got here via traffic accidents that their owners likely had no time to go through them before they were carted away. Perhaps their owners hadn't even survived. But we never saw blood.

The sun came through the clouds around then, and the junkyard spread out before us like some kind of twisted scrap Eden, a strange and alluring paradise. We smiled at each other and concurred this was kind of interesting. We began to move faster. Was it the photos, the spare change, the girl's phone number? I wondered if they'd ever had a date; if he'd had a collision an hour after he'd met her. Perhaps after his wreck in the Dodge, they'd gone out in her Cutlass where we found the condom. If he'd then purchased the Granada where we found the hypodermic, he was either diabetic or slipping into addiction, which couldn't be promising for the relationship. We junked one story for another as we moved from wrecked flower to wrecked flower, like hungry bees. We dreamed of contraband, stacks of twenties secreted in door panels, a brilliant unpublished novel, a kilo of weed. We were no longer hunters but gatherers. We ducked and scurried about like mice, while the scavenging hunters paced around us slowly and ominously, wrenches and crowbars for teeth and claws, gnawing and tearing at metallic flesh. A forklift lumbered by like an old dinosaur, an AMC Pacer in its jaws, Norteno music at top volume blaring from its orifices. It rounded the corner with a diesel rumble and a loud squeak, vanishing slowly into the metal jungle that, like a rainforest, seemed to endlessly spread in all directions, its horizon broken only by those odd primal totems.

I came upon a flooded trunk, a plastic-wrapped Hostess cake bobbing among the toxic liquids, protected by the same thing that threatened it, both being petroleum products. I could have reached down and retrieved it and had it for lunch. The Victorian curlicue white line of frosting across the chocolate icing had retained its delicate design, persisting like religion in a godless world, or perhaps us humanoids in a world headed toward climactic Armageddon, no thanks to the thousands of derelict autos and their gasoline engines that surrounded us.

Greedy for yet another find, I foolishly navigated between two listing Pontiac Grand Ams, and one of their doors came off the hinges and slammed into my leg, tearing my jeans down the shin and ripping into my flesh. Ouch. Just a deep scratch, fortunately, but an initiation of sorts too. I'd bled.

Ron tended my wound. He'd do just about anything for me. I mussed his hair as he wiped away the blood. His shy smile.

Eventually we arrived at the vans, definitely the trippiest part of the whole menagerie. People had clearly lived in these. There were refrigerators and beds and shelves, catsup and Lea and Perrins steak sauce, pepper and salt shakers, plates. A waterlogged Bible clung crookedly to a back bumper. Inside we found another volume titled *The History of the World*. There was a jar of peanut butter and a few slices of Wonder bread.

On one van, its owner had painted a little scene of a Viking walking ashore from out of the surf, a buxom blonde consort by his side, all scantily-clad curves and pin-up girl good cheer in her silly Viking girl helmet. There was an Indian sitting Indian-style (imagine that), grinning, holding his pipe. *Who was here first?* was written in big cursive black letters, and under it: *The answer: God!*

So much for junkyard politics. Regardless of who was here first, auto wreckers will likely be here last. And if cars are a kind of home – especially in L.A. – then this is our Pompeii. A record, a story. Something we love will be here one day, some part of us with it, no doubt: an old photo, someone's phone number, an attempt at birth control or safe sex, our identity, a cupcake.

Outside the gates (like an ancient city, hawkers sold

clothes, tools and auto parts in an impromptu flea market amid the hustle and bustle of parking cars and Spanish shouts), I found a rack full of old shirts from air conditioning companies, Ford dealerships, auto body shops. Each of them had a name: *Greg, Jesus, Angel, Dan, Walter.* I bought the 'Greg' and 'Angel' in honor of lost boyfriends, the wreckage of my own life.

Ron laughed at me. "I got a *Ron* at home if you want that."

"Not yet, man," I joked. "Not yet."

Lolito

I.

Yeah, he'd look good in one sock, and likely monosyllabic on the dotted line like most boys his age. But there was nothing as creepy as marrying his mother or living in a boardinghouse with him. Well, not really. But if the Internet is the grandest Chelsea Hotel there ever was, a tower of Babel a billion stories high, full of secret rooms and stairwells, then I was no different really.

Lo. He didn't appear there at the Chelsea at first. He came old-style through print media, which made him all the more sacred. He got reduced to 1s and 0s like the rest of us by necessity, but before he did, he was in the good old newspaper. On a lark. Lo. And out came the scissors, up vertically across the newspaper type like a starved termite, a sharp turn left, another, then one more, and finally the straight ahead final sprint and I had him square for the bulletin board, where he joined the other objects of my affection: Sid Vicious, Kurt Cobain, Marky Mark.

We collected beautiful junk, Chandra and I, and Lolito was no different. He wouldn't like to be referred to that way, I'm sure, but we were older, we knew the immensity of beauty, the shocking commonness of it. Which didn't make it cheap or valueless. No, just the opposite, the blessed paradox, the irony that is the only god. If one tree is beautiful, it is no less so in the enormity of a forest. It is, in fact, enhanced by the beauty of its surroundings, the abundance that exponentially multiplies its grandeur toward infinity to full extravagance – like a belly laugh or a lust insatiable.

Fire indeed. Sweet smiling Lo with the big Chiclet teeth, the bright whites of his eyes amid all that beautiful brown skin, looking up at me from newsprint as he whittles two sticks in his Eagle Scout outfit, shorts and all.

We called him our son in time, smiling down upon us from up there on the bulletin board, appearing in print for all the world to see as a recipient of some sort of commendation in the nearby town of Granada Hills – he'd saved a cat or a Little Leaguer, or scored a 2400 on the SAT, or won a spelling bee – something responsible and good-role-modelesque. No matter what it was, it was that face and smile – life like a huge blossom, seventeen and unstoppable.

My sin. I hoped his birthday was real soon.

Chandra and I had no children of our own – me for obvious reasons, she for want of a worthy man to raise one with. We'd fallen together in the way of frustrated independent-minded women and middle-aged queers who'd grown tired of the parade/charade. A kind of marriage. And so, our dear Lolito was a kind of kid we had together. Slow afternoons, I'd troll the web for mentions of his achievements: soccer goals, recitals, certificates.

In our three-bedroom ranch house in La Crescenta, packed to the nines with crap. We were eBay people; we thought ourselves purveyors of antiques. But we were rag pickers really, unemployable types. We just had a good eye: Chandra because she came from a long line of merchants; myself, because I'd spent twenty years cultivating an appreciation for the beauty of men and the essential blemish that made the masterpiece.

Oh yes, indeed, Lo had precursors. Legions of them. Bright-eyed Mexican Indian boys with ragged appendectomy scars by the bushel, sullen JC students with acne and embarrassing tattoos in spades, and all manner of damaged goods and slightly off-kilter beauties from the near and far reaches of the earth.

Lo had his blemish too. He was cockeyed. Just slightly, but I studied him close, though his features were so eclipsed by the grand and overarching beauty of his smile, it was hard really to notice the finer points. But there it was, the left slightly lower than the right.

And so it is. "Our son is the most beautiful son on the block," I'd blurt apropos of nothing, and Chandra'd humor me as she bid on a teapot or purchased a ring she'd resell tomorrow for double the price, her fingers skittering over the keyboard, making the rent.

I made the mistake of befriending him digitally. I even tried to explain it all when his father got involved along with other authorities. Lo. Lo and behold, a handsome stranger. In one gym sock – and later a jockstrap to go with it. I never asked for that picture, he sent it off on his own volition. He referred to me as MILF, but I went by Jenny. I never lied about my age.

Jenny who infiltrated his Facebook page through a Granada Hills classmate named Tiffany who had involved herself in Mary Kay and Avon and the like. She had a billion friends and was a clear security breach on the road toward Lo, for as 'confidential' and private as Facebook allows you to be, it just plain broadcasts your friends, which is really no different than fighting Al Qaeda by keeping an Alsatian in your backyard, while the airports dispense with x-ray machines, the TSA, the whole nine yards. I didn't even have to remove my shoes.

Tiffany and her 6000 friends. Sure, I'd had to buy some eyeliner, some foundation, and I flattered the girl with thanks and good wishes before I scrolled down and sent my invite to Dev Singh who then sported but one photo of that bent-up beaming handsome dork of a face no doubt from his high school yearbook photo. Even if he were the paranoid type and went and asked Tiffany about me, I'd prepared the ground. Tiffany'd share my normalcy: "A really nice lady, single mother, and beautiful – look at her pics. I think she has a son your age."

He accepted. And the photo album fluttered open like a bird's wings taking flight. Devvy with friends, all crazy smiles, hands on shoulders in group shots; he was plain Dev, strumming a guitar, looking pensive out the window; in yet another, sporting a blue blazer with one of those cheesy patches on the breast which said something like Winslow or Exeter or some waspy word followed by "Academy," he was Devonshire Singleton, promising young civil serviceman of the great British Raj. But he was lo-lee-to as he 'one-two-three' juggled his soccer ball, in his green and white soccer outfit, the ball airborne above one foot as he effortlessly keeps it aloft (a charming cut on the hairy right knee, the left shin wrapped with an athletic bandage). And always, the hair gelled into little spikes and the Adam's apple placed just so. Lo. Lo and behold. Beautiful Lo. Laid me low. My ruin.

I went to work on the friendship. But I kept all this from Chandra. That was my sin. My only sin. I kept certain things from his mother.

Chandra had started to tire and scold me once the joke had begun to wear thin. And it had been a good joke for a good long time. We sat in two different rooms trading – she in the dining room, me back in the den. We found this not only more productive as we avoided bullshitting all day, but it also added an odd intimacy for, since we could not speak to one another without getting up and interrupting the other, we would send occasional emails to humor one another. More often than not, these missives would veer toward intimacies in the way of small talk, more easily shared across that comforting digital divide than face to face.

I might start with jokes about the neighbors, but it would inevitably lead toward a discussion of something in one of the jokes, perhaps someone's mother or father, and then a series of emails would go back and forth about her frustrations with her mother and mine with my own. And of course, references to Lo, aka Dev Singh, whom I googled ad infinitum. It was surprising how many photos could be found of a relative nobody, but then again he was of that narcissistic generation that "posted" everything, and what's more, he saved cats and Little Leaguers besides – a real budding overachiever – so in his way he was a "somebody" for his station in life.

All teeth and Adam's apple, with those big bright brown eyes slightly off and goofed, his coffee skin.

We called him Jorie, the wife and I, and he longed to travel. He had an older sister and a little brother, he was hard on household appliances, he endlessly schemed to borrow the station wagon. The story just spun out between us in Twitter, text and email:

CHANDRA: Don, Jorie is at school and wants to stay for a play rehearsal. Can you pick him up later, like at 7?

DON: I told him he can't do model U.N. and the play and soccer. He has to choose 2. I hate how he goes around me and tells you cuz you're the soft touch.

CHANDRA: I am not the soft touch. I just think theater is important. He knows that I appreciate the value of the arts. Unlike yourself. Model UN and soccer? How is the boy ever going to explore his more civilized side. Feminine side?

DON: Chandra, we've been through this a thousand times. He's not that good an actor. He'll get a bit part and waste all that time. And achieve nothing. The boy's strengths are in more academic pursuits, and of course soccer. Btw, he said you failed to wash his socks.

CHANDRA: Wash them yourself. He's 17, he doesn't need his mother to launder clothes.

DON: Poor thing, he's already posted himself in one sock on his Facebook page as a joke to his friends that his mother is a lame housekeeper.

CHANDRA: What?

DON: Never mind.

Because Dev and Jenny were getting to know each other.

JENNY: No, Tiffany is mistaken; I don't have a son your age. I have a young son, just 9. I hope he grows up to be as handsome and smart as you are :)

DEV: Oh thanks, Mrs. Carmichael, that's a really nice compliment coming from a pretty lady like yourself.

JENNY: Call me Jenny, Dev. I'm a just a regular person and I think it's important to treat young men like yourself with the respect they deserve as adults!

DEV: Don't make me blush! I'm just a kid. Have a good one.

I sold a Swedish chair, and Chandra finally moved the antique Stickley hutch. We celebrated with dinner at a local bistro, and well into our cups, she brought up sweet Jorie. "You know his friends are razzing him that his dad is kinda faggy."

"Oh really, and you want him to get into theater? The poor kid is desperately trying to hang on to his masculinity. Let him play soccer."

"Oh please, Don."

"I'm not kidding. They're razzing him about you being a MILF. He has to punch them to defend your honor. Let him play soccer!"

He grew dear to us – and all the pictures got printed and pinned on the big corkboard. He was our Jorie, complaining about our lack of food, our curfew, our rules. He bargained in the way of boys: "I'll wash the car; just let me stay out till twelve – please."

An innocent delight it was before he grew wings of silicon, wholly unbeknownst to Chandra. Then Jorie was slowly made Frankensteinian flesh. He was Dev and then Lo and behold, there was Lo, and not long after, a Sherriff named

Ruben Ramirez at the front door.
But first there was the pool party.

DEV: Hey Jenny, how are you?

JENNY: I'm great, enjoying the warm weather.

DEV: Me too. We're having a pool party. (Visions of Lo in his baggy board shorts riding low at his tummy trail).

JENNY: Fun! What's the occasion?

DEV: My 18th birthday!

JENNY: Oh my goodness, you *are* a grown man! :)

DEV: Yeah, it's kinda crazy. Cool, but crazy.

JENNY: How come crazy?

DEV: Some of my friends are being kinda rude about it.

JENNY: Oh, that's no good. Sorry to hear that.

DEV: So, can I ask you a question? I could never ask my parents this.

JENNY: I'm your friend, Dev. Shoot.

DEV: Well, my friends are like razzing me for being a virgin.

JENNY: Well, boys do that. Just ignore it. It all happens in good time.

DEV: Yeah, I guess, but I wish I could just get it out of the way sometimes, cuz I'm the only one in my group who hasn't done it.

JENNY: Oh honey, don't feel bad. It's a special thing and should happen with the right person in the right time.

DEV: Do you think I'm cute? Maybe I'm just ugly.

JENNY: No, no, honey, you are a really handsome boy. Let me tell you, a single woman like me, at my age? I know what a handsome man is, and you are one! :)

DEV: Are you attracted to younger men? What's your email?

Like I say, I didn't answer and I didn't ask, I only provided my email when he asked for it. What poured in shocked even me. Lo in one sock and not much else. Well, a jockstrap.

DEV: Is my body hot enough?

JENNY: When's your birthday?

DEV: It was yesterday actually. Oh shit, Dad's here. Gotta go.

Meanwhile, my jaw was somewhere mid-chest, zooming in and out, astounded, ruined by his beauty, which transfixed me for the next fifteen minutes, flipping through all his photos and then back to the email crowning it all. Then Chandra behind me at the door. "What are you looking at?"

A tragic look on my face, Lo's package zoomed up to life-size on the seventeen-inch screen in front of me. "Jorie, it's Jorie."

Chandra just stared at me like I'd lost it. "What?"

Then the Sheriff's Crown Victoria pulling up. Putting my cup of coffee down. The dread. I considered my route of escape: out the backdoor, over the neighbor's fence. Me and the gangbangers chased by helicopters.

"Go back to work, Chandra, I'll handle this."

"Don, what is going on? What have you done?"

"It'll be okay, trust me."

She was astounded, her brows furrowed. "You Face-booked him?"

What could I say? I never told her I'd even found him on Facebook, let alone "friended" him. I kept that part to myself as I'd noticed she was getting, if not tired, a little disturbed by my constant rambling on and on about Jorie. I'd gone too far, I knew that.

He was our Jorie, sure, but he was also my Lo, and then he was Dev in real life, and I guess John Doe teenager to this Ruben, and a vulnerable son to old man Singh and God knows who in the final analysis where none of us have names.

I answered the door determined to face my fate.

"Good afternoon. I'm Officer Ramirez. Is there a Donald Victor here?"

"That's me."

"I'd like a word with you."

"Yes?"

"Can I come in?"

"No, I'd rather you not."

"Would you like to come down to the station?"

Leave Chandra out of it. "Sure." And in a louder voice over my shoulder – "I'll be back in an hour, Chandra. I'll call if I need anything. It's just a misunderstanding."

She was weeping somewhere, I could hear it.

"Oh, and get your laptop, please," Ramirez said, waving a warrant at me.

I went back and got it, unplugging it quickly without shutting it down with some vague hope it would crash and die.

You know the drill. The little interrogation room, lots of posturing by Ramirez and his detective colleague, Mack O'Connor. Questions like: "Are you aware of the punishment for child pornography."

"Why would I be?" Guffaws.

"Does statutory rape mean anything to you?" Ramirez said.

"Personally no, but I've heard the term, yes."

"How about contributing to the delinquency of a minor? That sound familiar, Victor?" O'Connor got in my face now. "Do you think that's a crime? Not that it matters what you think, of course. The law's the law."

"Yeah, and people don't like creeps like you talking to their kids," Ramirez said.

O'Connor leaned closer. "Have you ever been charged with a crime?"

They turned on the computer and had a bunch of laughs at my expense. Dev wasn't the only boy in one sock, a jockstrap or less.

"They're all over eighteen," I said.

"What, by a week or two?" They both laughed. "You're a sick fuck, Victor. Do you know how old young Mr. Singh is?"

"I do. He's eighteen."

Another laugh shared between them. "That what he told you?"

I didn't answer them.

They both walked out and left me there to ruminate for about two hours. Then they said I could leave. I can't say I was surprised or relieved or anything. I was just sort of taking it one step at a time.

"Can I have a ride back?" More guffaws. Ramirez walked away, quipping, "Door's down the corridor on your left."

I had to go to the Ralphs six blocks down the road as it was the only place left in town with a public phone. To dial Chandra. In the rush of being abducted, I hadn't taken my cell phone with me.

But he turned out to be eighteen in the end just like he said he was. By a day. Mr. Singh just had some pull at the Sheriff's Department, that's all. He was an attorney, kind of a shitty one, it turned out, in that he wielded the power it gave him inappropriately. It made me feel sorry for Dev/Jorie, who it turned out now thought me "some sick perv" in that callous dismissive way of teenagers. Oh, you just wait, Dev Singh. One day, when your looks fail you, your desires won't, and you'll be the dreaded "other," which will either wake you up or destroy you. You're a bright boy, and I love you in my sick pervy way, so I'm betting and wishing you'll wake up. I want only the best for you, dear Dev. Don't end up like your father. He's far worse than what I am. Me, I'm just pathetic, a bit creepy, but harmless really. Your father is an abuser of power and history groans under the weight of the rubble and tide of blood men like that leave in their wake.

"It's just wrong, that sheriff coming over here, trying to intimidate me. Plain wrong. Singh should be exposed and lose his license to practice."

"So, what, you're gonna sue him?" Chandra said.

"I've half a mind."

"Just half, because you'd be suing the sheriff and Singh for abusing your rights and you're just some innocent middle-aged man flirting with a high school boy under false pretenses. Who would award you anything? Why would you expose yourself through such a case? That's a lose-lose."

"Why? To destroy Mr. Singh's career, of course – for his corruption, for dishonoring his son's beauty."

"Martyr yourself for Jorie. Such a good father."

"For Dev, yes."

She rolled her eyes. "You're insane."

"He's eighteen."

"Is that all you have? I mean think about it. I'm a woman, I'm a human being, a good friend and citizen, a helpful neighbor and sister and daughter – I have a BA in Art History even. But all that pales, of course, under the bright lights of a single number: eighteen."

"Oh come on. I'm not a woman, a daughter, sister, all that, but I'm a human being too. I'm not a perv. I'm not saying eighteen is everything. It just is in this case, legally speaking. But this isn't about legality since I've done nothing illegal. It's about beauty and the reductiveness of a person who turns it into a number, which is Singh, not me."

"He's just protecting his child, Don."

"Whatever. Protect him on your own time, not mine. I'm at play in the fields of theLord. Let me be."

More eye rolling. "The fields of the Lord, eh? You're a liar and a predator."

"So was Eve."

"What are you talking about? You misrepresented yourself. Child or no, you did wrong."

I shrugged.

"Anyway, count your blessings and don't do it again. Now, have you thought about dinner?"

"Yes, my dear Chandra, I'm taking you out. I've put you through too much today."

"We lost our son," she chimed in.

"No parent should have to experience that."

II.

But of course, they weren't experiencing that, were they? Of course, that's how the story goes if you get it from Don's twisted mind. All's well that ends well. Sort of. Like any perv, he's skilled at making it all sound on the up and up. But what if it went a little differently than how Don tells it? What if Jenny had been a tad more pushy? What if they'd actually planned to meet? Where would Don have suggested? There were no Enchanted Motor Inns in the valley. He'd probably suggest meeting in the mall.

He'd go and sit in the food court and when Dev arrived, he'd eye him, watch him waiting and looking for Jenny. Oh, and Dev would be so cute, all dorky, cock-eyed and brilliant white at the teeth and eyes, the bobbing Adam's apple as he swallows nervously, looking about innocently. So, so cute. Lo-li-to. Don might gather the courage to walk by and drop something – keys, a napkin, anything really to help him linger for a split second – or maybe he'd ask directions to the Abercrombie & Fitch store in order to break the ice before continuing on to "What are you doing here in the food court with nothing to eat, son? Waiting for your friends?"

"Uh, yeah, waiting for someone."

"Ah, I see, me too. My ex-wife!" And he'd chuckle, which Dev would be forced to join in on. "Always wants to meet me on neutral ground. Never get married, son, it's a tragedy."

More embarrassed laughter. Don's treating him like an equal; like a man.

Don, who's not totally sure whether he's hoping for bisexuality or he's just enjoying pawing at his prey. This is the place where Don no longer really knows what's happening. It's all in the hunt, and Dev's proving a great hunt – the doe-eyed fresh deer with just nubs for horns, skirting foolishly along the edge of the herd when it passes the forest.

But Dev might give him that knowing precocious look too, like he knows how to handle the edge of the herd and likes it there. And together they'd head off to the restroom and maul each other in the furthest stall. Dev would walk out and never say goodbye. Don would pull out his cell phone and speak loudly so Dev would overhear him. "Jenny, where are you? I've been waiting twenty minutes. Don't be a Carmichael and arrive a half hour late."

What would that feel like for Dev? Or would his brain still be so full of the adrenaline of orgasm that he'd never hear it? On to the next thing. Or maybe he'd already be so overwhelmed with guilt at the fact he'd lost his virginity just like he'd planned, but not quite in the same fashion as he'd hoped, that nothing could enter his mind just then.

Or maybe it wouldn't go so smoothly for Don at all. Maybe the two were captured on camera and that's why Officer Ramirez ends up at his door the next morning. Don would meet old man Singh then. They'd have called him down to the station to pick up his son. Now we know why Don hates Singh so much. Singh would read him good and put him on notice.

Troubled Dev, who'd still be eighteen and once again with Daddy getting him out of a fix.

They'd both end up sex offenders anyway, because that's the law. Public gay sex will get you on the same register with the child molesters, consenting and "of-age" be damned.

I'm no Nabokov, so I'm not gonna kill Singh or have Chandra run over in the street either. No, this story is going nowhere, like most desire. But speaking of Chandra, what about Chandra? The witness. Or was she? She ran a harder bargain on eBay than Don, and maybe she did the same with Dev. Maybe Jenny Carmichael wasn't the only friend Dev had made outside his high school circles. Maybe there was a grad student at UCLA who'd noticed on Dev's Facebook page that he'd been admitted there for the fall; a grad student who took advantage of their common ethnicity to invite him to the Southeast Asian Students mixer to welcome the class of 2014 to UCLA. Even old man Singh would have liked the idea of that one. And where would Chandra have coaxed the boy? Chandra was a charmer, after all. She could throw out the name of some hotel in Westwood and wait in the lobby and play dumb when Dev arrived and it didn't seem anyone else was there, and the concierge knew of no such mixer. And maybe they had the wrong hotel? And "I'm so sorry, let me buy you something to eat." And the slow calculated flirtation, and Chandra in a sudden tizzy as they wrap up their meal because she's lost her Blackberry and Dev dialing away and no sound coming from Chandra's bag or pockets – the two laughing – and her understandable and panicky request for him to come upstairs with her to her room and try calling her there – she's just sure it must be somewhere up there. And where would it be – under the pillow? And would Dev or Chandra give one or the other *that look*? And the bed is right there, and Chandra would thrill that her parents would be so happy she'd finally found the elusive East Indian man – and so would Dev, you bet! MILF! SCORE! as he ravished her boy-style. Only afterward would she think about the two dozen years' difference in their age and the fact that Dev was now totally freaked out and just wanted to leave. But it beat that weird experience at the mall. Chandra was a girl, at least, and there was the comfort of their common culture. And this tale he could brag about to the boys back home.

And what if Chandra ended up with Don's chlamydia via Dev, and they'd get treated at the clinic by the doctor who always thought they were a married couple anyway. And wouldn't the three be family then?

And who's gonna tell Jorie? Jenny Carmichael? Who is

Jenny Carmichael? Did Don use pictures of Chandra in building her profile? And if so, what must Dev have thought when she showed up at the hotel for the mixer?

"Someone needs to tell Jorie," Chandra would weep, admitting to everything in the face of venereal disease.

"He's an adult, Chandra; let him wash his own socks."

Pedro and the Mark

The plump gringo waddled into the cantina and hoisted himself onto the bar stool next to Pedro. Theo watched him, always curious about his fellow gringos – how self-contained they were – and wondering whether this one would show a little more life.

The man looked around at the cheap posters of Chichen Itza tacked to the walls and ordered a Negra Modelo. This wasn't the tourist district, so Theo figured he was either lost or maybe even knew the city well. Eventually the man regarded them, and Theo picked up a gay vibe and maybe even a little condescension as the man gave yet another middle-aged gringo with his young Mexican companion the once-over. He coughed, said hello, and announced he was looking for fauns.

The pair just looked at him.

"You know ... fauns? Do you know what a faun is?"

"A deer, right?" Pedro gulped from his beer.

Theo was impressed that Pedro knew such an obscure English word, but the stranger clearly didn't feel the same; he impatiently responded "No, that's a fawn with a 'w.' I mean 'un fauno' – like a satyr, a creature with hooves and little horns."

"Oh." Pedro clearly could care less.

"They're mythological beings, right?" Theo said, leaning forward to cover for Pedro's disinterest.

"Yes."

"So, what makes you think they're around here?"

"And not just in your head," Pedro added without looking at him, checking his cell phone messages.

The gringo chuckled. "I thought like that too before I met one."

"Where did you meet one?" Theo asked.

"L.A."

"That seems either the strangest or the most obvious place to meet such a creature. But how do you know it was real?"

"There are ways."

"What ways?" Pedro turned. "And why are you asking us anyway?"

The stranger glared. "Well, I've been here a day. You looked like you had a clue."

"What does a clue look like?"

The stranger was clearly losing patience with Pedro and answered with a hint of anger, "Tired and weary. You've both been here a long time. You know it, see it for what it really is. You probably think about leaving every day."

Pedro grinned. "That's jaded, that's not a clue. Besides, I was born here," he said.

"Well, then, you should know if there are any fauns about. That's why I asked you."

"I thought you said you asked us because we had a clue."

The man hefted himself off his stool and turned to leave. He threw his card on the bar. "If you want to, contact me. I'm willing to pay."

Theo reached out and grabbed the card to read it as the fat stranger lumbered away: "Dwayne Vanderbilt, Consultant." It had a phone number and some little paisley-looking things above and below the name for decoration, but nothing else.

"How much?" Pedro called after him, before smiling and looking at Theo. But the man didn't turn and proceeded out the entrance.

* * *

Theo had been in Oaxaca a year, watching these Americans rolling in and out like the tides – having their experience, seeing Monte Alban and the pyramids, buying their pottery, their rugs, their art and whatever else. Coffee. Mezcal. Guayabera shirts, for chrissakes. Spanish classes. Skulls. Americans either looked right through you or averted their eyes the minute you looked at them. They were having *their* experience.

Though Oaxaca was a real city, and not a beach resort, it was sullied by all the tourism, so much so that 'the poison trade' had essentially compromised the city's character: there were pedestrian malls where local businesses sold t-shirts for fifteen American dollars, along with all number of knickknacks – mystical Zapotec masks, soaps, jewelry, arts and crafts, coffee, mole, chocolate, and little bottles of mezcal. The city had even gone so far as to force local villagers out of the plazas and squares, where they'd once sold fruit, herbs, chapulines, homemade mole. Litter was rarely if ever seen downtown, but as soon as you hit the highway leaving the city, the creeks were so full of trash they could barely flow and their banks were covered in avalanches of refuse.

And there weren't just tourists in Oaxaca, there were also retirees. Lots of them. Maybe they'd started as tourists and kept coming back until they were too old to follow a traveler's itinerary and shifted to an elder's routine. A stroll around town, a midday nap, a little to eat, a struggle to shit, all the while forced to wear sunscreen, shades and a panama hat over their thinning white hair. And since they had time, why pay the rising hotel rates when you could sign a lease and stay for a year at $200 a month? A few started educational foundations and the like which, because he enjoyed kids and benefitted from the Spanish practice, Theo had volunteered with.

It was due to the largesse of one of these retirees, in fact, that Theo had ended up in Oaxaca in the first place, before getting wrapped up with Pedro. He'd been offered a house to write in for the summer, rent-free, and jumped at the chance. During that time, he did very little writing, a fair amount of drinking and quite a bit of dallying with local boys, along with the volunteer work with the kids.

When the homeowner returned and met Pedro, he called Theo a "chickenhawk, just like the rest of them," meaning all his gay retiree "friends" whom he gossiped about and dissed endlessly. Theo lectured him on Greek love, told him he pitied him his lack of wisdom, thanked him and left for a nearby hostel. Better a chickenhawk than a philistine. Theo was forty, Pedro twenty-six. They didn't qualify even as Greeks, but American puritanism being what it is, once the gap between lovers crested a decade you were suspect. It's why Theo didn't miss America and hadn't gone back: the endlessly neurotic moralizing which made every SUV-driving, coffee-swilling, sanctimonious resource hog an expert on what to do about the ravaged planet that apparently wasn't *their* fault. He was not going to join the inane chatter that made up the so-called "serious" culture – read Facebook – of America-in-decline.

Pedro was the antithesis to all that, a Mixe from high up in the mountains who knew where he came from, what he was, and what he wanted. Theo loved it when Pedro spoke in his native tongue. Mixe was tonal and singsong, and lovely in a way that helped Theo to understand the romantic idiocy of tourists who'd try to go native.

Pedro was a teacher but had lost his job in the ongoing annual strikes and street battles when he'd fallen in with a radical communist group and was implicated in the kidnapping of a rightwing militiaman during the height of the tensions in 2006. Pedro swore he never met the guy, who was ultimately released, although beaten pretty badly. Since then, Pedro'd been trading on his looks, doing odd jobs for the retired gay gringos who overpaid good-looking young men like him and gave big tips when the boys proved eager to remove their shirts or swing their uncircumcised dicks around at parties. The old guys rarely wanted more than that. And since few knew more than rudimentary Spanish, Pedro learned

English by default.

Pedro had been sitting in the Parque de Llano counting hundred peso notes from a recent drywalling job for a Texan couple up in Colonia Reforma when Theo walked by and did a double take. Ten paces further along, Theo turned and looked back for a third time. Pedro saw him this time and offered his Cheshire cat in return. Theo strolled back and sat down. They chatted, and within minutes Pedro had determined this gringo had no money, but he seemed open and somehow present. *What would it be like to know a gringo for real?*

They ended up walking around and talking, drinking coffee, laughing at children, lame advertising efforts and the general clownishness of people. Pedro told Theo he had a wife and kid but he liked being with men too. And that answered that question. They hiked up the hill to Theo's and finished what had started with the smiles in the park.

Later, Pedro told him he'd fooled around with other boys while a kid, like a lot of others in the village, but once he'd reached manhood, he'd married and had the kid. Pedro was smart and work was scarce up in the village, so he'd come down from the mountains to Oaxaca to study, become a teacher, and hopefully teach back up in the village. It hadn't quite played out that way and he'd ended up in a school in Mitla, in the opposite direction, where he'd gotten political while his marriage tanked and he began seeing other women, until a gay gringo couple picked him up one drunken evening out near the ruins. He'd liked it, more for how it felt and how much they worshipped his beauty than for any real attraction to men. They offered to fly him up to Puerta Vallarta where they'd be spending Christmas. He demurred, but, enlightened about the obscene wealth of gringos and their willingness to share it with a handsome young man – and what with his now dubious future as a teacher – he did what any young man would do.

Soon enough he'd jumped into the gringo retiree community, and since then had been painting, chauffeuring and doing whatever else needed to be done – and for double the wages offered by Mexicans. He soon learned that putting out would compromise his position, however, when he met the boys who'd unwisely spent their capital, so he became a tease – thus sticking to shirt removal and dick wagging – and kept his dalliances outside the local gringo economy with European tourists or other Mexicans.

He never dated men, of course. They were strictly for taking care of business and defibrillating his ego. But he found Theo interesting somehow, and his affection for him grew. On his days off, he'd find himself thinking about him. Ah well, a buddy. You could always use another buddy to party with or have your back. So they started going places together. "You're good to hang out with," he'd say when they went into the Sierras, or down to the coast. Sex was something they did when they went to bed and when they woke up. But they never talked about it. They were like two potheads. They had a common habit.

Pedro kept working for the gringos, many of whom Theo had met, as they had come around to visit during the past summer knowing he was one of their kind's houseguest. Theo wasn't particularly interested in hanging out with other Americans, so he'd avoided their social circle – the monthly parties, the weekly brunch. Sometimes he wished Pedro wasn't so tied up with them as it increased Theo's own interactions with them. There were all kinds of them, of course – Theo admired those who'd started nonprofits and schools and he'd befriended them. But some were not so savory. When they spotted him and Pedro at the Café Arabia on Plaza Zucatti, they'd talk one way to Theo and another to Pedro, peppering their inquiries with innuendo and flirtation. Theo had the urge to say "Pedro ain't one of your boys." But Pedro didn't need looking after.

* * *

One of the more wrecked of the gringos was the one looking for fauns. He was known in the gay retiree community. "Oh,

Dwayne. He comes and goes, he's gotten into trouble with the rougher boys of the zocalo, been robbed and all that. Once he dodged a prison sentence when he diddled the wrong boy who was young enough to make legal trouble – the son of a cop, no less. Tsk, tsk."

Pedro asked around and learned the others hadn't seen Dwayne in several years. It was said that he'd been in Bolivia and Paraguay and had some kind of trust fund that allowed him to wander about. He was a seeker of experience and mystery, and he wasn't afraid to lose himself in jungles, even risking illness and death in some remote place he'd been told in no uncertain terms to avoid. He'd been held by both Colombian and Peruvian rebels, had endured cholera, dengue, malaria and yellow fever, done ayahuasca with the shamans of Peru, peyote with the Huichol outside San Luis Potosi, and even lugged himself all the way up the Inca Trail to Machu Picchu. He was not a particularly healthy-looking man, but he must have been strong as an ox to survive all that.

But apparently he'd only revealed his current hunt to Pedro and Theo. The retirees all speculated on why he was back, complaining that he'd been vague. So, why ever had he asked Pedro and Theo? Did they really look like they had a clue? He'd certainly been correct in that they looked tired. Theo'd been burnt out on Oaxaca for some time now, after that long fruitless summer, followed by a chaotic September moving from one hostel to the next until he convinced Pedro to get a place with him down near the zocalo. Pedro'd been living rent-free in a roof apartment above one of the retiree's houses, but was eventually pushed out by the retiree's niece who'd come down to work on her Spanish. Offers poured in from a dozen seniors once word got out he needed a place. But Pedro knew better and surrendered to Theo's entreaties. "As long as we're doing it just to save money," Pedro said.

"We both need to get out of here and you know it, Pedro. There's no future for you as a "boy." They'll throw you over once you get older." Which wasn't necessarily true. The old gay retirees were incredibly loyal and employed these boys well into their forties, at which time the retirees often dropped dead and left their estates to their loyal assistants. Besides, Pedro had his son.

"I'm not leaving here. I've got my boy to raise." Not that he spent much time raising him. He and the mother couldn't get along for more than an hour at a stretch and she was hoping he'd just lose interest in the child. She had a large extended family that was more than happy to keep the boy for themselves. And she'd heard the rumors about Pedro and the gringos, which could only mean one thing. Well, two actually, and that secondary monetary consideration was nothing to scoff at. So, little Rodrigo spent Sundays with his father.

Theo was selfish and wanted Pedro for himself, but he begrudgingly accepted lost Sundays (three-year-old Rodrigo was an adorable child with a ready smile). But he certainly didn't want to share Pedro with the retirees who had nothing better to do than lunch and dish each other, and demand the company of their assistants, who always ate for free. A baby rival was tolerable, but men with money? It was too much, and Theo suspected the old guys must critique him viciously: the "writer" who doesn't write; the aloof forty-year-old who thinks he's too young for us. That's not what Theo thought, though. He just found them boring. If rejecting lunch and home decorating was ageist, then he'd accept the accusation, but he didn't think that's what aging was, and it wouldn't be that for him. He hoped. He fancied himself like the nonprofit set, but other than volunteering, he was doing nothing to create such a future. Well, he was flat broke and somewhat lazy, what could he do?

* * *

Pedro wouldn't leave it alone. "I have an idea, Theo."
"About what?"
"About el gordo."
"Dwayne. His name's Dwayne. What are you thinking?"
"Let's show him a faun."

"Do you know of one?"

"Of course not, they don't exist."

"Who's to say, Pedro?"

"Come on, he's been eating too many mushrooms."

"Ayahuasca maybe."

"It would be so easy to play it out. We'll take him up to my village, wine and dine him, bring out my tio who's got that wise old Indian look the tourists love. Throw in a rattle, a drum, a few shots of mezcal."

Theo smiled. "But it's cruel, Pedro."

"And your disdain for him and all of them isn't? Which is worse – giving him an experience or writing him off? You don't think people notice your arrogance and aloofness?"

Theo's smile widened. "I'm just sincere and honest. I don't pretend to like people."

"It's your bad gringo manners. When's the last time you met an aloof Mexican?"

Theo couldn't think of one. There were probably a lot of them in Lomas de Chapultepec or Polanco back in Mexico City, but out here, not a one. "Are you saying there are no aloof Mexicans?"

"I'm saying there are plenty, but they're smart enough not to let on."

"Well, there's nothing wrong with honesty."

"Other than it makes people hate you and spread rumors about you. Which is something, believe you me. It could get you killed, compadre."

Theo had never thought of it that way before. But then, come to think of it, he was generally only aloof with Americans. Why was that? Because he knew them? Wasn't afraid of them? Or was it just self-loathing projected on to those most like him? Lost souls, wandering the earth.

"What are they saying about me?"

He smiled widely. "That you're Pedro's whore. Honesty," he winked.

Theo threw up his hands and laughed. "Fine, let's do the faun thing."

"I'll talk to my tio Sunday."

* * *

But Sunday was too late. Dwayne had already hooked up with Vaughn by then.

Theo didn't know Vaughn except via gossip and by sight, as he'd been pointed out crossing the plaza once months ago when Theo was lunching with the seniors. But that particular Thursday, he and Pedro had spotted Vaughn at a table in the zocalo with Dwayne. They looked almost like twins.

The story about Vaughn was that he was a wreck of lust and greed. He'd come to Oaxaca twelve years ago, an overweight, fading homosexual, well past forty, his desires well-honed and specific. He'd lived most of his life in California, though he came from Missouri or some such unnoteworthy place. He developed a taste for Latin boys while doing hair in Los Angeles. As his looks faded, he'd realized he'd need more and more money to hold onto the young men he fancied, and money was something he seemed to lose as fast as he procured it. He'd ultimately gone into a partnership on a hair salon with a friend who'd spun out of control and crystal meth-ed himself into rehab, ruining and bankrupting the business in the process. Vaughn had lost everything and once again found himself at loose ends. He got work here and there but felt humiliated so far into his career begging for opportunities, all the time seething with resentment at his partner Troy's excessive and destructive behavior. He'd been to Tijuana like most Southern Californians, but it wasn't until he visited Puerto Vallarta, something of a gay mecca, that he realized there were boys not just for the taking, but at close-out prices. His girth and cynicism didn't seem to be the liability they'd become back in the states either. His blue eyes alone could snag some of the most gorgeous boys he'd ever seen. He had a brief spasm of conscience, which quickly passed as he allowed himself to be smothered in the glories of smooth brown flesh and the aggressive need of these young open-hearted souls. No one knows when or where he got the idea to perfect his craft in Oaxaca, but it being another gringo hot spot, it's not hard to guess – likely, some other traveler of like mind had informed him that the boys were even poorer, prettier and more exploitable down there than in Jalisco.

He didn't even bother staying near the zocalo in a hotel or looking for a little bungalow in the better parts of town. No, Vaughn saw the boys in the street washing windshields on the road in from the airport. He shouted for the driver to stop, but the driver told him that they weren't even in town yet, he must be confused. There were, after all, nothing but tire vulcanizers and body shops on this stretch of traffic-clogged thoroughfare.

"I'm not confused," Vaughn stuttered in broken Spanish. "Let me out."

The driver pulled over to stop. "Are you sure you want to get out here?"

"Yes!"

The driver shrugged. "Be careful."

Vaughn tipped him a ten peso coin and trundled his little wheeled bag down the broken sidewalk in his threadbare espadrilles, resolved to find lodgings right here, ground zero for the boys. He lived in that district still.

The other thing about Vaughn was that he was constantly borrowing money. "Goddamn that Troy," he'd always say in place of thank you. He'd alienated nearly all the gringos with his empty promises of paying them back. Rumor had it he'd taken to selling mushrooms to tourists. The drug cartels were not terribly active in Oaxaca and mushrooms weren't their game besides, which was essentially the more lucrative cocaine moving north through Acapulco. But on occasion, they were known to pass through town. And if they didn't get wise to Vaughn, the police likely would, as he already was on notice for his occasional pederasty. In other words, he had plenty of good reasons to tell *el gordo* Dwayne where to find a faun and how he could make that happen, and at what price. So much for Pedro's tio.

"We've been outmaneuvered by Vaughn, I'm afraid."

Pedro laughed. "That's even better. That creep does nothing but make promises he can't keep. If we play this right, we'll get rich, I'll buy Rodrigo and we'll leave together."

"For where?"

"I don't know. DF? LA? Isn't Obama about to offer amnesty? Besides, you know as well as I do that with enough money …"

Theo finished his sentence "… yeah, yeah, I know, Lady Liberty always lifts her skirts."

"Who?"

"The statue?"

Pedro looked vexed.

"Never mind, it's an East Coast thing." As it was, all they had in California was a fence. They'd never welcomed anybody, huddled or not.

Pedro and Theo sat together in the zocalo for three days, taking occasional sex breaks, waiting for Vaughn and *el gordo* to appear again. "His name is Dwayne!" Theo kept razzing Pedro.

He tried to tell Pedro about a Marx Brothers routine, but he feared it came out all wrong in his dubious Spanish. It was a scene from *Duck Soup* where Harpo and Chico were supposed to find some guy, so they went to the baseball game on Monday, but the guy tricked them and didn't go. Tuesday, the guy did go, and "we tricked him, we no show up," Chico proudly proclaimed. Wednesday was a doubleheader, "nobody show up."

Pedro not only didn't laugh, he got up and went for cigarettes. Theo figured he'd probably lost interest about halfway through. They both did this, so there was no reason to feel sore. When Pedro talked fast in Spanish, Theo ignored him, and when Theo mangled the language, Pedro did the same.

At the end of the third day when they'd grown so bored and anxious that they'd actually had full-on sex five times, the two appeared.

Pedro watched like a predatory cat as they sat down and

ordered. Then he sauntered over, all smiles. "How have you been, Vaughn? Good to see you," etc.

Vaughn was blushing, as he had a thing for Pedro, which says less for Pedro and more about Vaughn's relentless attraction to young Latin men. Theo thought then how Pedro wasn't actually that cute, what with his acne scars, his too-low hairline, his bullet-shaped head. Oh, but he loved him, his intelligence, his capableness. All that was sexier than his looks. Theo was even a little shocked at how attached he felt to Pedro. What would he do if it fell apart?

Vaughn then attempted to introduce Pedro to *el gordo*. "This is Dwayne."

"We've met," Dwayne replied in a clipped tone with his customary glare.

"Has he asked you yet about young deer?" Pedro asked.

"Very funny. He means fauns, Vaughn, get it?"

Vaughn smiled. "Faun and Vaughn, that rhymes!" He guffawed. "I'd never thought of that before. You've obviously come to the right place." Pedro could see Vaughn's shifty little mind at work. He'd likely heard all about the faun search in the past few days as he got acquainted with Dwayne, and would of course be assuring him he could find one while wracking his mind for how to do so. And then Pedro enters stage left. "Everything happens for a reason," Vaughn was fond of saying.

"Dwayne, I don't know what Pedro told you last time you spoke."

"Nothing, and he was rude, dismissive." He glared again at Pedro. Whatever pangs of conscience Pedro might have had were rapidly diminishing.

"Well, you have to understand, Dwayne, there are secrets" – and he leaned in close to Dwayne across the table – "the locals keep very close to their chests. The fact that you're on to one of them clearly made our Pedro here a tad nervous - hostile even."

Dwayne looked unconvinced. Pedro nodded gravely.

"But now that it's all out here in the open," Vaughn continued, "and do forgive me, Pedro, but I can vouch for Dwayne. This is not your run-of-the-mill American tourist. Dwayne is a –" And he fished about: *Professor? No, that was no good, those creeps had ruined it for Maria Sabina and psilocybin. A rich man? Well, true enough, but that was better left unspoken, considering.* He finally settled on: "– a very spiritual person with the utmost discretion." And he nodded to himself as if convinced. "I do think, Pedro, this is a man we can work with."

Pedro shrugged. "If you say so, Vaughn. I trust you completely, as you know. If you are comfortable with him, then I am. Mi casa es tu casa," he then said, looking at Dwayne with a big smile.

"I speak Spanish, don't condescend."

Pedro turned to Vaughn. "He's difficult. And that is going to raise the price."

"I'm not difficult, I just don't like being toyed with."

"You will not be toyed with," Vaughn interjected. "Pedro, let me do the negotiations with Wayne – Dwayne, I'm sorry – and you talk to ..."

"My tio."

"Yes, Tio Angelino." Vaughn was desperately trying to sound in-the-know and wasn't above making up a name out of thin air. "Next week; is that enough time?"

Pedro screwed up his features as if he were thinking, calculating. "October, the rutting season, the whole corn ritual and all, uh, I don't know, it's not ideal right now. Next June would be best."

"June! I won't be here in June," Dwayne protested.

"Well, it all comes down to how my tio feels about it."

"Tio Angelino," Vaughn announced as if to remind him of the mysterious powerful fixer.

"Well, listen, I need to get back to my friend." And Pedro motioned with his head in Theo's direction. They both looked over and Theo flashed a smile and waved.

When Pedro returned to their table, he bounced his eyebrows up and down and grinned. "We're back in business."

"Oh really? Well, you know what Vaughn wants, Pedro.

And he can deliver nothing without you and your tio story. So why deal with him at all?"

"*El gordo* hates me."

"Dwayne. His name's Dwayne."

"Yeah, well, Dwayne hates me. Vaughn's got an in with him. And he thinks he's got one with us. Let him think so."

* * *

Theo had seen the groups of men dressed up as devils who danced in the Guelaguetza, the cultural festival that happened each summer. Vaughn told them Dwayne knew all about that too, which is why he was here. They were out at Chavalos, a high-end Argentinian place, popular among the gringo retirees. Vaughn was picking up the tab. They didn't ask.

"So they're the bait," Vaughn announced with assurance.

"The bait for what?" Theo asked.

"The faun, silly."

"That doesn't exist? That faun? I'm just saying."

"Oh, honey, we can whip up some young faun. How hard could it be?"

Theo didn't like or trust Vaughn and was having second thoughts about what he'd previously thought simply an entertaining diversion. "I don't want any part of this."

"Oh, for godsakes, Theodore, do you have any fun in your little melodramatic writer's life?"

Theo rolled his eyes.

"All I'm trying to say is that this is not just for money. You don't write just for money, do you? Ha, ha – obviously not. It's for the ages, my dear. Immortality. A contribution to the human spirit. What we're creating here is a legend. Why, you could write the script. We'll do a movie if it all plays out right. Ha, ha, ha."

Theo just looked at him.

"Goodness, we're serious." And Vaughn motioned to the waiter for another bottle of Malbec, winking at Pedro, who silently popped another olive into his mouth.

"And broke, which is your real point, right?" Theo said.

"The elephant in the room, ha ha ha."

"So what's going on with you two anyway?" Theo asked.

"What do you mean?"

"I mean, are you romantically involved?"

"God no – is he nineteen and Zapotec? I think not." And Vaughn guffawed.

Pedro smiled, but Theo looked pensive. "So he just pulled the same stunt with you as he did with us, asking about the faun."

"Oh no, that came later … we bonded over the boys. And once I saw his ability to pay, shall we say, I found all sorts of common ground. Did you know he likes Stickley and Fiestaware?" Like most queens, Theo thought to himself. Was Vaughn being sarcastic? "Anyway, I've been pimping out loads of boys and getting the seconds." And he howled. Pedro laughed with him, but Theo looked disapproving.

"Oh, Theo, don't be such a philistine. I'm not a real pimp. I just do a little upfront. I'm the middleman for the newbies. Once they've made a few connections, I'm cut out in a jiffy and I don't protest. I'm not broke for nothing … ha, ha, ha."

He paid the bill with a stack of Benito Juarez twenty peso notes, and caught Theo's ogling. "Oh honey, I just love that Benito's looks. I go to the bank and turn in all my 100s, 50s, you name it – all those stern-looking Aztecs and arrogant Spanish criollos, you can have them. I like my Benito – el presidente indigena!" And he laughed away, endlessly entertained by his own wit.

On the sidewalk, they waited for a cab. "So he told us he met a faun in L.A. Is that for real?"

"Well he met some Ukrainian who claimed to know one. A whole song and dance about the fountain of youth. This 'Yuuuuri'" – Vaughn drew out the name in a faux Russian accent – "claimed he'd met fauns in the mountains of Rumania or somesuch."

"With the vampires?"

"Right? That's what I was thinking. But anyway, you know

the drill about Balkan old age, all that nonsense about eating yogurt and living to 115. Well, it isn't the yogurt. It's the fauns. But you need to suck them off, and then you'll be beautiful and young forever. The Ukrainian wasn't a bad-looking guy and told Dwayne he was 167. Looked about thirty-five, as Dwayne told it."

"Who would ever believe such bullshit?"

"Well, don't get your panties bunched up just yet. I'm not even near finished, dearie. Said Ukrainian took him up into a canyon outside of L.A. and showed him one."

"I don't believe it."

"You don't have to. Dwayne says he saw him with his own eyes – hoofs, horns, and hung like an Arabian. And I mean the horse. Or do I?" He laughed.

"So did Dwayne blow him?"

"No, the Ukrainian claimed this faun was on his last leg … or hoof, as the case may be." He smiled at his own joke. "His potency was, shall we say, badly diminished. He spoke with a Spanish accent and claimed he had relatives among the dancing demons of Oaxaca. The rest is history."

A cab pulled over and Theo asked one last question. "Is he mentally all there, or are we exploiting a disabled person?"

"Oh Theo, puhleeze. People get what they deserve, and if the usual depressed homosexual syndrome counts, yeah, he's mentally challenged and probably so full of antidepressants and Klonopin, et al, he lost touch with reality a long time ago. Now all that's left is to lose touch with his trust fund." Peals of laughter as Vaughn shut the door and the cab sped off.

Theo turned to Pedro. "So what exactly is the plan here?"

"Vaughn's angling for ten thousand dollars U.S. He wants half."

Theo's eyes bugged out before asking, "But why offer Vaughn half?"

"It doesn't matter, Theo, we won't pay him half."

Theo raised his brows and looked at Pedro. "Pedro, you have to live in this town."

"Vaughn will get over it. It won't even bother him that

much. He'll learn from it and realize he's got to be a little more cunning and that there's no such thing as easy money."

"Are you listening to yourself?"

Pedro just looked at him.

"I'm not a criminal, Pedro."

Pedro nodded, smiling.

"I'm serious, I don't want any part of this."

"Theo, this is Mexico. A fool and his money are soon parted. There's no crime. No one gets hurt. Just a little fun. Vaughn doesn't need the money as badly as we do. And if it doesn't work, what's he gonna do, press charges?" He shook his head, grinning.

"You're crazy."

"You're the one who wants me to go with you. The coyote will cost me at least five thousand."

"So you're serious? You'll come with me?

Pedro shrugged.

"And what about Rodrigo?"

"Well, I need to make a little more money for him, don't I? That's why we're cutting Vaughn's take."

"And what, you're just going to buy Rodrigo from his mother?"

"Yes. She's going nowhere fast. She needs the money. She'll have another baby with some guy she likes more than me. I know her."

Theo shook his head in disbelief.

Pedro sighed and hugged him. "Poor Theo. It'll be O.K. You don't have to do anything. Just be by my side. I like it when you're with me."

But still, Theo thought of Mexican jails. He wouldn't be able to stay in Oaxaca if they did this. He'd be completely paranoid. Fine then, he'd leave for the States as soon as the job was done and hopefully Pedro would be with him within the month.

* * *

The fateful day arrived. Pedro and Theo walked up to Dwayne's hotel - the Grand Oaxaca, or some name like that, he couldn't remember. But he knew where it was and that it was an old convent that had been turned into a five-star hotel which seemed sacrilegious on some level, but then the Catholic Church and the power structure were one in Latin America and no one seemed to care whether you were worshipping money or God or whatever. It was a church and now it was hotel, but it was a colonial building. It was "theirs," in other words – the conquerors. They could do whatever they wanted with it.

Dwayne had rented a Land Rover for Pedro to drive up to the village. Dwayne was all business.

"The money is in this purse. You get it when we meet the faun, and not a minute before, capische?"

"Si, yo capische."

Vaughn waited with a picnic basket at the vulcanizer's on the corner of Emiliano Zapato and Simbolos Patrios on the way out of town. He waved and smiled as they approached.

"Good morning, everyone." He hopped into the back seat with Dwayne and opening the picnic basket. "I've got tamales, empanadas, churros." He laughed.

"What kind you got?" Dwayne asked.

"Well, the tamales are pollo, and the empanadas are guava. The churros –" He broke out laughing again. "– just grease!" Theo was suddenly glad that Vaughn was part of this. He'd be able to keep things light, keep the tension down with his friendly banter and wit.

The road began to climb and Dwayne nodded off after noshing two tamales and an empanada, Vaughn next to him, still grinning ear to ear.

"Pull over," Vaughn said.

"Why?"

"Why? You ask why? I put a roofie in the tamale." He held up Dwayne's little purse and unzipped it like a stripper wearing a pair of rubber shorts. He pulled out his rubber-banded five thousand dollars and shook it, "We're done here. Let's head back to town or leave our little Dwayne here."

Theo looked at Pedro. Their whole plan was now completely unnecessary, and it had seemed so brilliant. So fun, right? Didn't Vaughn say they were going to have a little fun? How fun was this? Where was the legend, the story that Theo had slowly grown inspired to write?

"Why aren't you pulling over?" Vaughn said crossly, the smile vanishing.

"I'm thinking," Pedro answered.

"Well, that's not your job, sweetheart. You're the pretty one," he said sarcastically. "Want a tamale? Ha, ha, ha," he cackled.

Pedro looked at Theo. Theo remembered the script, the whole beautiful choreographed adventure Pedro had laid out for him a week ago. The one Vaughn had agreed to: the pleasant drive into the mountains, the arrival at Tlahuitoltepec, the Mixe village, impressing Dwayne with the women in their traditional outfits and Pedro's uncle Jaime. (He'd need to call him Angelino to tip him off.) Then the trek into the woods to the little clearing below the cave where they'd do the little faux ritual with tobacco and mezcal, all sitting Indian fashion in a circle. Tio Angelino would look toward the cave. "He's there, he's listening. Now we wait for him to come out." When he didn't, Angelino, with gravity, would tell Pedro he must go in to find him. Pedro would protest, grow pale. "I'm not going in there. I don't want to see any faun. He does." And he'd point at Dwayne. Angelino would speak softly and calm his nephew, placing his palm on his forehead and looking over at Dwayne. Pedro would nod and get up, as would Theo. Angelino would look at Dwayne and nod. "What does he want?" Dwayne would ask nervously. "The money, silly," Vaughn would prod him, elbowing him in the side. Dwayne would hold the little purse close to his chest: "It's for the faun." They'd all agree and reassure him that Pedro and Theo would risk life and limb to bring him out. This was dangerous work. Angelino would be nodding all the while and then shrugging and getting up to leave when Dwayne gets stubborn and won't give up the money. This is where the option to overpower him and just rob him came in. Theo had argued vehemently against that approach. "He'll give up the money. He wants to see the faun." And Theo and Pedro would tiptoe up to the cave, hesitating now and again, pretending to hear things – growls and snorts. Eventually, they'd make it to the cave entrance and gingerly enter. Then they'd run deep into the mountain through the cave's passageways that Pedro knew so well from his childhood. They'd reach the underground lake where they'd have to swim, holding the money purse up in the air while they made their way through the water. Then more passageways and finally out the other side into daylight and a way back out into the forest, far, far from the clearing where they started. Dwayne would be feeling *had* by now, tricked, taken, made a fool of. Would he lunge at Vaughn? And why would Vaughn agree to such a plan? To be left with the mark and none of the money. Pedro had assured Theo that Vaughn would go along with *any* plan, and he'd dropped his pants and shook it at him the day before just to seal the deal.

"But Vaughn's not a retiree. That'll never do. He'll want more," Theo had warned him.

"It'll do for now," Pedro had reassured him.

Vaughn would play dumb, be the brave one and venture up to the cave when the boys didn't return. Angelino would mutter prayers loudly in Mixe. Vaughn would return with a terrible fright on his face. "Blood everywhere. Oh my God, oh my God, he's killed the boys! Run!"

The three would then descend rapidly down the trail, terrified that the faun might be in pursuit. Dwayne would stop them. "Why didn't you grab the money, Vaughn? We've to go back for the money!"

"Are you crazy?! Murder and mayhem. I'm not going back there. What is money in the face of such tragedy? Go back yourself!" He was quite sure Dwayne would not call his bluff, especially with Angelino running ahead of them.

But none of that was happening now. And Vaughn had

five thousand dollars in his hand. Actually he had ten. And a pistol. They were entering a village along the highway. "Pull over or I'll blow your cute brains out," Vaughn announced. Pedro pulled over. Vaughn hopped out, but before closing the door advised them, "Don't eat the tamales, ha, ha, ha." Then his brow furrowed and his eyes flamed with hate. "Fuck you, Pedro." He slammed the door, looked both ways and crossed the street to a little bus shelter.

"Is he fucking kidding?" Theo asked Pedro. Pedro pulled a U-turn and parked alongside the bus stop, knowing Vaughn wasn't stupid enough to pull a gun in broad daylight on the street of a Mexican village.

"What are you doing?" Vaughn shouted, annoyed.

"I'm leaving Dwayne with you."

"The hell you are."

"Well, it's that or you're both coming to town with us."

"I'm not getting in that car."

"I know people in this village," Pedro informed him.

"Oh, really?"

"Yeah, with machetes." Every gringo was afraid of the legendary machete murders favored by the native population when someone didn't play fair. "So what'll it be, Vaughn – Dwayne and death, or my half?"

Vaughn sighed, and a smile crossed his face. "Dwayne *and* death? Don't I get to choose one or the other? Ha, ha, ha." He pulled the purse out of his baggy pants and pulled out half the wad of cash, handing it to Theo through the window. "Here's your five. You do have to give me credit for trying, ha, ha, ha."

"Thanks, Vaughn," Pedro said. "But I still think I'll tell my friends you're here and what you did."

Vaughn looked pale. "That wouldn't be fair."

"Oh, we're way past that."

Theo was nervous. "Come on, Pedro. We got our take, let's go."

"I want all of it, Vaughn, or I call out the machetes." That's when they heard the bus coming down the hill.

"Whoops," Vaughn smiled, gloating. But Pedro hopped

out of the car then, and before Vaughn could react, he kicked him hard in the balls. Vaughn doubled over and Pedro yanked the purse from his hand, hopped back in the car and gunned it.

Theo said nothing.

"Vaughn is a piece of shit."

Theo didn't want to stay in Oaxaca another day. A group of dogs appeared in the highway. They scattered to the shoulders when they saw the Land Rover coming – all except one. Pedro didn't even brake, and ran over it.

"Pedro!"

Pedro shrugged. "They're strays."

"You can't do that when we're in L.A."

Pedro just looked at him.

"So what the fuck do we do with Dwayne?" Theo continued.

"We'll take him back to the hotel and put him to bed."

"What if he wakes up? Or, what if he doesn't?"

Pedro and his default shrug.

* * *

They parked the car near the zocalo where they could watch it from a café. Eventually, Dwayne stumbled out. Pedro smiled. "Free and clear."

Theo breathed a sigh of relief. "Okay. I'm ready to get out of here. Bus station?" He stood up.

They walked back to the apartment where Theo's bag was already packed. He never really unpacked when he was traveling. He liked to think of his suitcase as his rolling dresser.

"I need a little money for a bus ticket."

Pedro peeled off five hundred dollars and handed it to him.

Theo's paranoia reared its head and he stared at the money in his hand. Were they marked bills? He wished he'd never gone along with any of it. Well, a rich man got robbed and no one got hurt. It certainly could have been worse. Still, he felt nostalgia for yesterday, for all the months they'd spent innocently together.

Pedro seemed stoic in parting. Theo hugged him and took a deep breath. There was a chance he'd never see him again. It wasn't that easy to cross the border, contrary to all the propaganda. And it was dangerous. And …

* * *

Theo rode the bus five hours to Mexico City, nervous and watching at each stop for Dwayne to hop on. When he got to the airport to find a flight to LA, he fumbled in his bag for his passport. He couldn't find it and had to step out of line. He dug and dug, but to no avail.

It was gone. Someone had stolen it. And he knew exactly who. He blushed. And then he laughed. He could get a replacement for cheap at the consulate. But couldn't Pedro have just asked him for it?

Theo sat down in one of the multitudes of chairs in one of the numerous waiting areas. He wasn't sure how to feel. Encouraged? Betrayed? A fool? Well, he'd know soon enough.

He looked around and the world felt vast. Awesome, yet predictable. He felt elated and sad all at once. And then he thought of fauns, and how they'd mocked Dwayne's search for one. How uncanny, it occurred to him then, that Pedro seemed to be the very thing.

The Pancake Circus

Clown Daddy bussed dishes at the Pancake Circus, a tacky breakfast joint on Broadway in Sacramento, and well past its prime. There were potholes in the parking lot and the clown marquee's paint was peeling atop the desiccated tar roof. I only went there when I was depressed and, in my half-baked noncommittal self-destruction, craving food that would kill me if I ingested enough of it. I wanted a steamy stack of buttermilk pancakes with that whipped butter they use that melts slowly and thoroughly, sort of like my psyche does when it's heading south. (It does not have the same effect on your arteries, however, which slowly harden like dog shit in the sun.) And I wanted that diabetes-inducing syrup, of course. Two or three shots of it – lethal as sour mash – surreptitious, sticky and sweet as it vanishes into the spongy cake, absorbed like a criminal into the social fabric.

Clown Daddy began as a tattoo of a tiger jumping through a ring of fire – a tiger with a pacifier in his mouth. A tiger caged in a mess of plump blue veins – veins like the roots that buckle sidewalks. Straining as they held the pot poised over my cup; straining like my throat suddenly was; like my cock caged in my drawers.

"Coffee?" It was Josh Hartnett's voice.

In an effort to compose myself, I drew a breath and followed those veins up that forearm, down through the dimple of its elbow and up across the creamy white biceps, firm and round as a young athlete's butt cheek, before the blood-swollen tubes vanished into his white polyester shirt, reappearing at the neck and passing the Adam's apple, which was nothing less than a mushroom head pushing boy-boisterous out of his neck-skin like a go-go dancer in Tommies. "God have mercy," my soul muttered, as my eyes, having lost his veins somewhere under his chin (and damn, what a beautiful charcoal-shadowed chin), slowly crept up his clean-shaven cheek, savoring the pheromonal (and I mean 'moan'-al) beauty of him. Especially his eyes, which looked like a junkie's as he tightened the belt. And bingo, like apples and oranges lining up in a slot – oh my God, I won!

I'm a homo and you know where I'd look for the coins. I felt my sphincter dilate, and my butt cheeks were suddenly like open-cupped palms, holding themselves out to him.

I came in my pants. And then, a bit unnerved to say the least, cleared my throat. I'm not sure I would have been able to even answer him if I hadn't relieved the pressure somewhere. Fortunately, God had mercy after all.

I whimpered: "Yes, please." I couldn't even look at him, so I watched the cup as he filled it to the top, and then some. It crested the brim and ran down onto the saucer – and then I watched the pot move away, off to the next table.

Jesus H. go-go dancing Christ. My drawers were soaked and cooling. I felt like a kid who'd wet his pants. This had happened to me only once before, in jr. high, when Greg Vandersee had stretched, lifting up his arms and revealing a divine cunt of underarm hair that made me lurch forward as my cock emptied its boy-fresh copious fluids into my little BVDs.

Fortunately, Clown Daddy was a busboy and not my waiter. I could handle "yes" and "no," but "the buttermilk stack, with sausage and one egg over-easy" wouldn't have been pretty – or perhaps even possible.

"Hi, I'm Edna. What'll you have?" She smiled.

"A bed, some lube and an hour with your busboy" would

have been the honest answer. Or a fresh pair of undergarments. But this wasn't about honesty, this was about self-destruction. Wasn't it? I ordered the low cholesterol eggbeaters in a vegetable omelet with whole wheat toast. Say what you will – lust leads to healthy choices. Doesn't it?

What I hadn't realized as I sat back gloating, my penis clammy in my damp, semen-soaked briefs, was that when I'd looked in Clown Daddy's eyes my days as a law-abiding citizen had abruptly ended. Choices? Choices had nothing to do with it.

But ignorance is bliss. While it lasts. And while it lasted, my head wobbled like one of those big-headed spring-loaded dolls that look just like Nancy Reagan, swinging this way and that, watching for him, rolling up and down and around like an amusement park ride, taking in the Pancake Circus as I did so, its paint-by-number clowns adorning the walls, its circus tent décor, its uncanny ambience of a sick crime waiting to happen.

I watched him move about while my fly tightened like a glove over a fist. A wet fist, sticky and greedy for whatever it had just crushed to sticky pulp. My mind played the sideshow song as I imagined Clown Daddy behind the curtain, Edna up front barking for him: "Step right up, see the man who makes you cum in your drawers!"

I gulped the coffee down, which drew him back to my table like a shark to wet, red, bleeding bait.

He didn't look at me until I thanked him, and then it was just a shy straight-boy grin. God, but his features were sharp, angled and clean. His dark, deep-set eyes, the long lashes, the wide mouth with its full lips, the arresting pale blue-white of his skin and the night-black hair – that goddamn shadowed chin. And his eyes: dark as crude oil, raw out of the ground. He was undeniably, painfully handsome. Prozac-handsome because he cheered me up. Wellbutrin-handsome because one saw one's sadness disappear like a wisp of smoke – and those pesky sexual side effects? Gone. Every woman in the place blushed when he cleared their plates. I probably wasn't the only one stuck to the vinyl seat in my booth. Thank God my cock has no voice or it would have been barking like a dog.

But I felt the letdown all the same. He's probably straight. Though he ignored the blushing dames. He seemed even a little annoyed by their attention. But we knew who each other were, the girls and I. I eyed them and they me. Did I look as greedy as them? Like there was one cabbage patch doll left and they'd kill to wrest it from whatever fellow shopper had his or her eye on it. Fact was, we all had holes we wanted his cock in. Simple as that. It was like there was one tree left in the world and the ditches yelped like graves to be the chosen one.

I gulped my food like a scat queen falling off the wagon. Delirious, my diaper soiled, I paid my check and left, one glance over the shoulder to see him bend to pick up a fallen fork. Damn, Clown Daddy had a butt like a stallion. My dog leapt, knocking over the milk dish again. Jesus H. cock-hungry Christ. I lurched out the door as my piss slit opened like a flume on a dam.

Clown Daddy sent me home in a frenzy is what he did.

I rushed home, needing to get naked. Onto my back on my bed, my legs kicking like an upended insect as I pulled like a madman, again and again, on my slot handle, hitting jackpot after jackpot until my bed was plain lousy with change.

From then on, he filled my nights and days like a cup, brimming over.

I went for more pancakes two days later, but he wasn't there. On the third day, he was, with a beautiful zit on his cheek. Clown Daddy looked right through me when he recognized me, and then he pulled himself back out.

I lurched. Shit – I came again.

"Coffee?"

I half-coughed. "Uh, yeah."

"Cream?"

I nodded. The greed. My shorts were already full of it.

"Sugar?" He's talkative today.

I regained my composure. "No sugar – sugar's for kids," I answered flirtatiously.

I don't know why I said it. I had to say something. I wanted to hold him there, even if for only a few seconds.

He smiled the brightest smile and walked away.

My head swiveled. What was that? Had he flirted back?

While I waited for my waitress, I read the ads urethaned into the tabletop: vacuum repair, van conversions, derogatory credit, body shops, auto detailing, furniture, appliances and bail bonds. The clues were everywhere. It occurred to me then that he was the only white busboy in the place. The rest were illegal Latin guys who didn't have a choice. What would a citizen take a job like this for? Maybe he was Rumanian or something. But he had no accent. What could he be making? – four, five bucks an hour? Hell, his looks alone could get him ten doing nothing for the right boss. He could hustle at two hundred, do porn for a few thousand a feature; he could wait tables and fuck up and they'd still forgive him because the doyens of Sacramento would return for the way he made them feel against their seat cushions. *What* was he doing here?

Who cares? Just let me fuck him. Shoot first, ask questions later.

He was as aloof as ever when he came back with the coffee. Three cups later, I asked for sugar. He smiled again. "Sugar's for kids. You like kids?"

"Sure, kids are all right."

He nodded and raised his brows with just a hint of a grin as he said, sort of stoned-like, "Kids are all right." And he walked away.

Go figure. I scribbled my phone number on the coffee coaster, with a little cartoon kid, waving.

* * *

And he called. But he never left his name.

"This is the guy who likes kids, down at the Circus. I can't leave a number, but meet me at the Circus at 3 p.m. Wednesday."

I jacked off at 2:30 p.m., not wanting to repeat my little Pancake Circus habitual jackpot when I sidled up to shake his hand. My knees might buckle, and then what? Would I hold onto his hand and pull him down with me? Would I beg him to clean up my shorts with his tongue? Would he do it?

I needed to get hold of myself. I turned the key in the deadbolt as I left the house. I pushed the key in hard, my mouth agape. In and out went the key. I reached for the knob. Good God, I've lost it.

I saw him from two blocks away. He sat on the low wall of the planter that had endured, neglected and falling to pieces with its ratty bushes and weeds, between the sidewalk and the parking lot.

He wore black boots, Levis and a camouflage winter coat. Not a promising fashion statement for what I had in mind.

He nodded when he saw me coming, but ignored my hand when I put it out to shake. He just said, "What's up?" And then, without waiting for an answer, added, "There's a playground about five blocks from here."

"What?"

"Come on, I'll show you."

I feigned having a clue, but I really didn't until it occurred to me he might be suggesting a place to have sex – some doorway maybe, or a clump of trees out of view that schoolyards were notorious for. But it was 3 p.m., school would still be in session.

I could see the schoolyard fence from a couple blocks away as we approached. Stepping off a curb, he grabbed my arm by the biceps, and my cock leapt like a Jack Russell terrier.

"Stop here."

He dropped his gaze and I followed it as, with his left hand firmly in his pocket, he lifted his pant leg to reveal a plastic contraption surrounding his ankle. A small green light pulsed intermittently. He studied it, then backing up three feet, got it to stop pulsing and simply glow a constant green.

"This is as far as I can go," he said.

It took me a minute to realize he was under house arrest. What does it mean? I didn't know anything about law enforcement. Drunk driving? It must be some kind of probation. He's probably a rapist or a killer, a thief or a drug dealer. Nah, too cute to rape. But if he's fucked up enough, what would that matter? Too smart to kill. Thieves are a dime a dozen and I'm only carrying twenty bucks. Drug-dealing? Humbug. So what. But none of these possibilities were in any way convincing. He was just too sexy to fit any criminal stereotype, which shows you what a dumb fuck I was.

I may have misread him, but I wasn't completely foolish. Not completely. I knew he was a criminal, so I figured I'd need to find out about the ankle bracelet before taking him home. Just in case he was going to murder me or steal my stereo. The logic of queers. On top of all that, I assumed he'd tell me the truth, which was preposterous – except that he did. More or less.

He retired to a sloping lawn in front of a house on the corner, offering, "This will be fine." I was getting more and more confused. Sex right here?

Within minutes, we heard them: the cacophony of tykes, who were now streaming down the street in gaggles. They reached the far corner, stopped, looked both ways, and then proceeded across. Group after group of them: little Koreans and Viets with rolling book bags; Mexican kids burdened by overstuffed backpacks; white kids on skateboards; little black kids strutting.

"Aren't they beautiful?" he said.

"Sure they are. Kids are like flowers."

"Flowers?" He looked at me like I was stupid.

"You know ... colorful things? New life? All that?" He wasn't buying my poetry.

"I mean beautiful like meat," he said.

He ran his tongue across his full upper lip and it occurred to me, amidst my throbbing erection, that he was a convicted pedophile. My cock was like a poised spear now, but not because of what he'd just confessed about his sexual orientation – it was his tongue and what it had just performed. Take me, you beast. I must confess, the moral repugnance was not the first thought that entered my mind, nor the second. The tongue being the first, what followed was my sudden disappointment that not only was I possibly the wrong gender, but I was most definitely not the right age. I hadn't a chance. My cock still reached for him, fighting against the binding of my jeans – not to mention the limits of his orientation – like a child having a tantrum, refusing to let go of a cherished teddy bear. But I felt the sweat on my asshole cool.

He lay back, a sprig of grass in his teeth, smiling at the kids – a pedophile cad. They smiled back. Jesus Wayne Gacy, we were cruising!

I tried to get a foothold. "Uh, would you like to go grab a coffee?"

"Nah, I'm happy right here."

I said nothing more, paralyzed with ineptitude. We sat there for just fifteen minutes, until the herd had passed. "Damn, I gotta jack off. Come on."

Speaking of come-ons – was this one? I'm not sure I was interested anymore, but of course my cock still was, throbbing like a felon in chains. I followed.

Back to Broadway to an ugly stucco motel-looking apartment building streaked with rusty drain runoff, its windows curtained and unwelcoming. Clown Daddy said nothing. He simply keyed the lock, and I followed him into one of the saddest apartments I'd ever seen. A mattress lay in the middle of the living room, with a single twisted blanket on it. There was an alarm clock on the floor, and in the kitchen, fast food trash in the sink.

The toilet was foul and ringed with dark grime. There were no pictures, no kitchen utensils, plates or cups, no toaster, no coffee maker, no books, no phone. Other than the bed and the roof and plumbing, there was but one thing that made the place habitable at all: a television with a VCR.

He pulled a videocassette out of the back lining of his camouflage hunting jacket and placed it in the VCR. He sat down on the bed, suddenly eager and animated. "I just got this from a dude I met. It better be good; it cost me thirty bucks." There were no credits, no title, not even sound. There were a lot of kids, though, doing things that got people put away.

"I think I better go," I muttered, when all at once, with his elbows now supporting him on the bed, he leaned back and yanked his jeans down, revealing an enormous marbled manhood which slapped back across his taut belly like a call to prayer. His eyes fixed on the television, never even acknowledging his handsome cock as he grabbed it full-fisted. "Jesus God" I muttered to myself, staring at one of the most stunning penises I'd ever seen: nine inches, wired like the backside of a computer with mouth-watering veinage, and nested in the blackest of hair, which right now was casting deep forested shadows as it worked its way under his well-stocked jumbo-sized scrotum. I never had a choice. It was down my throat before I made any decisions or even considered whether he wanted it there. He didn't protest, bucking his hips and driving into my whimpering mouth as he glared at the television set. I shot in my pants without so much as touching myself, just moments before my throat filled like a cream pastry, hot gobs of his god-juice leaking from the crust.

I tongued it clean before he quickly grabbed it like a hammer, or anything else I could have been borrowing, to put it away. He didn't even look at me as he hopped up to his feet, yanking up his jeans in one fluid motion. It wasn't fear of intimacy like I'd seen with other guys. He was simply done, and more or less emotionless – in his own world. God knows what he'd been thinking as he bucked his manly juices into my craving body, which for him had become just one big hole to propel his anti-social lusts into. I can't call it my mouth; it was just what was available. I'd have torn my skin back like curtains if it were possible and let him drill through whatever part of me got him off.

"That tape sucked," he casually related. I was still sitting on the bed, stunned, not knowing what to do, licking the remnants of his now cooling semen off my chapped lips. "I gotta go to work," he informed me, pulling the videocassette out and handing it to me, without making eye contact.

'Uh, I don t want this," I said as my hand opened to accept it.

"No? Don't you like kids?"

"Uh, I think you know what I like."

For a while he said nothing. "Keep it for me till next time." He grinned.

"Next time?" I was in a daze, but hope springs eternal.

"Yeah, next time I see you."

I lit up even though I was consumed with dread from what, other than the amazing cock action, was a profoundly depressing social interaction. "I'll just leave it here," I said, balking.

"No can do, guy. I'm on probation. Can't have that here. Keep it for me."

"Uh, yeah, sure, till next time."

* * *

I didn't think myself an accomplice as I walked home. What did I know about such legal machinations? I only knew I was no longer depressed and had just had one of life's peak experiences. Had his cock literally trounced thousands of years of science that had eventually developed selective serotonin reuptake inhibitors? Imagine the clinical trials. I'd seen a lot of cocks, a lot of naked men, like any fag. But Jesus H. Priapus Satyriasis, I had never seen such a beautiful manifestation of the male organ anywhere – in print, on film, in my bed, even in my fantasy life, which was no slacker when it came to cock. I imagined what it must have been like for explorers coming upon Yosemite, Victoria Falls, the Grand Canyon. Unimaginable and sublime beauty. I leaned against a wall at one point on the walk home, needing to catch my breath, my cock once again tenting my jeans. The fact of the matter was: I was strung out on his cock. And I didn't even have a phone number.

No matter, he called, thank God. It was either that or I was in for a lot of pancakes.

"I got some more tapes. Wanna come over and check them out?"

I didn't hear any of it but the "come over" part. "When?"

"Now."

"I'm on my way."

The door was cracked when I arrived. When I opened it to step in, I lost my breath. Splayed across the bed was Clown Daddy, his substantial manhood like the clock tower at some university – everything converged toward it.

"Oh baby," was all I could think to say, which was oddly appropriate considering what was happening on the VCR where his gaze was fixed. My brows furrowed. Good God, they can't be more than three.

"Come to poppa," he said with a fatherly grin.

I was like a panting puppy with the promise of a walk. He held the leash. I leapt and was sucking on his teat like a hungry lamb before you could say "baahhh," drooling and lapping up and down the hard shaft, savoring the throbbing gristle of his veins, weeping at the sweet softness of the massive velvety helmet. I was aware of what felt like a tear rolling down my inner thigh. My asshole was sweating like a day laborer short on rent: more baskets, more peaches.

I knew I needed to strip but balked at taking a time-out for fear he'd lose interest or lose control. I hopped up and stripped quickly. He didn't even notice, his eyes locked on the romper room shenanigans stage-left like a baby enthralled with a mobile.

I knew all I had to do was get into position, and in no time was on my knees on the bed, blocking Clown Daddy's view of the television. He didn't miss a beat as he hopped up on his knees and grabbed my waist, answering my plea for "Lube, Clown Daddy, lube," with a hawk into his palm.

I opened like sunrise, pulled him into me more than he plunged. I heard him as he vanished into my sleeve: "Uuuuuuuuuuuuuuuhhh." And I matched him like a chorus: "Aaaaaaaaaaaaahhhhhh." I dropped my face into the mattress as he pounded me, knowing I'd be unable to maintain any balance with my arms, which were not only shaking with excitement but were seriously challenged, considering the slams he was delivering and the fact that my body's focus was pretty much solely directed at the contractions of my rectum as it greedily grabbed at what can only be described as the bread of life. A baguette of it, no less.

He sent me onto the floor by thrust ten or so, and then he emitted an enormous Josh Hartnett, "FUUUUck," as my ass-hole filled with his ambrosia.

He pulled out with an audible pop and wiped off his cock with the blanket and fell backward onto the mattress. "That's a great age," he muttered while staring at the ceiling.

I felt a momentary sinking feeling as I looked at the video monitor, realizing all at once the makeover I would need if I was to hold onto Clown Daddy past the duration of his probation.

"I gotta go to work," he said.

I nodded; I knew the protocol. He popped out the tape and handed it to me. I staggered down the walkway of that shitty apartment building past dried out cactuses in pots and a pair of roller skates – good God, did his or her parents know who was living next door? What about Megan's Law? I was lost in a strange milieu of overarching lust, revulsion, horror, responsibility, and that unique post-fuck feeling of "that was great; everything's gonna be just fine."

* * *

At home, I fumbled through my bathroom drawers for the Flo-Bee and set to work shaving my body clean of hair. While my mind remained a stew of anxiety, and I winced at the razor nicks I was inflicting on my balls, I reveled in how I was going to finally incite his lust as he had mine.

Next, I got out my sewing machine and set to work on a new wardrobe: a sailor suit, a Boy Scout uniform, a large diaper, Teletubbie briefs.

I put on the briefs and sailor suit, looked at myself in the mirror. Ridiculous. "Don't be so negative," I self-talked back. I did a striptease, attempting to be convincing. I worked on my little boy shy look. But when I finally dropped my trousers and gazed at my hairless cock, I was sorely dismayed. I had a big dick, huge really, and the shaving had only made it look bigger. How am I gonna convince Clown Daddy I'm a child with this thing? How many grade-schoolers are packing eight inches? Then there were my chest and arms. I worked out, for God's sake; I was a mess of secondary sex characteristics. I needed to gain fifty pounds, maybe take some hormones. "One step at a time," I calmed myself.

I'd done what I could and I wanted to see him, to show him how I'd be whatever he wanted me to be. I don't think at that time I was considering saving him and reforming him. I just wanted to please him, make of myself a gift. Woo him.

Chocolate. I bought a box of Le Petite Ecoliers and went for pancakes in the sailor suit. He smiled big when he saw me. The hostess looked askance. The crowd wondered. It occurred to me I was exposing him. I blushed red as a swollen cockhead. I left as quickly as I'd come, racing back up the street. Whatever happened, I didn't want to hurt Clown Daddy. Goodness no, I was interested in his pleasure.

* * *

There was a message on the machine when I got home: "Nice suit, hee, hee. 8 p.m. Wear it." Click.

The shirt never came off as Clown Daddy's maleness hovered over me and he ominously climbed up on top of me, his lead pipe of a cock bobbing like a tank gun, my legs held behind my ears like the spring-loaded pogo stick I would soon be playing the part of as he bounced me off the mattress.

"You look fucking great." He smiled and he kissed me this time, full, his tongue like a tapeworm, bent on my intestines, determined to reach all the way down to where his cock was reaching from the other end to meet it in a hot sticky mess of saliva and semen.

"Daddy, daddy, daddy," I said in a series of yelp. We growled, we lost ourselves and rode our dicks like runaway horses. His final thrusts were downright divine, my hands digging into his firm white butt cheeks like talons holding their kill. He split me like a piece of wood and my cum hit his chest so hard it bounced and splattered like blood would if the axe of his cock had buried itself in my forehead.

I'd brought the diaper in my backpack.

"Daddy ... please ... diaper me."

He guffawed, and then with an eagerness I'd never seen, cried out, "Yeeeeaaah!"

He diapered me. Patted my ass. Told me to pack up and get out.

My God, I'd done it. I'd seduced Clown Daddy.

He didn't kiss me goodbye of course, nor invite me to brunch. But I walked away without a videocassette this time. Progress.

* * *

I guess that's when it occurred to me I could save him. And maybe not just him. Maybe I'd just found the treatment for pedophilia. God knows, no one seemed to give a damn about these people. The last sexual minority. I could rehabilitate them all. My shaved asshole, a rehab center.

That's when I saw the squad car. Parked in front of my house. Next to the undercover white Crown Royale. Three men in dark suits. It was the Matrix and I was Neo, standing on a street corner in a sailor suit, my hips bulging from the diaper that swaddled my manhood.

I knew what they'd found. I knew my chances. I ran. It wasn't much of a chase. I had nowhere to go. All I had was a shot at making it back to Broadway where the great voting public could witness four cops tackling a child – a rather large child, to be sure – in a sailor suit.

I felt the tug as one of them got hold of the back of my shirt just as I reached the intersection of 23rd and Broadway. I screamed as high-piercing a preadolescent scream as I could muster.

I was interrogated at length. I assumed they had Clown Daddy somewhere. How else would they have nabbed me? I drank coffee, got knocked around, but through it all I endured by dreaming of meeting Clown Daddy – when I was finally convicted – in some filthy prison cell where we could pursue our love affair in peace – me trading cigarettes and gum for razors to keep my cock and balls soft as a baby's behind for my Clown Daddy and his meat-Eucharist, truly a transubstantiation of all the misery around us into an Elysian field of bliss.

"Where did you get the tapes?"

I refused to tell. "I found them."

"Where?"

I had to place them as far away from Clown Daddy as possible. "In a trash can in Vacaville."

"What were you doing going through trash in Vacaville?"

"Someone on the Internet told me he'd put them there." I was indicting myself. I thought I was saving Clown Daddy. If I had to lie, even to the point of destroying my own future, I'd do it for Clown Daddy – blinded by love, or myopia for his cock. Same difference. And to think, I didn't even know the details of his crime. We'd never discussed it. I didn't want to know.

"Who?" the cop demanded, but in a boring, annoying, non-sexual way. Why couldn't Clown Daddy be my interrogator?

"It was one of those throwaway names."

"What was it?"

"Bob."

"Goddammit! Bob who?"

"Bob1 at aol.com."

He backhanded me across the face. *Whack!*

They threatened me with a stiff sentence if I didn't give them something. I only considered that their sentence could never be as stiff as Clown Daddy's meaty member, so I was unimpressed by their threats.

They sentenced me to five years.

Clown Daddy did not appear in my cellblock, though I looked and waited and pined. It had been explained in my trial that the videos found in my home had been coded with a tracking device, leading the authorities to my house. Not unlike an ankle bracelet such as Clown Daddy wore. It had even been suggested that Clown Daddy was a narc, or had used me as a patsy. The judge put a stop to those conjectures, admonishing the defense: "Whoever gave him the pornography is not on trial today. Another day. Right now, we're trying this man." And he pointed at me like Clown Daddy's member used to do.

Clown Daddy never appeared. Only Vernon. He was my cellmate, and as a skinny white fag, he informed me I'd be wise to do his bidding. I've done it, though he lacks both Clown Daddy's girth and length, not to mention all the other characteristics that gods wield over man.

Ah, but the gods are kind, for they have blest us with imagination. And so when Vernon slicks his member with Crisco I steal from the commissary and mercilessly impales me, I close my eyes and see a circus tent, and the circus music begins, and all the clowns drop their baggy pants, and then the tigers and lions turn, lifting their tails, and the dwarves and ape men offer up their tight behinds, hands firmly gripped to their ankles – and the crowd cheers, and then goes "AAAHHH" as Clown Daddy in all his naked huge-dicked grinning Josh Hartnett-throated glory comes swinging through on the trapeze spraying his jism all over the clowns and animals, dwarves and freaks, and the whole damn crowd, who bathe in it like the blessed waters of Lourdes.

And Vernon is proud. He thinks he's made that mess all over my chest and belly. Let him think it. The truth is hardly important at this point. I'm an innocent man doing time for kiddie porn, the police are fools, Vernon's a chump, and my asshole's just a 7-Eleven that he holds up every Saturday night. As for the cash, I hand it right over. In fact, I leave the register open. No way to run a business. But I, unlike Vernon, am not proud. For I have seen God.

I spend all my time with him. Vernon, that is, not God. We even eat pancakes together. I stuff my face. I'm fattening up for Clown Daddy, while Vernon goes on and on with his theories.

"The earth is a plate," he says. "Mankind sat down and is eating. When he's through, it'll be over."

"Where are we now?" I ask.

"Somewhere deep in the mashed potatoes; maybe halfway through."

"Are you gay, Vernon?" I like to get a rise out of him.

"Not at all," he explains. He tells me men are pigs, and this is why you can't call him a faggot. Vernon says if it were legal, most men he knew (and he knew a certain kind, though he always meant every man) would fuck everything in sight, and what's more, they'd never let their sex partners survive to betray them (as they always will, by his reckoning – something to remember when I get out of here). Therefore, he's of the opinion that men "would drill holes in their sex partner's skulls if they could, and fuck their brains out. They'd drill holes in backs and arms, thighs, through the bottom of feet, right through the front of 'em, core the motherfuckers like apples," he says drolly, "leave them like the dough after all the cookies have been cut out of it. But the screaming would be annoying, so you'd do the brain first."

"Do you like the circus, Vernon?"

He shrugs his shoulders. "I don't like those clowns. Creepy."

"I knew a clown once."

"Shut up and eat."

I pour more syrup on my pancakes and watch it vanish, watch it run away and join the circus.

Queer Theory

Blow, baby, blow," I yelled into the maw of orgasmic bliss as the angel-headed Marco bobbed up and down on my sad ghostly-hungry shaft – long after beers drunk too swiftly in sultry afternoon of San Francisco July when the boys take their shirts off and temptation is around every bend and I couldn't help myself, and into his little overpriced studio with beads hanging in the doorway and needles full of crystal meth atop the stereo and an old half-empty bottle of red wine echoing the joys of nights spent long before this too-bright afternoon – when, I'd later learn, Marco'd been fucking Cody and Alvah and all the gang before I even got here. But it's a long, long story and I'm so tired and impotent now, I'd have to go all the way back to that forlorn summer of groping bodhisattvas and the white, milky sunbursts of Marco, Marco – it was San Francisco in the summer of 1989 and there wasn't a boy I couldn't make, and did make them all until the final foggy days of August humping their way through the Golden Gate and I was sad and Cody and Alvah gone and Marco too, gone, gone – and me with a stubborn case of clap to boot.

And Marco, Marco – angelic-choired, song-singing orgasms of sweating summer nights in Oakland Hills and Alvah going on about Cavafy and Rumi and all the other long-dead, buggering poets of antiquity and beyond. Cody said right out: "I'd sooner suck your cock than read your damn poetry, Alvah!"

And Alvah pulling off his belt and letting it fall heavy out of his pants – he wears no underwear, old Jew of the desert, sackcloth and ashes in his baggy pants, uncuffed and unpleated. It's in the first stars of evening in the Berkeley backyard and Cody falls to his knees, genuflecting and paying homage to the sad religion of a desert people that predated our own and sent us on this long sad journey of unredemption and fear of an angry God out to prove we're nothing but a bunch of deadbeat winos, sloppy with our sacrifice. And he must be appeased.

Cody'd gotten to turning Alvah around now – and after fumbling impatiently with a condom – proceeded to expertly put it in him with a groan like a camel passing through the eye of a needle. And so I went inside to find Marco, who'd fallen into a tea stupor watching *Jeopardy* on the television and muttering sutras or koans – I couldn't tell which, but it was holy, as are all his ruined words.

And not two days later, Marco'd nearly overdosed on crystal and so was gathered up by his mother and father in sad, dusty, mauve Oldsmobile driven all the way down from Sacramento on a lonely Sunday wherein no one went to mass and traffic snarled in hated, heated lack of love – and Christ would have been disappointed even and was probably a tired Mexican field hand gathering strawberries or kiwis unbeknownst to all the lost wanderers on the American going-nowhere highway of it all.

He'd said he'd be back in a week, calling me from the loud, noisome corridor of S.F. General, above the din of crying mothers, their babies shot in drive-bys, and old folks choking on their own phlegm, amidst the shivering withered homosexuals dying of a plague that terrified us all into compulsive fucking and denial and death wishes, and sometimes even caution, or at least the rote ritual of condoms like lit incense and invocation, appeasement – and then too, there were the harried doctors, Christ-like trying to love their neighbor, heal the sick – and giving up sometimes even – as green lines ran straight across cardiac machines, echoing the sad end of us all in white corridors and mopped tiles of disinfectant-stinking floors ripe for death and decay.

So, a week gone, I went looking for Marco, who'd sent me a sad little postcard of Old Town Sacramento, with pictures of broken brick wino alleys refurbished into the horror of a suburban tourist mall. I came stumbling off the tired mule train of the underground MUNI dying its slow death at a dollar-a-ride – "Hey bud," I yelled, as it stalled for the eighth time, "what's this, a subway worse than Amtrak?!"

"And you can get off then!" he snapped, and turning to glare me down I recognized him as a sax man from the little club on 3rd Street and apologized profusely, like confession and "Bless me father, for I have sinned. A poor sinner, I know not what I do ..." I hopped out then and there and tripped up the steps to Market Street, busy with suited, booby-prize, lost American working man and woman rushing madness and the Gabrielic shouts of bike messengers warning them all of impending disaster and imminent destruction. Sweet rapture hanging from their waists.

I wanted Marco to make sweet love to me. His bejeweled, flower-decked, bodhisattva sphincter would opens for me like a lotus flower. It would sing sutras while I ride latex-clad and swollen through the old hobo rails deep in his groaning rectum, sad and forlorn with loss of another turd that very day.

Last night I'd nearly given up the ghost, drinking wine with Cody, ambling our way down Folsom Street, missing my sweet nineteen-year-old boy/man who I told everyone I met was a saint for sure, an angel sent from the lonely nowhere of Central Valley California where the railroads died and gave birth to a messianic hobo boy, name of Marco. Bartenders yelping at me to get out and carry on my crazy lovelorn rantings somewhere else, which I did until waking up on the floor in a pool of my own vomit and not a small number of men's wads in the backroom of some bear bar where I was later told I sucked off the whole house (the debate of whether oral sex were safe or no obliterated six throbbing inches at a time, all but forgotten in the missing of Marco and the desire for his manhood and any and all takers) – and all in a half hour's time, accomplishing some of the finest blowjobs many of these men had ever known. All for the missing of Marco.

And the other nights with my dear Marco gone were the same and unhinged, seeing mirages on street corners and in dance clubs of the golden locks and smile of my man child, my very own Antinous, who'd been the sweet boy lover of the Emperor Hadrian in the honey-colored ancient world, forever smothered in the old greasy olive oil of time. And I'm one sad Roman emperor with no empire but an old bottle of Port and a limp cock, HIV lurking everywhere like a dying Gaul – and maybe in my very own throat – weaving my way down Howard Street looking for an all-night market to get me a refill of this here nectar, hoping the alcohol will obliterate any disease, but all it does is bring before me visions of Marco and deep dreamings – even while I walk – of Marco, Marco Antinous, golden favorite of Caesar and dead all these long years in the Nile. And it can't be he's gone. And what if he's got it and is right now withering among fruit orchards in the Central Valley, their blossoms fallen, rotten fruit like a fouled offering from a mocking god scattered at his feet, his body curled in fetal position, and fear fills me at the whereabouts and condition of my guardian angel lost satyr born 2500 years too late for our destined acropoliptic love-fucking cumblasts in the dawn of civilization.

But it's all premature and delusional and Marco returns on schedule, his head hung low with a big bag on his back at the Greyhound station, and I run to him and hug him hard in my arms, witnessing his sad visage because he's disappointed the folks and before now they didn't even know he was gay and knocked out on a dozen different drugs, living in the Haight-Ashbury and making his money doing massage and selling speed.

"And it's okay, Marco," I say. "I still haven't come out to

my mother. But she'd send me money anyway, I think. And it's not important. What's important is the apple-red in your cheeks and that we get back to my hotel room down on 6th Street and I drive this train into your empty Wyoming of droughted ranchlands and cattle skulls staring at the highway – and you'll forget, you'll forget Marco, you'll forget the pain and your parents both."

Marco nods his head and is soon shooting speed in an alleyway while I run to the corner for a bottle, and then me and Marco are arguing with the guy at the desk because this fleabag residential hotel has a big *No Guests in the Rooms* sign in the lobby. And I want to tell him that this fine bodhi boy emanation of the very Buddha himself who loves all beings endlessly and without preference is a different story altogether from a guest and will in fact rain blessings of flowers and rainbow light on this very nowhere sad hell of a hotel, but I'm drunk and in my own way sort of closeted so I jabber a few pleas and fall silent. And I'm unself-confident now, especially on 6th Street where you need to be a transvestite or a violent son of the devil to get any respect, and I'm certainly not either. I'm just another broken-down wino.

But Marco persists: "Oh, come on, dude, be a bro."

And the manager finally agrees, throwing his hands up. "Go ahead, do whatever you want, the world's a sty and I can't stop it from falling apart before my eyes. I don't care anymore. I'll give you twenty minutes!"

And I find relief and a crazy kind of satori with Marco as we get stiff and sinfully hungry and I beg him to bareback, and he nods with just a tad of reluctance, and I think I see the host as he cums – he's arrived too soon for the Millennium and my heart's not ready yet – and he's weeping now and I give him a drink and more speed and he calms down, burdened by the demands of buddhahood and the certainty of being a reincarnation of Avalokiteshvara, the Buddha of Compassion. And it's hard on young Marco, just a boy from Sacramento become the one under whose very footsteps lotus flowers bloom, falling asleep in the arms of a horny old wino.

I rouse him and we head out. "Not twenty minutes!" I call to the man at the desk. Off to the Stud to dance and drink a beer or two, and forget, but before we get there we see a fight and a drag queen is left lying in the gutter, her forehead bloodied and her cheap wig a crown of thorns. The tough guys have run off and Marco, my dear St. Francis of Faggotdom, rushes and I think I see his wings briefly, but I was drunk and can't be sure. But I know he's an angel – I'm sure of that suddenly, for the drag queen is bleeding and Marco doesn't care because he is a Buddha and immune to AIDS, he has to be. And Marco, Christ-like, helps the drag queen to her tottering high-heeled feet and she's a mess and probably was before they jumped her, but now a real mess and so we know we have to take her somewhere but the twenty minutes are up and they'll never let us back in the hotel and even though I said a transvestite gets respect that doesn't mean they let them in hotels, especially if they haven't paid for a room and they aren't local. And this girl we've got looks the Castro type. She's no Tenderloin tart, but a well-bred college-educated young man on his own delusory road of fame, mimicking Judy Garland or Patsy Cline. And I'm muttering as I gather up her heels and scattered costume jewelry: "Why are so few of the great jazz singers inspirers of drag queens? Where is Bessie Smith and Billie Holiday, singing their plaintive broken-hearted nowhere and nobody and left-again-by-another-lousy-man blues? And where are they?" I ask Marco.

And he snaps, shaking with adrenaline and the last of the speed. "Why don't you do drag as one of them if you're so obsessed with it, Sal?!"

And I'm taken aback and hurt at upsetting Marco, and I get to weeping through my wine and falling on my knees in the drag queen's blood and smeared makeup on the sidewalk and begging Marco to forgive me, and Marco storming away with the drag queen, flagging a cab, and gone. Gone.

I figure Marco will take the drag queen back to his pad and like Mother Theresa herself in old dusty Calcutta where the funeral pyres burn on the Ganges, he'll put her back together again, bandage her wounds. And me, I'll go find Cody to get my mind off Marco – give him some time, but I know I'll endlessly obsess on him and what could have set him off. And why would I Judas-like betray his holy rectum with my infected seed – and not even for thirty shekels of silver, unless you count his beauty which would run into the billions – whole economies, GNPs of manly attractiveness and virility, abundant and copious wealth, enough to retire the scroogiest of misers for life and make of them spendthrifts.

And sure enough I find Cody not an hour later in the back of my place on his knees sucking a big bear cock expertly, his tongue moving like how he'd perfected moving cars around the parking lots in Manhattan where he worked the summer I met him and we first fucked each other. He's sure oral sex is safe and now anxiety knits my brow on my ruminant face, which Marco calls soulful and doomed, fascinated to watch as death enters him.

I order a beer and wait and soon enough Cody's back on his feet, leaving the man shuddering still with pleasure, licking his chops with satisfaction, and Cody's hitting me on the back and saying: "Sal, Sal, why'd you run off like that the other night?"

And I can't even remember the other night or running off or anything, but Cody's always seeing things in his own epic way so I explain I must have left on account of Marco which leads him to logically ask me just where Marco is and why not here, and I say, "Drop it, Cody, he's mad at me for fucking him raw and ran off with a drag queen."

And Cody, undiminishably enthusiastic and cheerful, crazy cumshot of a crazed bodhisattva, pulls me off the barstool and says, "We're going out to get supremely laid!"

And I huff and tell him *"I don't wanna,"* but Cody can't be appeased and off we go to more bars and sex clubs and I land a twenty-year-old Latino boy at the Detour who beats me off until I see Matthew, Mark and John in their lost Mediterranean madness of centuries past, and he's uncut, and as he spills his swollen yam-like member in my belly hair, it brings to mind Marco, sad little messiah, Christ-like and written of by them all.

The young Chicano boy grunts loudly as he spurts string after string of milky horchata and cherubs fly furiously around my own genitals, inspiring me to spill my sad drops of heaven on the empty, unloved pavement. He disengages himself from me and sighs the breath of a lost angel, attempting but failing to climb his way home. Disheveled, I thank the young Aztec prince and wonder about the lovely floating gardens of Lake Tenochtitlan he must dream of ere he rests each night, and I go on my way. And having lost Cody whom I left in the bar pissing on a troll in the bathroom, I go back in to find him and now he's arguing with some redneck-looking nelly queen in a baseball cap, plaid shirt and construction boots, who looks like he might have worked lookout on Sourdough Mountain with me and Japhy last summer but there isn't a speck of dust on his new America-promising-cleanliness-for-ever-and-no-pain boots. Cody reached out to pull his hair but the queen had none under her cap – her pate was wholly shaved. And she hissed and spit at Cody and he slapped her face, turned and stormed out, me on his heels.

"I've got to find Marco," was all I could say.

And Cody ranting and raving into Market Street about how he can't find anyone to lay and these Castro clones will be the death of him. And now the police are flashing their lights after Cody as he runs along the median toward Castro Street, screaming and carrying on like a madman. I lurk back in the shadows of the Detour's black doorway, hoping I won't have to bail him out again at 850 Bryant where they know him too well now he's been here in San Francisco six months. Cody darts and dodges and loses himself in the crowd on the sidewalk running down Castro Street and the cops give up and leave him alone. I'll never catch up with him now and besides I need Marco.

So I head across town to the Haight-Ashbury to his old yellow apartment building, the shade of old dark urine left too long in the pot and the sad fate of all nectars and liquids, including dear Marco's cum that splashed against the back of my throat not even so much as a broken-down quarter of a day ago, all of those strong young wiggly sperm beastly dead.

He's not home, it turns out – I can tell by the light – and the buzzer goes unanswered. I head across town to maybe catch up with Cody but go this time by way of Buena Vista Park that looks out on the whole bay, down to San Bruno Mountain and all the way up beyond the fog-shrouded golden bridge to the Marin Headlands, which crouch like a great Chinese dragon. And then the sea beyond which folds in all the lights and makes of the great San Francisco peninsula a lost prick deep in the asshole of time unending. A long sorry fuck that leaves the world spent. And the universe is casual sex as it is here at Buena Vista. The big bang perchance was an orgasm without love, and so we sad mortals wander in search of that which the universe is not premised on. The universe is premised on wine and a fast fuck in the toilet.

I find a lean cowboy type who jacks off in my face, and as my cock explodes in my pants I imagine the cowboy cum to be my Marco's and whiningly demand in prayerful stations of the cross, begging for mercy and forgiveness, that the universe not be about meaningless sex and venereal disease but about Marco and love and Billie Holiday being treated right by her man.

I wake at dawn scruffing in some bushes on the slopes of this very same Buena Vista, dried cum flaking off the grizzled beard of my unshaven chin. There's no telling who followed the cowboy but I think I remember a young Indian boy who whispered to me that he was the entire continent of North America, its distilled essence, come to me like a phantom angel of a hundred years ago to deliver the seed of understanding, to shoot it against the back of my throat and so leave me to swallow the truth, the truth – even if it kills me – and become from thence on the lonely bard storyteller of stiff cock and colonic laundering in the long forgotten washerwoman blues laundromat of the emptied warehouse of the unremembered heaven and the celestial Buddha realms rife with boyhood.

But just now I've got to find Marco, I mutter, drifting back down the hill to the Haight having unknowingly abandoned my last night's search for Cody which brought me by way of this brush-strewn promontory and nob of devastated earth and volcanic sorrow, Buena Vista.

Marco wasn't home then and not for days afterward. Never home when I called, and I drank more and more and wondered and wandered, thinking of no one but him.

Then one afternoon, strolling down Haight Street like a couple of dandies – it's Marco and the drag queen, all dolled-up like boulevardiers or cheap, thrift-store Oscar Wildes. They've got on floppy hats and long coats, wild-colored scarves adorning their Adam's-appled necks.

"Marco, Marco," I said, "I've been missing you something terrible!"

But he cut me off. "You need a twelve-step program, Sal, get out of our way." And he brushed me aside, the clone drag queen's nose so high I could see straight up her nostrils into the heavenly firmament itself. I stood slack-jawed as they hurried off, wondering why I'd messed things up with my insistent and manipulative needy raw fucking and my talk about Billie Holiday, and maybe I've gone and cursed everything with her sad, man-done-left-me dirges flickering about the halo of Marco. *Give him what he wants,* Marco'd probably figured. He's just another young stud on the make, I conclude, not an angel at all – a trick, and the universe is a cheap fuck anyway. I'll just duck into this here bar and get myself royally soused.

The next time I went by Marco's apartment, there was a man changing the name on the doorbell. And though I asked him, "What, has Marco gone and gotten married and changed his name?" I knew Marco'd left.

The man moved the toothpick around in his mouth. "I'm only the manager, I don't know folks' business. The whole world's goin' to hell. If I were you, I'd check there for your friend."

I hoped my Antinous hadn't thrown himself into the bay for love of me. A sudden regret he's had I imagined, strung out on speed, young Marco realizing my love for him and his for me and he's gone and thrown himself in the drink unable to wait out the drug's haunting voice. But I think better of it, Antinous and the rest. I was no Roman emperor, and besides, Marco didn't love me anymore. I was a damn fool wino in need of my mother's money and he was just another speed freak with a sweet body and golden locks.

I found Cody a few blocks away on Hippie Hill scoring some tea. He called to me from out of the bushes when he saw me ambling forlorn along the opposite sidewalk.

"Sal, yo Sal, we've got a plan to turn this whole park into Big Sur! We want you to be the old Chinese hermit living up on Bung-Ho Mountain in the mist, dripping down poems on the people like leaves and feathers cherry-blossom-drifting down through the fog."

I crossed the street, my head turned plaintively toward the pavement. "Cody, I can't be anybody on account of Marco's gone and vanished."

"Oh, forget about him. He's gone to New York with that drag queen who has illusions of making it big as RuPaul or Noel Coward or some such. Forget Marco."

I was stunned, and me having thought he'd thrown himself in the drink for poor broken me.

"Will you take me out there after him?"

He laughed. "No chance, Sal, I got me a nice little club kid with a big weenie; I ain't going nowhere for awhile." He laughed and inhaled a bong hit, neither of us knowing then he'd be picked up for possession of a gram of speed that very night to disappear into the county jail for another six-month gig, club kid or no.

"I gotta go."

"Ah, come on, Sal, we got big plans here," his voice rang out, diminishing in the wind as I walked back across the bright sunny street that was holding the premonition of a chill. And I turned to see a wall of fog spilling over the Golden Gate in the distance, thinking I'm nothing but a forlorn homosexual plying his hungry, sorry trade, wondering about Marco and hearing church bells and Latin verses from the mass just now letting out at St. Ignatius up the hill, and I imagine him lurching his pelvis up – this is my body – as he did so many times to shoot the hot white host and bless me with his seed – take this cup and drink it – loaded like a Spanish galleon of old it was, having taken the long trip from Manila to Mexico, across the land route to Vera Cruz and then all the way to Spain where golden ingots spilled from the palms of Spanish boys, their big uncut Mediterranean dicks roused like snakes from slumber, every potentiality of Marco's dreams and longings, his sad meanderings to come on this dark earth harbored in the sweet chromosomic code of his DNA-laden genes. And he was gone, and not a jumper from the bridge, though I would be yet I moped. And I called out into the dying day, "Go in peace," like a lonely priest or half-baked St. Francis in love with the little bird boys, though Marco was more like my St. Michael who'd pitchforked me into a mean depression that would require a lot of drink and Western Unions from Mom to resurface from. And so I said goodbye to Marco, the white fog spilling as I wished him peace, a wall of my golden boy's jism drowning me in the reverie of our short lost summer – and life's a sad, mean trick by an impotent card shark laughing at our premature ejaculations who's colored a boy's seed the same color as ice and snow and fog and keeps on saying 'Got Milk?' and laughing. And Cody's got it and I don't and I realize I love Cody and he me, but we'll never admit it and besides there's a whole new army of cute boys spilling into the city like that fog bank every day and we both want a taste of it.

But Cody's in jail now anyway because I'm telling you all this long after it's all over. But I thought of Cody then as I shuffled down Page Street, and the relationship we never had, and the endless string of boys we'd shared and chased after like a long freight train bound for the West and its endless bounty.

And the train's impending whistle takes me back to Marco, gone and never come back. I thought of my lost boy, grabbed a bottle and headed to the old Greyhound Station thinking of Alvah who'd gone off to Mexico City to argue literature with old Bull in dusty cantinas, and hand out condoms to Mexican boys amid the crazy racket of Mexican street vendors crying "Un peso, un peso, un peso!" on the old ancient, muddied, earth-sinking zocalo, dilapidated remnant of once great temples to the sun and moon, stained with the blood of a thousand broken hearts.

I thought perhaps I'd find a new angel down at the Greyhound station just growing wings from his acne-pocked shoulder blades, tight-skinned in anticipation of flight and newfound gayboy fame and wonder. But San Francisco is always Marco's and I couldn't bear the beauty of any more of them, nor their dreams and the haunting thought that half would be stricken and die in the beautiful poisoned garden of boylove. So I hopped the first bus south to LA, too tired to ride the rails, resolved to give up male love once and for all, and full of despair besides for everything, weeping for Marco who I'd lost and Cody who I'd never have and dreaming about Bull and Alvah who would call me a damn fool and buy me a drink and babble me batty into the balmy Mexican night where the stars wink back at you with the promise of Quetzalcoatl, like the cure we wait for but worry may never come.

"Cortez brought the cross and the sword, but we'll bring the lube and condoms – preserve the temple instead of knocking it down!" Alvah had shouted into the phone, encouraging my journey, bent on his messianic agenda like any old Jew still waiting. "The boys are rife and randy here, Sal!"

My cock had leapt at his poetry like a dog wanting to play fetch with a big brown uncircumcised dildo – visions of coal-black-haired Indian boys clinging to my butt cheeks as I plowed my seed into their dark wisdom – and what better to wean me off my Greco-Roman golden-locked lost love?

"You need a change, Sal," Alvah had shouted, extrapolating his incantatory lustful longings and advice through the threadbare weepful wires of Ma Bell, who was nothing but a mean old whore who charged too much and always gave less than she promised, if she didn't cut you off completely. The phone went dead on my last quarter, and I resolved to go, because so what if the universe is a cheap fuck, it's horny all the time and makes me feel loved and wanted, staying with me through and beyond the night and into the dawn – me, the lonely bard storyteller of stiff cock and colonic laundering in the long forgotten washerwoman blues laundromat of the emptied warehouse of the unremembered heaven and the celestial Buddha realms rife with boyhood's blissful being.

Pilgrim Soul

*"But one man loved the pilgrim soul in you/
and loved the sorrows of your changing face."*

WILLIAM BUTLER YEATS

I can't say I'd met that one man, but I'd kept looking, well past forty. When I looked around me, most of my contemporaries had partners, jobs – as in careers – even houses, and certainly cars. I had none of these. I'd no sooner corner one than lose it. Maybe because the houses were all rented – or the small cabin left to me was saddled with a massive lien; the cars were old and soon presented terminal breakdowns; the relationships were with incompatibles or based solely on lust; and the jobs, well, they'd always been stopgap for my so-called life as an artist, which hadn't delivered the necessary funds to make it viable, let alone justifiable at this late date. When I'd learned the increasingly uncomfortable pain in my lower back was due to an inoperable benign growth, I considered that the jig was finally up. The doctor referred me to the pain management clinic, that dreamy blissful land of OxyContin, Demerol and other opiates, a purgatory of stoned reality. Who wanted that? I liked the vivid glassy brightness of *be here now* sobriety.

I'd always given alternative therapies a shot, as from day

one I'd been saddled with mysterious ailments that never responded to western medicine's slash-and-burn clear-cut neoliberal approach (illness, pain – it's a hall of mirrors, so don't roll your eyes at my mixed metaphors). Off I went along the circuit: acupuncture, massage, reiki, shamans, meditation, etc.

These alternative therapies ultimately and predictably ran the same course as conserving the environment, saving endangered species and protecting rare Amazonian languages, but at least their intention was on target and they generally didn't create more problems as they failed to resolve the ones they were supposed to address. The key was they worked for *awhile*. And *awhile* can be a long time if you use it right.

I'd always been good at *awhile*, and lacking the responsibility or attachment of a job, a car, a house, or a relationship that mattered very much to me, I could take full advantage of the respite that it offered and get right to it by gathering my meager funds, packing my backpack and googling for where the current cheap flights could take me.

Which is how I ended up in Oaxaca. Before Oaxaca there'd been Buenos Aires, Valaparaiso, Bogota, Panama City – even Hanoi, Phnom Phen, Delhi, Cairo, Halifax. But I'd learned that Latin cities were best for my kind of dissipation. Fun first, ask questions later. There might not be a later – what a deal. Make a negative a positive. Thusly was I wedded to the Latin road: live for today.

I could recount a long line of sweet-souled beauties with skin like silk and the lust of lions, but I won't bore you with the details. Suffice it to say: Enrique, Angel, Carlos, Jose, Pepe, Victor, Isaiah, Anastacio, Vlad, Kevin and Mateo, ad infinitum, to recall just those who'd offered a name. Oaxaca would likely be no different. And what was all that sex but an odd reassurance that everything would be okay? That was the drug, the OxyContin for me, if you will, and even if it was just as delusional, wasn't sweet Carlos lying naked across the bed with a grin on his face more charming than those orange little bottles with the bad font for directions? Pain was so lonely: that was the real problem with it.

Morning and night I did my stretches I'd learned from the physical therapist, which kept the pain generally at bay. For awhile. And I was living out whatever 'awhile' I had left. There were bad days, but more good ones during my stay in Oaxaca, even though she'd assured me I was fighting a losing battle and eventually I'd have to work with the drugs. "In awhile," I smiled. The side effects were always horrid with drugs and the defeat of them untenable. Why, they were like being saddled with a house, a car, a job. And I wanted to be free.

Which is why I must return to Carlos, even though I swore I wouldn't bore you with the details. But he was the last, so just like in history, he gets top billing. And when I say the last, I mean the last trip into the heart of another, which is better than any trip to some exotic locale.

He'd actually shouted at me as I walked by the little Internet/copy shop he worked at. "Chavo! Hablas ingles?" It was the "ingles" part that got me to turn. They all wanted to do language exchange to improve their English and Carlos was no different. "But I don't just shout at anyone," he reassured me later as we lay together spent.

"Yeah, and you don't just want to exchange languages."

He grinned. "There are many languages."

"You speak several well, Carlos."

He did not lose the grin. "I guess."

* * *

I'm not as bad as you probably think. Actually, maybe I'm worse because I fall a little in love with most of them. That's the tragic part. And I don't have the heart to say – not only what they already know: I'll be gone, back to L.A., in two months – but that you can't come with me. And not because I don't want you to, or because the assembled Congress which claims to represent me wouldn't for even a minute consider your visa application, but because I'll be in pain one day and I don't want you to know that; I don't want you to see it; I don't want to be your invalid. I want to be your glorious and exciting adventure, just like you are to me. That's why they say I'm incapable of true love. If true love is about the long haul, I don't qualify because I live in the *awhile*, which is the present, and which is far more precious than forever actually, and in many ways the same thing. I tell myself I'm being a good Buddhist, but I know I'm playing fast and loose with it. Well, I'm in pain, Buddha dear, cut me some slack.

But he won't. He can't. Not his m.o.. It's easier to cling then to the crucified black Jesuses and sad-faced Marys – they're all over town and slack is what they cut.

I had a bad week in mid-July, which I spent mostly in bed. Then my broken body rallied and I went on a bender. Carlos got sore with me when he found out about Miguel. How to explain the lust for life when chronic pain lifts for who knows how long? How to explain *that* to someone in the flush of youth, a young lion whose body is daily a source of joy? So I assured him that Miguel was just for variety, but Carlos shook his head. "How's his English?" he finally asked. "It isn't," I answered. He shrugged. Advantage Carlos. He forgave me. How to explain *awhile*. If you had six months, you'd be doing the same damn thing is what I wanted to tell him. But he probably wouldn't be. Most of these boys were all heart. And to me, they each and every one of them looked like they had an eternity.

It was the rainy season, but still I loved to walk (even with the pain), so Carlos took me all over by foot – the river, the churches, each and every barrio and Mercado, even some of the villages where they wove rugs and made clay figures, or painted wooden chimeras – skeletons with big breasts or penises, monkeys with fins, mermaids, demons with long tails and twisted horns, bats with the purple and green wings of dragons, all manner of enormous grasshoppers and praying mantis. I'd sit down a lot, take breaks, but I was stubborn and not stupid. Exercise kicks up endorphins, the body's private stash of pain meds without the side effects, and though the aching and stabbing never ceased, they had less power after walking eight miles. By afternoon, the clouds would gather to the point of threat, and down it came, sometimes like a hail of bullets, other times gently like a lovely warm shower. No one seemed to own an umbrella, or very few did. Carlos told me he liked getting wet. I was used to the Northern Hemisphere where getting wet and getting cold went hand in hand. But this was the tropics – the sun would return and dry you off. Or you'd just walk around wet until you had a chance to change.

Rain or shine, we scurried along the cobblestoned streets in the colonial center of town, past machine gun-toting soldiers and lazy beat cops, who sometimes actually dozed off on their perches. We'd sit in the Parque de Llano and watch the kids in their imaginary games, sword-fighting, chasing, climbing. We'd go for coffee or something hot and spicy. Carlos lived down along the river, and he took me to the store for a mosquito net, as the critters were fierce and he said that was how he dealt with living down by the river. I was up on a hill, but there were puddles of standing water throughout the city and avoiding mosquitoes was no easy task anywhere. I'd been battered by their little artillery night after night until my ankles were ringed with scabs, my hands pocked with welts.

I didn't have a proper canopy structure to hang the mosquito net in the way they usually do it, so I pushed my bed against the wall and simply tacked the net to it in a sort of half-tent fashion like Carlos instructed me to. The mosquito net worked wonders, but apparently a day or two too late. Carlos looked concerned when he saw how pale I'd grown and that my teeth chattered with fever. He tucked me in under the mosquito net and brought me bowl after bowl of soup, made me drink tea and water until I pissed blood. Bad sign. He said we had to go to the hospital right away, but I begged off: "It's a flu, I'll live."

"It's the dengue," he told me. I'd read about it. So be it. It was ugly, painful and long-running – they say usually about two weeks, and rarely fatal. And since I was used to pain after thirty years of one kind or another, I convinced Carlos I could see this through. He wasn't comfortable with my decision, and insisted on ministering to me, and this I appreciated. I developed a purplish rash that covered my entire body and made the previous mosquito bites seem like nothing, while my head pounded like a big racing engine full of pistons. My eyes hurt. One day Carlos looked to me like one of the winged monkeys we'd seen out in the villages – right down to the purple paisleys on his cheeks and the red glowing coals for eyes. He scared me for a moment, and I feared he might be some sort of witch. And yet a witch was probably what I needed right about then.

He grabbed my hand and started talking to me, but I couldn't understand him. And not just because it was rapid-fire Spanish. My ears were ringing. I tried to thank him and tell him not to worry. He look disturbed, frightened. He gesticulated something and ran out. It got darker. And then I felt things slow down. And I became short of breath. I wondered what was happening. I was so tired.

Suddenly I had the crystal clear thought that I was about to die. Whoa. So fast. And then I did. Just like that. Nothing particularly dramatic about it. Though I did feel a momentary alarm at the surprise that it had finally happened. I mean, come on, we all consider it kind of a big deal, right? But honestly, I was overwhelmed by the feeling of release – almost orgasmic. I floated around the room, completely relaxed, and was able to look back at my pale, lifeless body, which also looked emaciated; I'd clearly lost a lot of weight with that illness.

Carlos came back with two people pretty quickly, and all three were in a panic. Carlos screamed a terrible guttural cry and fell to his knees. I felt terrible to see his pain and guilty, as I'd insisted against him taking me to the hospital. *It's okay, Carlos,* I wanted to say, *I'm fine now. Much better.* I tried to go talk to him, but the others were crowding him and they took him away. Poor Carlos. I'm sorry.

But I was dead and there was nothing to be done. Fortunately, I knew I was dead and I tried to remember what I was supposed to do, according to all those Buddhist books I'd read. Choose the right light to go toward and all that. But there were no lights. I decided to leave the house and go take a walk through the city. Maybe I was a ghost. That disturbed me for a minute. I didn't want to be alone forever, following Carlos around, watching him fall in and out and love and have that wild cat-like sex he was so fond of. One could do worse, I suppose. I hadn't apparently gone to hell. Or not yet anyway.

There was the same door I'd walked in and out of every day. But no need now for keys and locks. I'd been a bit OCD, so that was a nice feeling – not to have to check the lock three times. Down the street, the same birds singing, dogs barking, the garbage truck and the man who walked alongside it with a bell, the other guys shouting 'agua,' and those annoying gas trucks with their loudspeakers repeating endlessly their little jingle with the mooing cows: "Gas de Oaxaca!" I said "Buen dia" to pedestrians who normally always returned the greeting, but not today. No one could see me, of course; my body was back at the house growing cold under the mosquito net.

It was strange, somewhat exciting and a little bit terrifying, this death business. I was like the invisible man, but like I say, I felt a kind of relief. A euphoria, actually. Like something had finally happened that I'd been waiting for for a long time. Like a plane taking off, a trip of some kind. I realized how tired I'd been of life, how worn down by the pain and confusion. I cried a little bit. There's a dam that builds up in life. And now death, the sea.

I tried to focus on what was in front of me. Which was still Oaxaca. But I didn't see it the same way at all. Because while I could feel it, taste it, smell it – all my senses still intact – I felt no gravity, and no pain. Which for me changed everything. It was dreamy. I'd never particularly liked being in my body, and rarely was, if the truth be told. That thing had hounded me constantly. I wasn't going to miss food or sleep or hot showers or any of that. I'd miss sex with Carlos and the endless parade of a thousand more as beautiful as him that the world seemed to have lined up for me from Mexicali to Ushuaia or Tashkent to Hanoi. But if you had to take the rest of the package that was life to get sex, I'd pass. Not worth it. Or not in my case, anyway.

Oaxaca's streets seemed more or less the same but strangely more colorful and brighter. There was an intensity and vibrancy to everything, sort of LSD-like: a glowing succulent plant, the edges of building as shiny and crystalline-sharp as knives, a hologramic dropped ice cream cone running down the cobblestones. And I saw the little boy who'd dropped it, his empty, sticky little hand. And then something strange happened. I could actually feel how he felt – his devastating disappointment when he dropped it, and his mother yanking his arm to move him along – and then how he forgot it quickly, distracted by a dog loping down the sidewalk opposite. Then an old man walked by and I felt his profound sadness about the two children he'd lost long, long ago. I watched him with his cane, mulling the memories over in his mind, remembering the boys when they were little, then teenagers – and then he'd think of something else: those flowers over there, that woman's print dress so like what his aunt used to wear back in the village. Then I saw a drunk in a doorway, full of that hopeless drunken sadness about all sorts of things – his foot, his family, his youth and the *where did he go wrong* that haunted him, the woman whom he blamed for so much of it. A good-looking young man captured my attention, and he was actually thinking of killing someone. And then I sensed that *someone* he was targeting and he was scared and hiding in a little house up on the hill, and he was full of remorse for what he'd done. Which I recoiled from when I saw the blood and heard the girl's screams. All a terrible mistake was the feeling I got about it. I quickly sought out someone else to avoid seeing more.

In this way, the city was taking on a sort of surreal and dreamlike quality – not quite solid and where everything was sort of appearing at once, sometimes in rapid-fire mode and at other times things all stretched and twisting around each other, membranous – and what did that make of space really? Sort of like a continually blossoming fractal, multidimensional and infinite. And all these emotions pouring in like a flood – it was all exponentially multiplying around me, and I felt a sudden terror. It was too much and too big to hold. I tried to contain it by focusing on just one thing at a time. Children were best, as they had less history and more simple concerns, their emotions less complicated and layered. It didn't completely work, since when you lit upon a little boy who'd been beaten or molested, the pain was greater by far than from any random adult. That feeling of having no resources to grapple with it or rationalize it, and yet at the same time, the immense strength and plasticity of the mind of a child to keep absorbing new and bizarre experiences, one after the other. I hopscotched from child to child and when I'd find one who was thinking blissfully of food or an itch on his leg, I'd try to stick with him. What if I closed my eyes? But I didn't have any eyes. Would I ever stop engaging with all these people and their stories? I wished then I'd practiced meditation more often.

Because it wasn't just space that was changing - it was time too. I don't know how to explain it quite, but you could look at someone or something and it would take you on a sort of ride into the past, telling its entire history, and then go tearing off into the future as well. I could stop it anywhere, fast-forward it, or rewind it. There seemed to be a natural tendency to let it take you to just where it wanted to go, which I suppose is no different from life. We all tend to see what we need or want to see in anything that crosses our vision or consciousness – which, I suppose, is why I followed this old indigenous woman, who'd been selling tamales all day on the zocalo. She got to a particular corner and waited for a bus, chattering in Zapotec – which I now understood – to some other lady. They were talking about how it hadn't rained, how she hadn't sold many tamales today, but that next week would be better as the Guelaguetza, a huge cultural festival that happened each July, would be accelerating into high gear and people would be jamming the zocalo from dawn to dusk.

The bus came in the usual manner, loud, belching smoke with squeaking brakes and a loud-hinged door. I got on and sat with the two women as they talked together about their families – children and grandchildren, and who was doing what and why and to whom and how. And that's when I recognized her as my granddaughter. I – some other I – long dead. But when we got to her village, it all spun out in front of me and the village receded back in time to her girlhood and me – there I was, a wiry old Zapotec farmer, and I gave my granddaughter a hug. And then the village was gone and there was just forest, and there were warriors dressed in elaborate feathered costumes crouching in the bush and far-off smoke rising. And I knew that smoke was the Spanish encampment, and I was terrified by those fierce ironclad men and their horses.

I was squirting back through time now like one of those squeeze-bottle mustard or mayonnaise dispensers, or like a lanced boil full of pus, unwinding back, back, back to the pre-conquest when all the diesel-fueled pavements and squalor vanished into an Edenic paradise of the New World. I'd only known its filth in this life, one squalid, litter-strewn dirty-watered Latin American capital after another. To think that that had all been imported, along with Jesus, technology, iron, industry and democracy – that hallowed term which had been exploited unto its demise like any rich vein of gold or silver by these westerners. They'd exploited everything: religion, land, intellect, ideas. How to describe it from the perspective of death? A mouth, that's what Western Culture resembled now, and it made you feel hungry, so you identified with it. Invest in the mouth to cure your hunger. Stay with the mouth. Something like that. And it doesn't just eat, it talks.

Money is speech sings that toneless boy judge – what's his name, Bob? John, that's it, John Roberts. What a name? Why wouldn't he have changed it? A high priest named John Rob-

erts, the oracle of their great dying god, Greed. So unpoetic for
an oracle. Well, greed and poetry, they don't mesh generally.
And to think I'd lived my whole most recent, short, desperate life under the thumb of that grim, ugly, mouthy god while
everyone kept telling me to be grateful. I was lucky to be living in the flower of civilization, they'd say. Bah. Something
overgrown. Not a flower. A big head of cabbage, chewed at by
vermin, perhaps. Some kind of abundance, no doubt, but not
a beautiful one. Fattened pigs, big-breasted chickens, SUVs!
So I saw from death, along with many other things. None of it
matters much. The dead are essayists, editorialists for a day.
Until it all painfully, gloriously expands – huge, timeless, vast.
Imagine swimming through the sun.

In the blink of an eye, Oaxaca and all its mountains and
timescapes and drama were all gone and I was suddenly on
the streets of Buenos Aires, walking in a solemn throng with
a black armband, and I knew Evita was dead and I didn't have
to work at the shoe factory that whole week and had come
to pay my respects. And flash, I'm on a ship on the high seas,
vomiting over the gunwales and feeling a terrible thirst. The
places I traveled became like all the boys I'd slept with, too
numerous to count and I won't bore you with them either.
Suffice it to say: Buenos Aires, Oaxaca, Valparaiso (a sailor!),
Bogota (a vile man who mistreated his own children), Panama City and thereabouts (a series of deaths by malaria), California (a fruit grower who underpaid his Mexican field hands
– say it ain't so!), Spain (a priest), Algeria (a cobbler), Egypt
(a tailor), yada, yada, yada. I lost interest.

How strange, I thought, that in each successive life we are
drawn back to all the places we'd lived in other lives. Well, it's
human nature, I suppose, to return to familiar faces, places,
foods, landscapes, etc.. Habits! We like the familiar. Maybe
that's the only reason we have habits at all, our need to remember, to keep in touch with where and who we've been. To
not go stark raving mad and lose ourselves. We're making the
rounds, trying to gather up all our lives as if they were fruit,
firewood, cotton. And why? Like luggage, really. I suppose to

contain time and space. But why don't we just stay put and live in the same place over and over again? Wanderers all.

I'm writing this in death. Who will even read it? A thousand souls in the form of empty green wine bottles float through the air above me like a school of fish. I pull one of them down to me instinctively and cram these notes into it and then toss it like a balloon back up to the rest of them that then speed off like a flock of birds, curving, feinting, fanning out, then diving as one off into the horizon. On the way to the future? Who knows if that bottle is the next me or just someone who will maybe tell this story?

And now, the bird bottles gone, lights are coming out of the sky. At first I thought they were space ships. First I was drawn to a red one, then thought better of it and went for the white. The closest thing I can use to describe it: When someone smiles with total sincerity – from love or just goodness – so that your heart can barely contain it? Well, imagine. The rib cage has to crack open, though, like an Apollo rocket lifting off, out of its launch cage. You don't want to explode. There's an *Oh no!* that you're expanding outward into endless space, losing yourself, but a joy too, as if to say, stop, it's too good, it's too true, it's too sad and happy, and not too fast, and easy there, and the rest of it – it overwhelms and thus obliterates emotions, which are things that happen in a contained space. And then it's just something else I can't ever explain. You'll have to die, I guess, like you had to be there. And you will die, so I'm confident you'll understand, and that's a good feeling to have as a writer. Don't worry, it's not hard once it's happened. It is the relief I sought. But it's hard going in (though my dengue demise was better than most exits), then crossing the threshold, being overwhelmed by all those other people and past lives, and then sorting through these lights. It demands all your attention. There's a definite fear of losing your mind, even though you don't have one, which tempers the panic a tad. But it's work to stay one step ahead of it. No, not ahead at all. I'm one step behind it. It's like you have to keep up with it. To run faster – I feel like a little boy – *wait for me*, running with all my might, laughing, but crying too. There's anxiety. I'm not sure I'm up to it. But I've got the boy's eager little spirit too. That's the ticket. Death's the man. The boy. I've been chasing him all my life.

Puppets

When he left, he told me he wanted to be with someone positive, someone who wasn't afraid, and someone who wasn't just screwing around.

He said it in an angry voice. And I took it. Because I *was* afraid, I *wasn't* positive, and well, I worried that in my life I *was* just screwing around.

He was a painter then, and he had painted me. I had painted him too, until he said: "I'm not gonna be your HIV project, your dying muse."

We stopped dating; stopped speaking. We both stopped painting. He started making puppets. I only knew this because I saw a playbill for a show. And I went. Because I was haunted by him and by what he'd said; by my own guilt; regret. I'd treated him like he was fragile after that frightening bout of pneumocystis. I hadn't meant to be cruel, but I'd treated him like someone who was dying. I'd painted him that way.

But he wasn't dying. Not then. And not now, twelve years hence.

He was, in fact (instead), being born.

* * *

I hadn't seen him in over a year, so I was apprehensive about the puppet show. It was in a small theater in San Francisco's Mission District – small enough that he'd see everyone who was there. It was the usual puppet stage, diminutive and intimate, about five feet across and three high, and just as many deep. He was a silhouette above the action as the puppets flounced about, throttled each other and flailed with their awkward limbs. I watched his shadow on the wall and don't remember much about the show, other than the puppets themselves: there was a clown, a Frankenstein, a couple buzzards, and a big daisy-headed thing that played the fool.

When the lights went up, I sat a minute as people clapped and slowly filed out; some stayed to linger and congratulate him on the show. He didn't acknowledge me, and I got up and left.

That was okay. I felt I'd hurt him, and so those were the consequences. Why then had I gone? Did I like puppets? Well, what's not to like? But no, I wouldn't have sought them out. I suppose I went because I was curious, because we used to have long angry arguments about art and which of us was the better artist, or even an artist at all. Competition. It was the tension that formed the glue between us. Or was it the other way around – the glue that created the tension? HIV had been part of that too. He was better than me for having it from one perspective (experience, our queer zeitgeist, real life), but he was also at a disadvantage, and though I didn't show it, I gloated about it to myself whenever he hurt me. *He won't be here to become the great artist he thinks he is,* I reassured myself, even as I winced with self-disgust at such cruel, callous thoughts.

So maybe I went to see how he looked, to gauge his health. A morbid fascination. Or was it fear? Did I only see Miguel selfishly, like a puppet of my own death? He was ashen. Almost blue. AZT. But he was more vital than I was. He was creating, and I, during that time, was not.

* * *

I started seeing his puppets all over the place – in shop windows, at galleries. And on handbills too, advertising his shows. He made puppets who took pills and were cathetered; he made demon and angel puppets; puppets of crack whores and drag queens, muscle boys and campesinos; puppets in gabardine suits and puppets in silk kimonos. He made puppets of political personalities – Jesse Helms, Reagan and Bush, the Pope – and he made monstrous puppets named HIV and PCP, KS and CMV – big ogreish things with arms to their ankles and enormous malformed dicks. With big, sad eyes. They looked back at me hungrily out of lit-up windows in darkened, empty shops on Guerrero or Valencia Street long after midnight, the fog sifting down, enveloping everything – all the streetlights like dandelion seeds. His puppets looked like abandoned children, and they made me think of Leonard Cohen's song, "Suzanne."

So what then? Are we supposed to love a disease? Death? What kills us?

It didn't help that it was October, bare branches and leaves falling. I kicked through them, alienated, unable to look at anyone for fear I'd see the strings attached to their wrists and shoulders, strings that would likely ascend dizzyingly into the clouds, as if somewhere way up beyond were billions of colored kites tangled out among the stars. It nauseated me.

* * *

On the Day of the Dead, I went to an exhibit and came upon his skeleton puppets sitting on bleachers on his little puppet stage. Some of them were pointing, and it was as if they were telling the viewer to look at the other altars on the other side of the hall.

I did. There were numerous altars to grandparents who'd passed and young people cut down by war, car accidents, guns and AIDS. Why were there always so many smiling photos on the altars of those who'd died of AIDS? Leaning out for love. Leaning out *like love. With love.* I felt a need to touch those altars, or something on them, to pet them like a cat. It was as if they purred.

He came up from behind me. "Hello."

"Hi, Miguel. "I saw your altar."

He nodded. After an uncomfortable silence, he said, "Wanna go get some coffee?"

Afterward, we went back to his place and sat on his bed, and he told me he was ready to forgive me. I didn't know what to say to that, and it actually made me sort of angry. We lay back on his bed then and he told me everything that had happened in the last two years: how he'd come out to his family; how the drugs always seemed to stop working for him soon after he began taking them, but how a new one would come along in the nick of time. How he'd been afraid. His hand found my hand then and we lay there silently.

He rose and showed me puppets he was working on and how he constructed them – the little wooden dowels for limbs, the Sculpey clay for the hands and faces, the little hooks and leather straps, hand-sewn outfits, the long reels of fishing line – and even fishing weights so the puppets could move more realistically. He showed me two running puppets he'd been working on, and he took off down the hall with them running next to him. I laughed heartily. I'd never seen a running puppet.

He smiled like a proud kid and then he dropped them, grabbing me around the shoulders. We hugged full-force, pushing our chests together, my heart feeling big and restless against his, like it too had flouncing, uncoordinated puppet arms rattling the cage of my ribs, trying to get to him. Reaching. Leaning out.

Then he was somber again and told me he needed to get to sleep. I averted my gaze after he opened the front door.

* * *

I didn't hear from him or run into him again after that for a long time. Until I chanced across another handbill. The show was titled "Romeo and Julio: An Anti-tragedy," and the two running puppets were pictured, one with a "plus" on its belly, and the other with a "minus."

Three days later I watched as the little red taffeta curtains parted, revealing the "plus" puppet up in a window at the back of the stage. A sign under the window said *Capulet Medical Center*. The N-Montague streetcar rumbled into the middle of the stage then and out stepped the other puppet.

The tale unfolded, with ACT UP demonstrations in the streets of Verona, mounted police chasing the running puppets up the walls, or off the stage entirely. Once Miguel donned a smiling Ronald Reagan mask and chased the two puppets up and down the aisles. The crowd laughed nervously. Puppets were slain and Romeo banished, and in the last scene in the crypt the friar made drug cocktails like a mad chemist and gave condoms to the star-crossed lovers, just as all the other puppets arrived for the final showdown.

Then the friar said, "Montagues and Capulets! Fear is your enemy, not each other!" The friar, leaning out.

I got up and left.

I went to several bars, one to the next, until I caught a stranger's eye that I fancied. We had a drink and then went home together. Afterward he talked, much of which I didn't listen to. I was angry and sad and felt like I'd learned some things about fear and love and about forever that were very different from what I had thought about them before.

I didn't seek out Miguel anymore after that. Nor that boy I'd gone home with.

And I began to paint again.

Trunk

Ending up in the trunk of a car headed for Houston was not what Bobby had had in mind when he'd come to New Orleans. Of course, he hadn't counted on vomiting on the shoes of the Reverend Norman DuMay either, nor running into the likes of Old Croc and his creepy mojo medicine. In fact, Bobby'd come to New Orleans in order to avoid such things (an ironically interesting choice for such an escape, isn't it?), to lay low, and get his life in order; to do the right thing. He'd come to volunteer, to help rebuild in the aftermath of Katrina, to turn over a new leaf for himself and his relationship to the world.

That's what he told himself, anyway. On a more visceral level, he'd been drawn like a magnet to the Crescent City out of an odd sort of identification. He wasn't so much appalled and horrified by Katrina as he was pruriently and subliminally intrigued with it. Perhaps it was a conviction that he was sinking fast and that what was happening on the flooded streets of New Orleans was a disturbingly apt metaphor for his own inundation – with booze, semen, crystal meth and all manner of unbridled desire. What was that old line of Hamlet's? *'Tis better to take arms against a sea of troubles, and by opposing end them?* Maybe he and this dear unfortunate city could help each other? Something like that. Bobby wasn't thinking too clearly. New Orleans as Yorick? Or was it all a fool's errand? Call it a sort of megalomaniacal codependence; call it a cry for a help; call it a cautionary tale for the neo-con dream or any other twisted sort of messianic hogwash. Bobby was looking for an anchor, and what better place to look for it than a place that had been swallowed by the sea?

Glued as he'd been to his television set and his laptop through most of September, he'd witnessed the National Guard in their speedboats rescuing dogs and obese women off roofs; he'd seen the Superdome packed to bursting; the president smugly attempting a riff on *"ich bin ein New Orleansian,"* though it came out "moron," or "asshole" – Bobby couldn't tell which. Neither he nor the leader of the free world could speak German.

Eight months later, channel-surfing the television, his laptop balanced on his knees, Bobby, once again blazed to the nines on speed, with no fewer than nine IM boxes open with such names as *9inchbliss, Gutterthroat* and *Gettheebehindmesatan*, it dawned on him that no one was really doing anything much about the fate of New Orleans – least of all him (he'd been too broke buying drugs and booze to even send the meager twenty-five dollars in response to that letter from the Red Cross that came with more of the return address labels he'd been using for the past year) – and that no one likely would. It had become a lousy reality television show with no plot other than *the government doesn't care, it really doesn't.* Katrina gave sink or swim a whole new meaning. Laissez-faire. Well, it was a French word and New Orleans was the Frenchest of cities, and America hates the French – even begrudges them their fries now that the holy war is on. Meanwhile the vice president belabors us with the intricacies of flood insurance fraud when he's not shooting his friends in the face with buckshot, and the president is too busy feeding Christmas trees into a shredder (wait, those aren't trees, they're young men!) to be bothered with such inconsequential things as chocolate cities – though he did call his white friend "Brownie." Hey, let 'em eat brownies. But who was George Bush, anyway – Willy Wonka? Did he look like Johnny Depp? No. He was a godly man; he had people to kill and nations to destroy. The Lord's work. He'd as likely rebuild New Orleans as he would Iraq or the Tower of Babel. Bobby snorted another line, muttering, 'Man, this country sucks.'

Moments later, he nearly choked as he quaffed another Sierra Nevada. Sink or Swim. A jolt of guilt shook him, and he looked around the room – at clothes strewn about, scattered empty beer bottles and tiny cans of amyl nitrate; fast food bags and wrappers; a hole in the wall where his friend Kip had punctured the drywall during a particularly out-of-hand sex scene. What on earth was going on? How many beers had he drained while watching the news reports of the devastation over those past nine months? How many porn sites and Internet chat rooms had he barreled into, ignoring the news stories of Katrina's wrath and aftermath on the portal pages on his way in and out, while the tragedy droned on at low volume from the television across the room? How many lines of speed had he snorted, brilliant white as a Katrina trailer? How many boys had flooded him? Had he flooded? – all while the levees sat unrepaired. How many times had his heart filled with horror and repulsion that he was comparing his pathetic, broken-down life – albeit one with a roof over his head, a job and three squares – to victims of a natural disaster? Was his life really an ongoing hurricane? Was it that bad? Was he that self-indulgent? He looked in the mirror, chipped the crusted scab of a speed bump off his cheek. Even FEMA wouldn't be able to help *him*. It was that bad. A line from back in the day when gay people had a political conscience flitted through his mind: *The personal is political.*

He thought of Father Robert, his Jesuit uncle. What had he always said? If things are really bad, and beyond help, go help someone else. Of course, that was easy for him to say. He had a vocation. What did Bobby have? A big dick? An AA degree? A habit?

There were lists of organizations on the *L.A. Times* website. He steered clear of the Christians, as he knew by experience that he'd always end up on the wrong end of a Bible quote with those geeks. He was a proud, out homo, and that wasn't something he was willing to put aside. This was about helping other people, not sucking it up and taking abuse from selfish fucks whose only motivation was their own sanctimony and a low point mortgage in the afterlife.

There were the Red Cross, the United Way, etc., but he didn't want to end up in some office in Baton Rouge. He wanted to be on the ground, knee-deep in it, just like he was in his own self-destruction. He chanced upon something called GUMBO (Greater United Metropolitan Betterment Organization) which looked sufficiently lefty and irreverent to be pro-homo or at least laissez-faire about such things (why, one picture of its volunteers had a group of dreadlocked hippie boys playing Hacky Sack in a park, while nearby little girls in cornrows played ring-around-the-rosy). No-brainer. He immediately filled out the volunteer application form to join a crew gutting damaged houses in the 9th Ward for poor folks with no insurance.

The minute he clicked to submit his application, he was ecstatic and felt newly self-empowered. He began cleaning up his room, the poppers and beer cans clanging together like the opening bars to some cheesy musical: *Poppers and beer cans and sweet apple strudel, faggots and rainbows and ...*

He felt – well – good, upbeat, upstanding, well-endowed and attractive; a sure bet to get laid. He was full of himself, a narcissistic federal disaster area that Mr. Bush would be wise to do absolutely nothing for. *I'm an activist*, Bobby congratulated himself; *a do-gooder; part of the solution; a relief worker.* He felt so good, he threw a going-away party for himself, got shit-faced drunk, and blew his friend Ed in the bathroom.

* * *

Of course, what Bobby found in New Orleans was anything but relief.

It started on the airplane, where a comely flight attendant named Bo scribbled his hotel room number on a cocktail napkin after shamelessly flirting and feeding Bobby free gin and tonics between Phoenix and New Orleans.

Bobby made a point to stop at three cocktails and took no speed breaks in the bathroom, telling himself he would simply make it a date and not do anything sexual.

He failed.

But he only had one bump, two beers, and he used a condom. Progress. And at least it gave him a place to sleep his first night in New Orleans.

He set out early next morning, as the steward had an 8 a.m. flight to Minneapolis and was clearly moving on to the next thing, showering and chattering on his cell phone while Bobby gathered his things together like a hobo, more or less ignored by his host.

He got a quick insincere smile and a small wave as the glorified waitress chortled on about the Denver-to-Dallas route with some queeny colleague, slamming the door behind Bobby as if he were putting the dog out, his gaze all but averted. In fact, Bobby barked, assuming of course that the joke would go unnoticed, as it did, to all but himself.

He stumbled onto the streets of Metairie, which didn't look half bad, considering what had happened a year prior. He'd expected worse. He hailed a cab for downtown so he could stroll through the beloved historic district and assess the damage on his way to the GUMBO office out past the Marigny in the Gentilly District. He wanted to wallow in his heroism a bit, which was markedly different from what he usually wallowed in when he visited New Orleans for Southern Decadence each year. He purposely avoided Bourbon Street, strolling along Royal Street at first and then cutting up to Burgundy, threading his way around the "trouble spots" which might derail his "new leaf."

To his surprise, the French Quarter looked downright passable – in fact, he wouldn't have even known there had been a hurricane if he hadn't looked for the broken windows and damaged, tarped roofs, which were incidentally loaded with hot-looking Latin boys, hammering about and being masculine. Thank God they had work to do or he might have lingered.

Then things quickly deteriorated as Bobby headed out into the neighborhoods. Enormous trees upended, piles of refuse up and down the curbs, Katrina trailers parked here and there asserting their ugliness while the charming houses desolately frowned with abandonment, shamed at their high water marks and concave porches like week-old diapers no one had bothered to change now that the waters had receded.

He checked in at the GUMBO office on Elysian Fields, a fairly undamaged area, if you ignored the blue tarps draped across every other roof, the boarded-up windows and the still ubiquitous red spray-paint graffitied on every other house with dates and numerical renderings of how many dogs or people were left inside in need of rescue or food drops.

He thought briefly of Noah – his ex, not the biblical character. Noah had been a contractor. He'd also gone off the deep end with speed and vanished into the digital divide – which meant he was either addicted to porn and Internet cruising or unable to pay his ISP bill, Bobby could never remember which. Regardless, the results were more or less the same. Man overboard.

The folks at GUMBO were smart, informed and not fucking around. "We're here because the government isn't, and we aren't surprised about that." Bobby felt that old dread of self-righteous lesbianism that every circuit fool gayboy feels when his Peter Pandom is exposed under the glaring lights of women who have moved beyond taking care of and making excuses for boys.

"Uh, yeah, great ... Uh, me too," he fumbled.

"Well, welcome, Robert," the pretty mulatto girl answered.

"Call me Bobby?"

She gave a quick smile, as if he'd cracked a bad joke, and

reached into a drawer for some materials he'd need to read.

His first order of business was to get settled in a house they'd recently had lent to them. He and eight other volunteers would bunk there while he completed his three-week volunteer gig.

It was only a few blocks away, so he hoofed it over there, and sure enough, it was rife with hippie boys in various of states of undress. New Orleans is hot and humid, not a place for clothing. But the thrill soon paled after he listened to them talk for a bit. Hopelessly straight and conventional and moralistic, like most hippie boys, Bobby was soon annoyed by their unavailable prettiness, their reggae music, their guitars and bongo drums, and knew he'd likely be keeping more or less to himself, and that none of these boys would likely give it up for the visiting fag, no matter how hip and cool they thought themselves. "Yo bra, nice dreadlocks, chocolate city, yeah," and the ghetto fist-play greeting.

He grabbed an empty bunk in the last room down the hall and headed to the bathroom, where he deposited what proved to be a traveler's turd, challenging the plumbing with its size and girth. As the water swirled and rose, Bobby felt a sudden shame, thinking that what New Orleans really didn't need, of all cities, was another turd floating down the street. He felt guilty; Californian; a fuckup; a bad omen; he panicked. He searched the bathroom for a plunger. He flushed again. The toilet water rose on his own private Katrina moment, nearly cresting the rim before it began to retreat. Thank God porcelain had integrity, he thought, as the water ebbed.

He went for help.

"No problem, dude, we all get traveler's turd on the road. There's a plunger on the back porch." Sheesh, what a frat house. He went to work with it, and as he plunged the third time, the plunger went inside out, and then quickly inverted itself, splattering shit across the walls, the toilet, and all over the front of Bobby's clothing. Welcome to "Chocolate City" he thought in disgust. An omen indeed. And then he heard the toilet drain, cough and swallow. Praise Jesus.

Back at the GUMBO office, showered and decked out in cargo shorts and a polo shirt, Bobby mustered up the best attitude he could. The place was a zoo and orientation was haphazard and fast. He was issued a white safety suit, as the dangers of toxic poisoning were substantial. He hadn't bargained for that. He'd heard of mold allergies and figured they couldn't kill him, but exposure to asbestos? Because what GUMBO did was gut and dismantle houses – something not covered by most insurance (and who had flood insurance anyway? Who could afford it?). And with a price tag of 7k per dwelling, GUMBO was forced to beg donations and volunteers in order to make a dent in what was otherwise an almost insurmountable expense for most people. Admirably and against all odds, thanks to donations, sheer will and an adopt-a-house program, they were getting people back into their homes, albeit slowly.

Bobby rushed home and modeled the white suit. It was made out of that weird sort of part plastic, part paper, part foil, part cloth stuff. The mask looked sexy at least – dangerous, sci-fi authoritarian – and like baggy jeans on a boy, the suit hung slack at the crotch and ass, so that if you could get beyond its clownish appearance, your imagination could conjure up tight butts and low-hanging balls, big uncut schlongs swinging pendulous and unimpeded like censers in search of a sanctuary. *My body is a temple* Bobby muttered. And he thought of Jared, Lars, Dylan, Josh and Bennett in the next room, and how loose and naked their bodies floated inside those suits, like astronauts in space, the thick foliage where the hair stood out above their oversized cocks, like a fecund flowerbox on some resurrected shotgun shack of New Orleans. Bobby's fantasy soon tented the gossamer fibers of the suit's fabric – and it wouldn't be the last time – forcing him in the days following to repeatedly pretend that he needed to squat down to get at low chunks of insulation still clinging or scattered along the bottom of dismantled walls.

On one such occasion, the Reverend showed up. "I swear you look like children of the Rapture in those white suits. And so you are!! Heh, heh. What you doing down there, son?"

Busted. Bobby looked up over his shoulder from his crouched position. "Uh, just doing what I came here to do, sir. To make these houses habitable again."

"Just in time for the next storm," the Reverend DuMay chuckled, ducking under a scaffold and making his way through the little shotgun house Bobby had been assigned to work on his first week, along with a one-week veteran, Tony, a Catholic boy from Boston – definitely not one of the hippie boys. Bobby did a double take on the Reverend as he moved on.

"How you doin', son, welcome to God's country," DuMay beamed, greeting Tony.

Bobby stared, rapt. He'd never met a southern preacher before.

"Has the Lord reached you, son, or are you lost still?" A grin crossed DuMay's face and Bobby's jaw went slack as he awaited Tony's reply.

Tony didn't miss a beat. "Jesus is my Lord and savior, sir." And they hi-fived. So much for avoiding Christians.

The Reverend guffawed. "Oh, son, you are ripe. Ripe as a swollen peach. I could just pick you off the tree." And he laughed and pinched Tony's cheek as if he were a small child. Then he turned and winked back at Bobby, before walking out the back and on to the next house.

"Who is *that*?" Bobby asked Tony, incredulous.

"Oh, that's the Reverend. He's harmless."

"As in the crazy being harmless?"

"Oh, he's into Armageddon." He shrugged his shoulders. "Takes all kinds."

Bobby scrunched his eyes. "Does it?"

"God works in strange ways. I mean, all the Reverend asks is if you've accepted Jesus Christ? Haven't you?"

"Sure, what the fuck, he's welcome along with everyone else. I don't play favorites."

"He's the only one."

Bobby glared at him. "Aren't you a *Catholic*?"

"Yeah," he said defensively, "we believe in Jesus too."

Bobby arched his brows but couldn't help smiling. Born of a long line of Marian heretics, Bobby thought it a dubious argument at best. But wasn't it just his luck that he got paired up with the religious one out of all the cute little humanist hippies, who were probably Wiccans or Buddhists? Then again, his chances of sex were probably higher with Tony, since a good 50% of Christian boys were major fence-sitters. *It's a fuckin' gay religion,* he thought, and he meant "gay" like a twelve-year-old meant it.

But Tony was kind of cute. In fact, he had a twinkle in his eye that Bobby was beginning to think was not the Holy Spirit. And there's only one other kind of man who has such a twinkle in his eye. Well, twinkle or no, Tony also had a fat, homely fiancée named Emily whose picture was tucked in the frame of the Anglo Jesus portrait above his bed, right next to the palm frond from Palm Sunday. Damning evidence. Still, Bobby saw him as several years shy of the self-discovery and reflection necessary to go down on a guy, but he also suspected that in time he would. Bobby didn't have that kind of time, and certainly didn't have that kind of patience – but then again, shouldn't he at least try to move things along for Emily's sake?

Lust springs eternal.

But how? He'd committed to three weeks. Oh, sure, one part of Bobby thought that was plenty of time. An hour was enough with a lot of men. But he'd need privacy and some downtime, a little booze – none of which were abundant, if available at all, in the bunkhouses of GUMBO.

They went back to work, lugging a stove out to the curb, hacking up some water-damaged furniture, and chipping away at more of the walls and ceilings. Quitting time came and they went out front to survey the Katrina pile they'd made, which they proudly compared to the other less towering ones up and down the street.

They unzipped their suits and climbed out of them.

"Damn, it's hot," Tony whined, stripping off his t-shirt to

reveal his excruciatingly perfect little chest. Ouch. Elvis Presley's "Don't be Cruel" lullabycd through Bobby's code-red-alerted brain. Good god, but lust was merciless. And never one to pass up even a semblance of opportunity – or failing that, just some good old-fashioned interactive homoeroticism – Bobby did the same. They looked at each other. "Dude, you're ripped," Tony shared.

"You too, man. You work out?"

"Nah, just lucky, I guess."

"Lucky, eh?" No, it was Emily who was lucky, Bobby thought. Tony, he was about to go home and step in a pile of karmic shit called marriage that was far more substantial than any Katrina pile.

Just then the Reverend came strolling by on his way back to wherever he came from before his visit. "Better keep those suits on, boys; the Lord comes like a thief in the night. Heh, heh, heh. Wouldn't wanna miss him." And he waved and hopped into a chauffeured blue Crown Royale parked two doors down.

"Can't they like get a restraining order for that guy?" Bobby thoughtlessly said into the middle distance.

Tony furrowed his brow. "It's a free country, dude. Jesus rocks." Bobby just looked at him and nodded.

* * *

Unlike Tony and Bobby, the Reverend wasn't part of GUMBO, though he took it upon himself to inspect their work often and "minister to them," as he called it. He ran his own outfit called BIO, which stood for "Bring It On," meaning the apocalypse. He was sure it was coming, and thus thought the rebuilding effort foolish. But he was doing a lot of good in his own fashion, through his soup kitchens and revival flea markets where people could barter all manner of goods, and the faithful could come down from Kansas or Missouri and do big giveaways with whatever they had to offer: clothes mostly, canned goods, soap.

No sir, he didn't see Katrina the same way as the lefties did. He was elated with the nearness of Armageddon and thought GUMBO a bunch of ignorant, godless liberals, suffering under the sin of pride, thinking they could avert the wrath of God, offering false promise and material assistance to poor wayward lambs. He'd sort of stroll around the GUMBO houses, shaking hands, clearly struggling with his own pride issues, a gaggle of sycophants at his heels. Tacky as Jim Jones, he had a thick white mane of hair and wore purple-tinted oversized aviator glasses and beige leisure suits that swelled with his girth and shook when he laughed. "You're not that different from a bunch of communists, really – and we know where they ended." And he'd burst out laughing. At times like that, Bobby wanted to snap back, "Yeah, well, you ain't that different than Il Duce or Hermann Goering, and they ended worse."

It's good he didn't, though, because everyone laughed along with the Reverend and, in fact, liked him. He had charisma, and a ready smile, a southern congeniality that made him basically un-hateable. Besides, some of the hippie boys were in fact *wearing* Che shirts, and the word on the street was the levees were in no shape to hold back another Katrina, which would in fact once again flood every single house GUMBO was repairing. So the Reverend had a point, whether you wanted to reflect on it or not, or whether you espoused his biblical paradigm. And on top of all that, as everyone at GUMBO knew, the man had been there from the start feeding and sheltering people in tents, and his credibility in terms of relief work was unquestioned. On some level, they were all in it together, and he was just betting on a different horse than they were. I suppose you could say the differences between GUMBO and the Reverend DuMay were along the lines of the friendly banter between White Sox and Cubs fans, although with far more dire consequences for the winners and losers.

But couldn't the Reverend put a cork in it? The hippie boys and GUMBO staffers weren't proselytizing about revolution, after all. But DuMay just chattered on endlessly, full of the confident bludgeoning rhetoric of an unquestionably dominant religion, while he meandered about the houses, his booming voice echoing off what was the left of the walls. "The President loves New Orleans, like he loves Jesus. We're the chosen people, and the President is proud of our witnessing. There's no city he cares for more…. Why, we're like the troops. In harm's way – no holier place to be. The President knows that; he supports us as God supports the righteous. He's in awe of the grace of our crucifixion, and when the great hurricane Lucifer Katrina the Second comes, he knows we will be lifted up like buoys. Oh ye of little faith, ye liberal devils, trying to drown us in your thirty pieces of silver. No, Lord, we don't want this cup to pass. We want to drink it down, drown in Your righteousness. You oughtta all go home and get your own houses in order, not ours."

"But, but …" Tony attempted a response. When conservative and liberal Christians collide.

"But nothing, son." And he guffawed.

Stern words, but the smile always spread across his face whenever he was most scolding, in effect emasculating and charming every audience that heard him. He was a preacher, all right, the likes of which Bobby'd never seen. After all, Bobby had been raised Catholic and Catholic priests were generally either white liberal wimps, corny yarn-spinning Irishmen, or besotted unimaginative English majors who churned out bad critical essays in place of sermons, outlining why the Resurrection made things different than if there'd been no such thing, or why it's better to obey your mom than to tell her to fuck off. No, duh. So Bobby had slept a lot during mass, when he wasn't fantasizing about the altar boys or other parishioners, while the priest droned on.

But he listened when the Reverend spoke. How he listened. The Reverend DuMay was an artist of the first order. He left people speechless, and Bobby found himself drawn to him.

"How you doing, Mr. Kennedy…Mr. Attorney General of

the You-nited States," he'd joke, "did you catch all the Mafiosi yet?! Heh, heh, heh. Mark my words, son, they'll shoot a proud man before they'll give him the keys to heaven. George Bush is a righteous man. It's written in the stars." And he'd gesture with his hand toward the sky.

Bobby would just laugh back, but he could detect the subtext, though he resisted the temptation to deconstruct the Reverend's balderdash to preserve his own peace of mind. What was the point with these people? When all was said and done, Bobby found it simpler to just treat the Reverend like a very good stand-up comic whom he didn't always agree with, but who, he had to admit, was very entertaining. A guilty pleasure. He wondered if the Reverend was aware that many people probably saw him this way – as a sort of clown. Bobby thought he was, and as if he were reading his mind, the Reverend soon enough eerily quipped, "I'm but a fool, Bobby, an instrument. Oh, His glory is great." And he smiled ear to ear.

An answer for everything.

Well, try this on for size, Reverend: Bobby was jonesing for speed, and though he'd on several occasions shared a beer or two with the boys back at the house, in between Hacky Sack sessions, he was determined not to fall back into drunkenness and debauchery, sex in alleys, and most of all the ever-destructive crystal. He'd fought the good fight for two weeks. A new leaf. God, but he was horny as sin, and he'd fought too hard to be queer and proud to classify good sex as depraved along the lines of alcohol and speed. But he'd vowed to only have healthy sex. But how does one find good, healthy sex? He didn't have the patience, and what's more, GUMBO was straight as the siding on a Katrina trailer. He was over outreach fantasies for the hippies, and Tony ... oh, Tony. Tony was ruining him with desire. Lately, Tony had developed an annoying habit of looking over from his ladder like a bro and smiling. Bobby had tolerated it at first, when he was still busy collecting the requisite masturbation material for later, like a bird feathering its nest – but after a week, every smile felt like Eros pulling back his bow: one, two, three – all day long, like Bobby was a hay bale or a sitting duck. He felt swollen and tenderized, sensitive to any touch. Tony just kept smiling and firing away, the heartless bastard. And then of course there was the "Jesus rocks" answer to any and all good news or common-sense truth shared with him – the Christian rocker's amen.

"Nice day,"

"Jesus rocks."

"I like these crowbars."

"Jesus rocks."

And the hugs. Oh, the hugs. "Blessings, dude." At the end of every workday. But never when they'd taken their shirts off. Oh no. Always once they'd put them back on. The cheap bastard. Bobby soon took to scowling at Tony's smiles and dodging his hugs. He knew it wasn't nice, but he couldn't stand the tease of it, even if Tony would never conceive of it as such. Tony was an idiot and a vacuous phony. But a hot one.

Tony eventually got the hint that Bobby wasn't into Jesus or his smiles – or was it more like he'd begun to feel that there was chemistry between them? That's when he'd start going on and on about his wedding to Emily, planned for when he got back to Boston.

"How old are you, Tony?"

"Twenty."

"Isn't that kind of young to be getting married?"

"Better to marry than to burn."

I prefer fire, Bobby thought to say as a luscious bead of sweat rolled down Tony's cheek and onto his smiling upper lip. As Bobby gazed at the beautiful boy, their eyes locked in Platonic love – or something – he knew what that night would bring. He'd had it. *Hell or high water.* Yeah, exactly. The water had receded, so he knew what part of that cliché was heading his way.

He'd stayed away for two weeks, but now he was dead set on Bourbon Street and the notorious Corner Pocket, where the dregs of the parish stripped for change, and the beer and speed breached the levee of whatever inhibitions remained in the poor lost lambs of the French Quarter.

It was Tony's fault, not his.

Tony did his bare-chested routine as usual at the end of the day, and this time Bobby just stared, quickly slurping up the drool that threatened to fall from his lower lip. And Tony said, "What, dude?"

Bobby just shook his head. Tonight he'd clear the slate. He'd go down to Bourbon Street and clear the slate. He'd held out long enough. He'd avoided drunkenness, drugs, sex, had even fallen for a clean-living Christian and done the Lord's work. *But God, I miss that old leaf*, he sighed.

"You wanna go out tonight? Like down to Bourbon Street?" Bobby chanced.

"No."

"Great. See you tomorrow."

On went the shirt. "Blessings." The embrace. A stirring in Bobby's crotch. They parted and Bobby waved, and it was all he could do to keep the digits surrounding his middle finger from dropping into a little fist.

* * *

Bobby didn't bother going home for a shower. He knew he looked enticingly blue-collar and he was in no mood for anyone looking for a clean-cut soap-smelling boy anyway. He was looking for another beast.

He marched down Elysian Fields, sweat cresting his brow, the humidity so thick the clouds and the sky sort of merged into an amorphous bluish-white-gray steam. He cut up Frenchmen, and crossing Esplanade – one signal-light post stuck like a tiki torch in the grass at a 45 degree angle (ah, the charms and grandeur of hurricanian ruination) – he had a laugh and thought of the River Styx. Whatever Eurydice he sought would be a sorry wreck of a slut indeed.

Sylvester was crooning at top volume when he entered the Bourbon Pub, and eyes swung about from the surrounding men as he entered from the street: some like babies toward shiny things, a handful like prowling cats, and still others like roused guard dogs who wanted a piece of his flesh or at least a good chase and tackle before moving on.

He glared back with his usual fuck-you-all visage, acquired among the clubs of L.A., and approached the bar. A sorry-looking go-go boy gyrated in a pair of boxer briefs, and Bobby momentarily wished the lad's pecs were as full of air as they looked so he could prick one with a pin and watch the boy fly around the room like a deflating balloon.

That's when he felt a distinctly reptilian presence at his side. He quickly glanced over out of a sort of animal watchfulness, and who did he see sitting on the stool next to him at the bar, but the Reverend DuMay himself, a pack of Marlboros and a cocktail perched in front of him like some flaming queen, his hair coiffed, dressed in a big oversized yellow-print Hawaiian shirt. He too looked at Bobby with the eyes of a hunter, but more like one with a long tongue that would strangle you in its embrace. Then he grinned, erasing all threat.

Figures the Reverend would be queer. Bobby felt so tired.

"It's Saturday night, son, and the Sabbath is just around the corner. What are you doing in this den of iniquity?"

"Oh, just a little R&R, Father." Bobby was in no mood. He'd felt like he'd crossed over at Esplanade and was through with the provincial squeamishness of do-gooders and hypocritical Christians alike.

"I'm not a Father, son, I'm a Reverend."

"Oh, sorry, I was raised Catholic."

"I suspected as much – you've always had the stink of popery about ya."

He clipped a quick smile. "And what exactly kind of stink is that, Reverend?" he shot back.

"Sort ah like sulfur, like frankincense and myrrh, but cooked a spell too long. Heh, heh, heh." And then: "Can I buy you a drink, son?

"Sure. Bud Lite. Thanks." Why not use the Reverend to get the buzz going, he figured.

"One Bud Lite and one 7-and-7." He turned to Bobby after ordering. "I drink 7-and-7 on account of the biblical references to the seven plagues, the seven angels, the seven days of creation and the seven seals of revelation, not to mention how many times Jesus asked us to forgive one another: seventy times seven."

"Well, I drink Bud Lite on account of it ain't Coors and they support the gay rags with advertising."

"I'll have to remember to boycott it. Heh, heh. Always preferred Coors myself. Heh, heh, heh."

"That's big of ya, Reverend."

"So you're a homosexual, eh, Bobby?"

"Yes, sir."

"Well, ain't you curious why I'm here?"

"You're one too, I guess. Frankly, it doesn't surprise me."

"Heh, heh. Not quite, son." And he leaned over to whisper. "I'm undercover. Heh, heh." Then he sat back again. "I'm here to save souls. Do you know how disgusted Our Lord would be to look down on this? I've started a new ministry because time is running out. The Rapture is gonna pass right over this place – and not Passover-style either, no sirree. These men here, they're all going straight to hell. And I aim to do something about it."

Just then "Stop in the Name of Love" blasted out of the speakers. And Bobby felt his political ire rising. He was taking a day off his good behavior, and besides, he was in his element. "Reverend, what makes you think that these guys here are interested in what you're selling?"

"I'm not selling anything, son; I'm revealing it. I'm offering it. For free. With a rebate. Money back guarantee. The lottery itself." He smirked.

Bobby drained the beer and set it down, wondering if the preacher would offer to buy him a second, or whether he should drag the man off his barstool and to the door. The Reverend looked heavy, though. A Herculean task. And didn't Hercules have *seven* labors or something? Maybe he should just start screaming, or blow a whistle ACT-UP style. But no one had whistles anymore.

"The Lord died once for your sins, son. Just once." And he pointed at the Bud bottle.

"What about the second coming?"

"You'll have to wait a spell, son. And better to be sober for it."

Bobby looked at him with disdain. "So how does this work, Reverend? You pick a guy up, take him home, tie him up, and convert him?"

"Whatever it takes, son."

"Let me tell you something, Reverend. Half the guys in here don't believe in your "God," and the other half do and they figure Jesus is either queer like them or he just feels the love and supports all this." And Bobby scanned his eyes around the room. "You won't find any souls to save here, Reverend, but you might find a knuckle sandwich. My advice would be to skedaddle."

"Though I walk through ..."

"Yeah, yeah ..." Bobby walked away, resolved to keep an eye on the Reverend, but also to get what he came for, which just then came stumbling down the stairs in a tattered wife-beater, tattooed like Queequeg, with the kind of scruff that made Bobby's balls tighten and tingle. The rest of the evening was more or less like most of Bobby's L.A. evenings of years past – a sort of time-suspended circus involving strange, leering, smiling faces; a gloopy techno soundtrack; the perusal and exploration of numerous male orifices; the feeling of cold brick against his face, his hands; the hardness of cement on his knees; the burning in his nose, and the rising of frequent belches; the anxieties of "Did he use a condom? I can't remember," and a chorus of "Sure, for a drink, I will. My name's Bobby," filling his head like a cacophony of advertising jingles. He rode the pinball night in the same way he always had.

It was as he was barreling out of the door of the Corner Pocket, his head swimming, sure that the cute boy taking off the discolored, faded BVDs up on the bar was none other than his dear Tony – no doubt full of the "gay-for-pay" excuse that he needed money for the wedding – when he bumped into Old Croc on the sidewalk. Old Croc was dressed in heaps of rags, and his face shone with sweat. He had friendly, uncannily familiar eyes, though, and when they met Bobby's they drilled right through Bobby's frontal lobe like an all-knowing mother's. "I been lookin' for ya," Old Croc smiled.

"What the fuck, leave me alone."

But Old Croc poked at him with his cane as Bobby reeled and leaned against the wall. "The mojo got you, and you'll be dead this time tomorrow if you don't take my mojo medicine."

All the superstitions of his Irish Catholic childhood were roused: black cats and ladders, broken mirrors and cracks in the sidewalk. Old Croc held out what looked like huckleberries, and Bobby suspected they'd likely kill him on the spot. Not such a bad thing, perhaps. "You better take these or your mojo's gonna finish you off. This time tomorrow. No time to waste. The spirit told me."

Bobby looked at him. He was scared, but his reason told him this man was just a bum looking for a dollar and preying on scared tourists from places like L.A. where voodoo and juju nonsense only appeared in the movies. Which was enough. Bobby leaned down with his hands on his knees, muttering something unsuccessfully to send Old Croc on his way.

"Bobby!" he heard someone call.

Without lifting his hands or torso, he craned his neck and saw a yellow mass moving down the sidewalk. DuMay. "Shit," he muttered, and then he pulled himself up, reeled, and grabbing the huckleberries from Old Croc's open palm, slammed them back like a handful of peanuts.

"Beware of false prophets, son," Old Croc whispered. "Now gimme a little something, and Ah promise you, the mojo will leave you be once and for all, and you'll find true love."

Bobby yanked a wad of bills out of his front pocket and proffered them to Old Croc, who quickly snapped the bundle up and turned and limped off with his carved wooden cane around the corner and down Burgundy Street.

"Get thee behind me, Satan ... or in front of me ... or what-ever." DuMay's voice trailed off as he hurried his girth up St. Louis Street. "Bobby, Bobby," DuMay called out like a love-lorn mother, "God bless you, my son, you are enveloped in the darkness, sick with the Tree of Knowledge and its foul fruit. But I'm here to deliver you ..." And just as DuMay reached him, Bobby's hands went down on his knees again as the Reverend reached out to steady his shoulders, and then out came an explosive spew of vomit which the Reverend was too slow to step aside from, his white loafers showered now in the orange and yellow regurgitated alcohol, Fritos, semen, beer nuts and huckleberries of Bobby's dismal fall from grace.

* * *

Bobby woke up in the megachurch, propped up in a pew, huge metal rafters above him, and DuMay up there at the pulpit, fully wired, his voice echoing and resounding off the metallic walls of what appeared to be an enormous aluminum-siding trailer the size of an airplane hangar.

"I'm down in the trenches with ya, boys. The trench, that's what your kind of boy likes, ain't it? Heh, heh. Face up to it, boys! It's a trench, a foul gutter, an irrigation ditch full of crocs and snakes – all manner of disease, slime and putridity. The Lord is gonna lift you up. These hands, my hands, will lift ya. And I ain't wearing gloves either. I ain't afraid of your filth. And I'll catch you when you fall, boys. I'll catch ya. I'm a catcher. Heh, heh. BIB, sons, that's what I call my ministry for you all. For the homo-sekshoo-all. BIB. Say it. BIB: Bringing It Back to the heterosexual fold. Bring It Back! Shout it out!" There was a lame muttering of repetition among the sixty or so tortured homosexual congregants. "We're bringing it on and we're bringing it back! And you know what *it* is, and where *it* belongs. The Garden, boys. That's what a woman is. A garden. That's what the hoochie is – a garden! Not some toxic superfund site like where you're puttin' it! And BIB's the way. Let me fasten that bib 'round your neck, like a bib of righteousness, and when that foul food of the devil drips from your mouth, the bib of the Lord will catch it and keep that pure white Sunday shirt of the Second Coming clean as mother's precious, holy milk." And he pounded the lectern with his index finger. Bobby tried to follow along, but all he could think of were DuMay's fouled white shoes, his sore throat, and the ache in his rectum; his pounding head and burning septum; his parched mouth. "And the Lord, he'll recognize you at the Apocalypse. And it's comin'. Mark my words. And there ain't no place at the table for the butt pirate. No sirree! Now get that Bib on! Get it on! Bring it on!"

Something in the Reverend's words reached Bobby then, and feeling the surge of energy, he rose, watched the building spin for a few seconds, and once he'd secured his footing, bolted for the door.

Two no-necks stood with folded arms at the entrance, and as Bobby felt more vomit rising, he saw the horrified looks on their faces when they stepped aside and he proceeded vomit-first into the cheap, aluminum-siding locked door, which snapped off its hinges and swung, collapsing like a space shuttle support platform backward to reveal the ruined plane of flooded Chalmette, Louisiana – its upended oak trees and ruined houses, a swath of destruction so immense Bobby could actually see all the way to Interstate 10 in the distance. He made straight for it.

"You can't run from Jesus, boys," he heard the microphone boom. "He's faster than vomit rising. You can't eat without a bib! The world is a trough of sin! You're pigs in it ..." But it all faded to an echo as Bobby ran like an escaped convict, ran with all he had, his temples pounding with hangover, his ass aching, tears streaming down his face. My God, maybe he had been born again. But into what he couldn't tell.

He was sobbing by the time he reached the interstate and saw the gas station and the couple arguing. There was only one other customer, a local in a pickup, who soon disappeared into the restroom. He looked back at the couple, the car loaded down with luggage. They were definitely on their way somewhere else. Far from New Orleans – its trailers and mold; its Hacky-Sacking do-gooders and closeted straight-boys; its traveler's turds and poorly-laundered BVDs sagging off the gay-for-pay strippers at the Corner Pocket; its fucking gumbo and jambalaya and beignets; its Christian preachers and old men like Croc – its omens and voodoo. It was true. Voodoo. And Bobby was pierced full of holes. And so what if a good number of the more recent needles were seven inches and made of flesh, or loaded with meth and Jack Daniels? He was poked so full of holes he had to escape or he'd sink like a little gay Titanic down into the swamp, never to re-emerge.

He was in deep trouble.

Old Croc had been right, and so perhaps was DuMay. Bobby had the sad realization then that when someone was as wrong as him, almost everyone else was right, no matter how hair-brained or stupid they were.

The couple kept arguing, the man now back at the trunk, pulling something out and flinging it at the woman. A dildo. She tossed it in a nearby trashcan.

"You happy?!" he shouted

"Oh Jeremy," she sighed, and he marched toward her, leaving the trunk open as she burst into tears and he hugged her close. Her head was buried in his chest and his back was to Bobby, who just then got a wickedly convenient idea. *I have to leave now* a voice said inside his head. Why ask for a ride? Two quick steps and he let himself roll sideways like he'd done in wrestling in high school, and he was in the trunk. But how to close it, and wouldn't they wonder how it got closed? But before he could figure a way, it slammed shut and he heard the man's muffled voice. "It's fucking six hours to Houston; let's get going."

He was elated to be escaping, and escaping seriously, far, far away like so many others had done from New Orleans not a year ago. But six hours in a trunk?

Fortunately, he passed out almost immediately.

He awoke when the car thumped over a dead possum

and the woman screamed out, "You killed it!"

"He was already dead," the man shouted back in a queer voice.

Bobby had no idea how long he'd been trapped in there, but he wanted out. The trunk was humid, claustrophobic and smelled like spare tire and Prestone. Within minutes of waking, Bobby decided that it had been a very bad idea to climb into the trunk and he resolved to get out as soon as possible.

The rest had done him good, and the hangover had progressed to the stage where a shot or two of whiskey would finish it off once and for all. But for that, he needed to get out. He searched for a latch. Not that he planned to bail out at seventy mph, but just to see if there indeed was one that could be opened from the inside. Perhaps next time they pulled over, he could climb out? Of course, they'd likely just peed and filled the tank when he'd climbed in, so it could be hours. But how long had he slept? He did the math: fifteen gallons at twenty-five mpg = 25 x 15 = ... close to 400 miles. At seventy mph, that was five-plus hours. They might be driving straight through to Houston. He hoped they'd stocked up on sodas and water at the gas station. Shit. A wave of panic jolted through him before it turned to dread. On top of that, he realized that unlike his captors, he now needed to pee. He held it as long as he could. An hour later, the trunk had another pungent odor.

"Good God," Jeremy grimaced, turning his head, "this trunk stinks." Then he saw Bobby curled up in it. "And there's someone in it!"

"What are you talking about, Jeremy?"

"Come here, look!"

"I can explain everything," Bobby muttered. "Please, please, I mean you no harm."

Jeremy looked at Jenny, Jenny back at Jeremy.

They helped Bobby out of the trunk, along with their bags, and they took him inside, where they bathed him. "I'll do it, Jeremy," Jenny said as he began setting out soaps and towels, unable to hide the big grin animating his face. "You go watch television or something."

"Geez, Jenny, I'm healed, remember?" he said, suddenly turned serious.

"Healing, Jeremy. Heeeee-ling."

He stormed past her to watch the *700 Club*.

Bobby was still dazed from hunger, fatigue and everything else, and he barely stayed conscious through the bath, remembering nothing but Jenny's beaming smile and somewhat disturbing over-vigilance with the sponge, especially in the nether regions. Then she folded him in a towel, doused him with baby powder and put him to bed, with a kiss on the forehead.

* * *

He woke up to their arguing in the kitchen, the sink running, and dishes clanging about.

"Are you gonna be okay here while I'm at work?"

"Yes, I'll be fine," Jeremy said.

"Can you handle this?"

"Yes, I can handle it!"

"Don't get so snappy, Jeremy, I'm just trying to help."

"Well, have a little confidence in me," he relented.

"If I had confidence in you, I wouldn't have done the intervention. You need support, not confidence."

"I need both, Jeanette."

"Just...remember what you learned. This is your Gethsemane. Your cup."

Jeremy thought of P.E. in junior high when he played goalie in soccer.

"My what?"

"This cup shall not pass?"

"What are you saying?"

"I'm saying, this is it, your crucifixion. Do you have what it takes?"

"I'm getting crucified now?"

"Temptation, Jeremy! It's your turn on the cross. God is

watching you." The soft rock station droned on in the background as Bette Midler crooned.

"I'll be fine. You're treating him like he's a murderer or something. I'm strong, have a little faith."

"Him? He has a name! Hello!"

"Whatever."

"See, that's the problem, you guys don't even bother remembering names." She audibly sighed. "I don't know. I don't like it. We shouldn't have had him stay."

"What?"

"I mean we don't even know him."

"Christian love? Hello?"

"Christian love? You're not Christ, you're a homosexual who's finding his way back to righteousness, Jeremy. You've got to be conscious of your fragile state. He might be Satan."

"Would you stop?"

"I'm trying to help you."

"Then leave me be to sink or swim!"

"Sink or swim. Did you look at him? He's a torpedo is what he is. Or a major iceberg. Now I know what they mean by handsome devil."

"I can handle it," Jeremy said. "Now what's his name?"

"I'm not telling. I feel like I'm leaving a drunk in the house with a case of beer in the fridge. It's insane." She paused. "I should wake him up and take him into town and drop him at the shelter."

"That is so cold."

"You like him, I can tell."

"Oh, please."

"Admit it; he's handsome."

"You clearly think so. How long did that bath run? An hour? Myself, I'm more focused on women and marriage right now. Reverend DuMay healed me, and I'm safe in my spiritual bib, thank you very much." And then he added, "And you're gonna be late for work."

"Okay, well, that's the spirit. Keep that bib front and center, Jeremy. I love you." Bobby heard a kiss. "I have faith and confidence in you. Totally. God bless. I'll be home at six."

Bobby waited for the door to close behind Jenny before he emerged, disheveled, in a pair of boxer shorts.

Jeremy turned, blushed and went back to the dishes, barking, "There's coffee and cinnamon buns on the table. Help yourself."

Bobby fell into a chair.

"Excuse me," Jeremy called out over the din of the faucet, "uh ... what is your name?"

"Bobby."

"As in Robert?"

"As in Bobby."

He turned the sink off and began sponging down the counter, his eyes locked on the sponge while he spoke. "Well, Bobby, um, this is a Christian home and we don't come to the table in our underwear. Do you think you could put something on?"

"Uh, sure, but I don't have any clothes, and I don't know what your wife –"

"She's not my wife; she's my sister."

"Oh. I don't know what she did with my stuff."

"Well, you can wear some of my clothes. Let me get them for you." Their eyes met, both of them blushing now.

"Wow, you're cute," Bobby said.

"Please. I'm not gay."

Oh, yeah, sure thing, Bobby thought. Maybe he hadn't escaped after all. Bobby suddenly felt trapped again. "You know, I really think I need some clothes and that I just gotta go, like now. I'm kinda confused and uh, a little stressed, and uh ..." And Bobby couldn't help himself. He started to cry.

"Hey, hey, it's okay." Jeremy took a step toward the table, then arrested himself. "Don't cry." But Bobby cried. Jeremy very carefully sat down in the chair opposite, out of range of any physical contact. Until Bobby reached his hand across the table. Jeremy grabbed it.

"I think I'm having some kind of breakdown," Bobby said between sobs.

"It's okay. "Why don't I call 9-1-1?"

"No, I don't need 9-1-1. Just hold my hand."

But Jeremy's pants were full to bursting. "Uh, I can't do that."

"You can't hold my hand?" Bobby looked at him with a face of total heartbreak.

Jeremy blushed, felt a bolt of something rip through his chest and looked down at the place mat in front of him. "No."

"Please," Bobby pleaded, gripping Jeremy's hand more firmly as he began to cry some more. Their hands tangled together until both chairs went skidding back across the linoleum as they lurched forward into a kiss. Bobby dragged Jeremy across the table and they careened onto the floor. Straddling him, Bobby stopped kissing Jeremy long enough to grab his cheeks, look into his eyes and asked, "Who the fuck are you?"

"I have no idea," Jeremy said. "Who are you?"

Bobby shrugged. And dove back in.

Pangs of guilt shot through Jeremy as Bobby once again smothered him and, throwing aside everything he'd just learned, Jeremy began lustily yanking back the boxer shorts Bobby was wearing. *They are my underwear, after all – there can't be any sin in that,* Jeremy rationalized.

They muttered and wept as they communed together and didn't really stop crying completely until they'd betrayed the books of Leviticus and Deuteronomy, as well as Paul's letters to the Corinthians and Romans – and arguably Timothy.

Spent, splayed on the floor together, Bobby spoke first. "I fuckin' need help."

"You need help? If you only knew."

"Oh, I think I know." And Bobby leaned up on one elbow. Jeremy looked back quizzically. "You were lost and wanted to be found – all that shit, right?"

Jeremy nodded. "Something like that."

"Yeah, well, me too."

"And so, what happened?"

"Well, until ten minutes ago," Bobby said, "I was pretty

sure it hadn't worked."

"What?"

"Well, you know, like, I'm not a religious guy or nothing. But like, you know the Lord works in strange ways? Or maybe voodoo does."

"Meaning?"

"Meaning I really like you. Like really, really, really."

"I'm not available."

"Uh, well, neither am I, actually. I never am. That's what I mean."

"I'm not really following this."

"Well, you know, star-crossed lovers, all that shit?"

"Romeo and Juliet?"

"Well, more like Romeo and Jude, or Jeff, or something."

"Romeo and Jeremy."

"Bobby and Jeremy?"

"I have a dog. He's pretty much my significant other."

"Well, I'm a speed freak."

Jeremy offered a tired smile. "I'm a Christian."

"I can't stand Christians."

"I want to be straight."

"I want to move in with you and get clean."

"I want to do what we just did," Jeremy said, sitting up.

"Me too."

"But I can't."

"But we will."

"No."

"Yes."

* * *

And they did.

Three Things I Pray

The Archangel Michael, Who Battles Dark Forces

A real Romeo, that angel was. And what better place for it – what with the balcony, the Italian ambience, the tragic air permeating the grimy old glorious architecture. Buenos Aires felt lost in time, Mediterranean, forgotten. The world and Evita had left it in the past, stewing in debt and unrealized potential. The usual suspects: sex and fate and the arbitrary slings and arrows of the gods, the IMF having been the most recent that seduced, loved and then abandoned them, like the Zeus that Europe and America were and always had been. Mount Olympus was up there in the Northern Hemisphere, and they were far down here ... below.

Calling up. Real Romeos.

And I'm some blue-eyed, pale-skinned, wrong-gendered Juliet.

I'd spent my severance pay from the circus on a plane ticket south, taking an apartment on Callao and Corrientes in the heart of the city, among the theaters, bookshops and all-night cafes. The palpable nostalgia of the place with its tango and old bow-tied waiters unnerved me, made me feel like a ghost.

Had I fallen from Olympic heights? Had Juliet's rickety

porch finally given? Balconies fell into the streets all the time here, crushing pedestrians. Maybe I hadn't fallen, but just expired and this place was no longer earth, but the underworld.

If it was, I'd say the dead have great coffee and they're rather handsome. And the rain comes in summer, warm and hard from big thunderheads. I liked sitting on the little balcony outside my tenth-floor room to watch it fall over the city among flickering lights, honking taxis and running-for-cover shadows down below. My room faced west, so I could watch the big clouds rolling in from across the pampas, having survived the long treacherous trek over the Andes, all the way from mysterious unknown Chile – and beyond there, Easter Island, where the big heads stared into the middle distance.

I slept fitfully. Callao is loud; the dead walk up and down it all night long shouting and singing – football songs and insults mostly: *hijo de puta, che boludo* and the national anthem. The cabs never cease honking, or the ambulances sirening, because no one gets out of their way – ever. The street dogs join in barking when the confusion reaches a tipping point, then hands are thrown in the air, and if one listens carefully, from among those shrugs and sighs is heard drifting up like Romeo's longing, the national forever-frustrated drawn-out ethos: *este pais!*

Pigeons roosted on my balcony, their characteristic flutter and low murmurs almost a comfort. Which is what I assumed woke me that morning: the telltale crash of wings against glass, the fluttering, the muffled high-pitched moan. Poor thing. They're tough, though. I figured it would be fine, thought no more of it and pulled the pillow over my head, hoping to steal a few more minutes of sleep before the bustle and noise of Callao woke me for good.

I mused languorously about the coffee I'd drink with *medialunas* or empanadas stuffed with Swiss chard and mozzarella as I drifted in and out of slumber. Soon I was falling headlong through the clouds of my subconscious, assailed by disturbing memories of the circus that then morphed into dreams of Juan Domingo and Evita Peron on the flying trapeze, Che clowning revolution below, chuckling and pop-ping candied corn into his mouth.

But I was soon roused from my reverie by the taxis and ambulances crescendoing ten stories below.

I stumbled into the bathroom and flipped on the light, looking at my grizzled face in the mirror. *Growing old, dear,* I muttered before twisting the knob and climbing into the shower. I heard the flapping again when I emerged from the bathroom. I'd need to pull up the *persianas* (I didn't know what they were when I got here either, but they'd proved quite handy: wood blinds that you pull up and down over your windows to keep out the sun, the cold and the *ladrones* – thieves – that Buenos Aires was rife with these days). I grabbed the rope next to the *persianas* and pulled hand over hand because they weren't easy. But I stopped when they were halfway up because, to my surprise, what I saw instead of an injured or roosting pigeon was a very, very big bird. Huge white wings folded over each other in the corner of the deck against the railing. An eagle? A condor? I'd heard they had those in Patagonia. The animals were all strange and different here: enormous guinea pigs called *capybaras* and llama-like *guanacos,* buck-toothed little rat-like deer-ish things called *maras;* and *nandus,* ostrich-like birds that ran around the pampas. I hesitated. Not one of those birds I'd considered had white wings. Perhaps a swan had escaped from one of the many turn-of-the-century parks reminiscent of the imperial cities of Europe. Even the birds were lost in time here.

Whatever it was, it wasn't moving. I pulled on the cord slowly to bring the *persianas* up higher without startling it. There was still a sliding glass window between us, so I felt safe.

My eyes bugged out when I noticed that under those wings was a human head – with curly hair to boot, like some overgrown cherub. *Ladron!* I concluded with a start, pulling the opposing rope to get the *persianas* back down before the cat burglar tried to get in. Imagine going to such lengths to rob a tourist. Had he hang-glided in or hopped down from the roof? They were dramatic, these Argentines, from kids on the street corner playing at *Maradona,* and that president who looked and carried on like a soprano in some Italian opera, to those nasty generals of thirty years past, who weren't satisfied with just exterminating an entire generation – they had to disappear them, steal their children and drop them from airplanes into the vast Rio de la Plata, and then claim they knew nothing, had no records.

I'd have to go down and tell the guard in the lobby. Though I'd heard the *porteros* were as often as not on the take and in cahoots with the cat burglars who sometimes went door to door *with* them – after paying them a handsome cut, of course – robbing and bilking the very residents who paid for the now colluding security so as to prevent just such a thing.

I heard the moan again. His ruse? It made sense if he thought I was a tourist – a moan is understandable even to a foreigner (no need for Spanish to comprehend that). Still, my curiosity was insatiable and I tiptoed back to the window and stuck my finger between two slats of the *persianas* to see if I could spy him. He'd gotten up and turned around and was now looking down off the deck, his naked back covered in blood where the left wing attached – and indeed it attached: blood and cartilage and tissue were showing. These were either some amazing special effects – maybe they were filming a movie? – or something stranger. I suddenly hoped I'd see a camera swing by on a crane.

He turned then, like he'd sensed me watching, and when our eyes met, I stumbled backward, letting go of the slats.

A friggin' angel? I didn't believe in such things. But those eyes: intense, fiery, penetrating. Maybe *I* was dead, and he'd come to remind me or carry me off to my hellish reward? I sat on the floor on my butt, considering the situation. Anything was possible. If it was a movie, he did need to get off the deck and back to the crew. I could go downstairs and find out if they were filming in the building.

Oh, what a cute butt he'd had when I viewed him peering

over the rail. It wasn't *just* that, either. Though I saw his ass only out of the corner of my eye when he'd turned, it was downright Roman, a real Caesar. He was incredibly hot is what it was, and I felt aroused. Which was crazy: fright and lust didn't belong together. Not that level of fright anyway. It was epic, awesome, Old World. Who was that character who'd turned into a swan? Holy shit, that was Zeus himself! I hoped not. Because if he was Zeus, that made me Ganymede. I fondled my grizzled, graying beard. I was no Ganymede.

I sat, trying to avoid panic. My curiosity piqued, I didn't want to leave, but I was terrified to stay. Then again, I wasn't here on vacation, hadn't come here to rest or tour. What did I have to lose? I'd come here to die or be dead is the honest truth. I was at the end of my rope – why not get on with it and explore the fray? What's the worst that could happen? I'd get robbed or condemned to eternal suffering. *Bring it on.* I got up and proceeded to the *persianas* and pulled them up rapidly arm over arm.

I stood and stared. It looked at me with those transfixing eyes, and then it smiled. A smile I couldn't forget: kind and welcoming when I'd been expecting a cornered animal, angry and afraid; a frustrated stuntman; a shifty-eyed thief; or an avenging angel come to spirit me off to hell for my unrepentant sodomy. But those fiery eyes turned to the warmth of a glowing hearth the minute its smile emerged.

I smiled back, but soon its smile lessened and a tear ran down its cheek. It was injured, sure thing; I could see now that the blood from its wings spread all over its shoulder. I felt tears then, too, which unnerved me further. Its eyes seemed to direct my every emotion. I opened the glass door and fell to my knees. Which brought me face to face with Caesar (and render unto Caesar what is Caesar's). The emperor rose to meet me, entering me like the host.

What was I doing? I felt possessed, unable to tear myself away or reconsider the course I'd embarked upon. I saw strange flashes of light in my mind's eye; I heard people speaking Arabic or Hebrew, or something like it; there was music and the scent of fruit. I muttered an Our Father and started in on the Hail Marys before I nearly choked.

I took a deep breath after Caesar had conquered me and returned to Rome, leaving behind his infinite legions. Then I looked up to meet the creature's eyes, which smiled again with that unbearable kindness. *What is it you want?* I implored softly, wiping the come off my mouth and chin.

It moved its great wings slowly, wincing at the pain. But it didn't answer.

I still had my doubts, but I was beginning to think he really was an angel, after those visions, his stupefying gaze and the bloody wings. But I didn't believe in such things. My mental health wasn't exactly stellar, I reminded myself, attempting to chalk up my visions to my usual paranoid fantasies. He was probably some artist or thrill seeker or pop culture icon filming some crappy movie. "You all right? You need help? Should I call an ambulance?" I stuttered in rudimentary Spanish: *Esta bien? Quiere ayuda? Una ambulancia?*

He shook his head with vigor.

"Are you an actor? A thief?"

He smiled again and shook his head slowly.

Well then. I didn't even have any Mercurochrome. I was an escapee, not a traveler. I remembered I had some first aid cream in a little kit I'd thrown in my bag.

"Just a minute." At least this way I'd find out for sure if they were special effects.

I stepped inside and bent down to my backpack, rooting around in the side pockets for my first aid kit, keeping a wary eye over my shoulder for any shenanigans from the chimera. I wondered momentarily if I really were in fact dead. Maybe my plane had gone down over the Amazon and these last few days were the wanderings of my lost ghost, wholly ignorant of its own death. Sheesh – and then the angel sent for me couldn't get it right either and crashed?

I didn't care either way.

I returned to the deck and ministered to the chimera, angel, whatever he was, dabbing his wounds – which, I was convinced, were clearly real – with Neosporin and a clean white tube sock, assuring him I'd get more supplies at the *farmacia* just as soon as we used up the tube. I dabbed him with the sock and laid a towel across the bed for him to recline on, so he wouldn't bleed all over the divan. His wounds weren't deep; it was more or less a flesh wound, but messy, as it had pulled his wing away from his back and torn the surface flesh.

He lay back and rested, and I left him there, proceeding to the elevator, off to get more bandages and antiseptic.

Archangel Gabriel, the Messenger

I'd left Los Angeles when the circus went belly up outside Palmdale. But I'd lost more than my dream job of clowning – I'd lost Anastacio, my lover. Like many of my compadres in the BubbleOpia Circus – or half of them anyway – he'd decided to stay in L.A. and hock his talents to the movie and television studios. So it wasn't like we'd had a dramatic falling-out or anything. We were just through and ready to go our separate ways. Or so I thought.

I'd been a clown for more than twenty years and had no illusions that I was suddenly going to be discovered by Hollywood – even if I were, it would probably be as some clown psycho with a butcher knife. That wasn't for me. Stephen King and Pennywise had done terrible damage to clowning, and I resented them for it. Myself, I'd been a sad and friendly clown – someone you could trust – a hobo philosopher of a clown in the time-honored tradition of Emmett Kelly.

And my paramour, Anastacio, was a real player, which made me the put-upon, down-on-his-luck clown even off-stage. I could take no more of it. Set loose in Los Angeles, there was no telling the pain I'd be in for at his hands. Just his infidelity among the traveling troupe, and in the numerous ostensibly non-gay Midwestern and Texas towns we'd performed in during those past two years, had been hard enough. The burning plain that was Los Angeles would make quick work of what was left of our love. I was through with clowning – romantically and otherwise.

Anastacio was a trapeze artist from Tamaulipas. He'd picked up with us when we'd played the fairgrounds outside Brownsville, Texas. "Not a legal bone in my body," he'd told me when I'd voiced concern for his status and warned him about Kim Sook, the enforcer.

"He won't take chances with Mexicans; he just won't." He'd driven off a dozen of them: roustabouts, clowns, cage-cleaners and cowboys.

"My English is superb," Anastacio informed me.

"True that, Anastacio. But Sook likes to see proof. He's a stickler for the paperwork."

Anastacio put down his book on the Kabbalah. A bright little bastard, he was the fourteenth child of an old sorceress from a dusty pueblo south of Matamoros, and like anyone with such a mother and thirteen siblings to dote upon him, he'd been overindulged and praised for his beauty and brains. Since then he'd spent all his free time reading and fornicating. A regular Lucifer. He'd studied structural engineering, neurosurgery, animal husbandry, herbs, numerology, physics and necromancy, among other disciplines.

He'd grabbed my hand, told me I had a problematic destiny and that he was part of it. Then he laid out a tarot and pointed to card after card. "That's me, that's you, this is what happens next week": a confusion of swords and princes. He shuffled and threw another reading, peered at it and shrugged. "It always comes out that way for you and me."

"I don't go in much for the occult."

"You don't have to." And he kissed me long and lasciviously. We were divinely naked in no time. And repeatedly and frequently during all the following afternoons.

I'd had half a mind to harbor him in Nadine, the private trailer that I'd commandeered when Lucy the Elephant Lady ran off with a telemarketer in Baton Rouge. But I was always wary of Sook and his eagle eye. He'd been after me just last week for mooching postage stamps to send Christmas cards to my dozens of nephews and nieces, snapping with a scowl that I'd lose Nadine if I didn't keep my drawers clean. Consequently, I reluctantly sent Anastacio packing after a mere five days of ecstatic gymnastics.

Not a week later, I was as surprised as anyone when I learned he'd been hired on among the acrobats.

How had he gotten by Sook? He must have gotten papers somewhere (it wasn't till later I'd learn he'd found Lucy's in my trailer, and after sacrificing a muskrat and mixing its blood with sage, he'd been able to erase all her information and put in his own). When I asked him about Sook, he said the dames of a nearby whorehouse had found favor with his substantial skills and beauty and adopted him, supplying birth certificate, social security card, and Texas ID.

The ladies would do that for him, charmer that he was. People lined up to do him favors. The boy had magnetism, and I didn't want to think how dark and winding the branches around that kind of beauty could grow. I didn't have to. Soon, half the circus was stuck on him. With his smile and his lithe, brown, acrobatic body, those big white Chiclet teeth and how he rolled his *R*'s. He stayed in Nadine a few nights each week and regaled me with pleasure, philandering only with women in the beginning. The Siamese twin girls wept in his arms and both swore their love; Betty the Buxom, with 56D cups, kept his cheeks rosy for three days running; the bearded lady shaved his pubes with her straight razor and diapered him as her own.

Meanwhile, stage left, Atlas and the lion tamer glowered in the way of lecherous men. Sure enough, when he got through the women, he turned to the main course and went man to man. First the roustabouts, then the cage-cleaners, ice-cream hawkers, popcorn concessionaires and finally the pole jockeys with their long sinewy arms.

But always he returned to me and Nadine. I prided myself on that, and I got the comeuppance for it, too. Became his fool.

He was as curious about bodies as he was about black and white magic and nuclear physics. After another blissful few days together, off he went again, taking up with Noah, the dwarf. Unlike the women, the men made me jealous. "He's thicker than you," he said cruelly when I'd asked what Noah had that I didn't.

"Why'd you move in with me if you love so many others? Just to torture me?"

"I liked your trailer."

Taken aback, my chin pressed back against my chest. "Is that all it is?"

He'd laughed then. "Don't be so melodramatic. You're my special one. We share destiny."

I looked at him suspiciously, the cad. "Can't it be just you and me then?"

"Destiny and monogamy? Are you crazy?" He laughed. "I'm a servant of larger forces."

Soon he disappeared for an entire week with Bennie and Adrian, the stilt walkers. *He'll ruin me,* I concluded. *Where do I sign?* I'd dream of us in midair. In waking he was acrobatic. We made love in the middle of headstands. I started taking yoga classes from the circus snake charmer to keep myself limber. To keep my Anastacio. My destiny intact.

Atlas was only a matter of time with his tattoos and muscles. A corny gay cliché.

As for myself, to keep my sanity, I pursued an erotic friendship with the bearded lady who told me, while she bathed me, that they'd threatened to cancel her contract if she ever showed up again in that black shift and pearls.

"You looked stunning." I shivered as she toweled me dry.

"I thought I was upgrading the friggin' circus. I bought it myself," she said.

But Mr. Sook, he liked to keep things as is. If it ain't broke, don't fix it. Still, she hated the frilly Victorian dresses they insisted upon. And she hated Sook. Sook was the vice principal, the enforcer if you will. A former Baptist minister who'd fled Seoul when the congregation and the authorities got wise to his trafficking in young girls to finance the church, the Lexus and the country retreat.

He'd defend himself angrily when the players muttered "pimp" under their breath. "They fled. I fled. You'll flee one day, too."

He was right about that, if nothing else.

The big boss was Gil Webb, whom I resented for how he made Sook do the dirty work while he enjoyed the chairman of the board routine, smiling and encouraging the players, handing out cheap compliments. He was an old carny with a gold tooth and a penchant for slugging Manischewitz, relishing the occasional knife fight when he came upon midnight intruders on the camp's perimeter.

He ran a tight ship with his first lieutenant Sook. It was said, in addition to the tooth, he had a heart of gold. But I'd never seen it. Not till the last day. And though I'd steered clear – I had no truck with him – he always paid on time and gave bonuses when the circus did better than expected. But on my last day, he paid me a fat severance, and looking in my eye, remarked: "You were the soul of this gig, Peaches. May the angels bless you." Then he spit out that tooth and handed it to me.

"That's very kind of you, Mr. Webb. I shall treasure this incisor."

"I just love me the circus," he'd enthused, staring into the night sky, his eyes glassy. "It's got me, it does."

"What'll you do now, Mr. Webb?"

He fixed me with a stare. "What won't I do?"

Last I heard, he'd been drinking steadily. They said he suffered from nostalgia. That he was from a long line of circus folk. Some said he was the bastard son of Emmett Kelly himself, and others that he'd escaped the Ozarks while just a boy, stowed away in the lion's cage, rationing off his beef jerky to keep the beast at bay through the long night and into Texas.

As it turned out, Atlas was a jealous lover and began to lay traps for me. Tiger cages left unlatched, parked kitty-corner to Nadine. I nearly lost my foot in a 'coon trap one Sunday on my way back from mass after Anastacio had wowed the choir with his a cappella rendering of "Ave Maria." Then Atlas put itching powder in my face cream. The crowd roared.

"Put a stop to it, Anastacio, or I'm bringing in Sook."

"A stop to what?"

"Bear traps, maxillofacial poison oak, the fallout from your philandering." I nearly raised an arm to him.

Out darted his tongue, and what followed was how he apologized and why he could do no wrong. He didn't leave Nadine then, except for shows, for three weeks running. Promised he'd be good. Even had two big midnight-blue angel's wings tattooed on his perfect brown back.

Atlas wailed after that in the alleyways between trailers. For weeks he moped about, despondent, drinking, and singing old gospel songs. But it was his giving lackluster performances that finally brought down the wrath of Sook. When the smoke cleared, Atlas was shacked up with a willowy lad of dubious majority whom Sook had commandeered from a local revival meeting.

After that, Anastacio moved on to the lion tamer. An insatiable hunger. Good place for him among those ravenous felines.

"You like nibbling on that little greasy moustache of his, do you?"

"You're my special one," he repeated, flipping the card off the top of the tarot: Wheel of Fortune. He put the bookmarker back in the *Gospel According to Ramakrishna* and pounced on me like a cat. I'd give him that. He was always upgrading his skills. A quick study, too.

Eventually he got a bad case of strep throat from one of his encounters at the truck stop east of Shreveport, and after oral sex I ended up with a prostate infection I couldn't shake. It would no sooner clear up than it would return with a vengeance. I felt like I was sitting on a stone, and sometimes when I peed I felt like someone was running a sharp knife along the inside of my urethra.

Doctors failed me, while Anastacio's efforts with meditation, herbs, affirmations, astrology and past life regression got me nowhere. He offered to take down one of the lions and offer him up. I told him in no uncertain terms that no creature should die for the relief of my glands. I learned to live with it. It came and went.

Love.

Once, soon after I'd arrived in Argentina, I'd gone to the province to meet a *curandera.* I could have done the same in L.A., but someone had told me this one worked with the legendary Gaucho Gil and I was encouraged. Gaucho Gil appealed to my clown's soul. A folk saint of a century ago, he was a regular Robin Hood and was credited with healing those near death. His little red shrines could be seen all along the highways, patron of travelers and thieves. Handsome, too, holding the bolas characteristic of gauchos. I can't have been the only one to think of his balls.

Across the dirt road where I waited in line at the *curandera's,* a boy sat atop a wall, watching the people and stray dogs and peering into the far distance from his perch. Now and again his mother yelled up at him: "Get off that wall before you fall and hurt yourself!" He smiled nonchalantly and waved back toward the house, which I couldn't see as it was somewhere beyond the wall.

The old man in line behind me muttered and slurped his *mate.*

I was ushered in and offered a wooden chair that faced the *curandera* in her stained old recliner. She asked me my name and then waved her hand over it once she'd written it down: I'd need to sacrifice a goat. "Only blood will cure blood," she'd stated. Then she went on and on about her dog from when she was a girl, how she'd carried it hidden in a backpack to school as her mother wouldn't allow her to keep it in the house. It stayed quiet, as if it knew its life depended on it. "I never had another human friend after that," she said. Then she looked me directly in the eye: "Do you have money?"

"For what?"

"The goat." She said it slowly like I was stupid.

"How much?"

"Well, the chicken, the goat, the candles: two hundred pesos."

"I don't have that much. And I don't want to kill a goat or any other creature."

She shrugged. "You don't have to."

"Did you kill your dog?"

"No, dogs are here to teach us about love and loyalty." She smiled.

"And goats?"

Her frown returned. "They're here for different reasons. They're not teachers. They're here to serve."

"What about Gaucho Gil?"

"What about him?" She looked me in the eye again, this time as if I were prying.

I shrugged.

The kid was still there when I walked out. Still smiling.

"Who is that kid?" I asked the old man who was going in next.

The old man shook out his *mate* cup in the ditch and pointed to a Great Dane dog loping down the street among the trash. "That's his," he said and disappeared inside.

As it approached, its enormity became more apparent. Half horse, it looked to me. The child cheered and called to it, and it ran to the wall and barked up at him. The boy had an uncanny resemblance to the angel I'd see later, with his curls and his good cheer. The dog was no Romeo.

The Archangel Raphael, Healer of Men

I nursed him back to health. It only took a day or two. Angels heal fast.

He told me that he'd come back to Argentina to drive off dark forces.

"I've got a dark force here inside." And I tucked my hand up under my groin.

That angel fucked me, wings flapping, and off flew the pain. No dead goat.

"Who says a spent penis ain't a dead goat? Where's your poetry?" he chided me. Then he tickled me, and wrestled and razzed me in Aramaic.

I wanted to thank him.

"You've thanked me. I love me a mortal." He winked and I swooned.

"Don't go," I pleaded.

He shrugged. *"Este pais."* And up went the *persianas.* He opened the sliding glass door and outspread his wings. My heart was ruined. It opened with his wings – too wide. I had to crawl to the rail, from where I spied him high in the sky heading toward the Casa Rosada.

I thought of the flying trapeze and what a clown he'd made of me, this angel. And oh, how I missed and longed for Anastacio then. Terribly. I curled up in the same corner where I'd found the angel, and I wept.

They devalued the peso the next day. The street filled with people. I almost thought they were celebrating as they banged their pots and pans with soup spoons. Then the banks all closed and windows began to break.

Only Evita could save them now, I lazily thought, watching it all from above. Eva had apparently promised she'd come back, though that was endlessly debated. But if there were angels about, why not her, too?

I watched from the balcony, looked for her. There were blondes, but none with magnetism or riding on a half shell. And then I saw the curly headed boy and the big loping horse-dog running through the crowd, and Gaucho Gil on a mount swinging his bolas in hot pursuit. The boy just laughed and dodged and eluded him through the teeming crowd.

Soon, clouds gathered and there was rain, and all among it white feathers. There was a murmur that slowly replaced the shouts then. And it wasn't *"Este pais."* They were whispering "Eva ... Eva Maria."

The crowd grew more and more quiet; they stopped marching and rioting, and instead loitered. Night fell, and candles appeared, flickering. Then everyone went home.

In the street it looked like snow had fallen. Not a soul. Then the little boy, head a mass of curls, running and kicking his way through the down, the dog loping and barking behind him. I yelled down and he ignored me as he had his mother, laughing and smiling as was his wont.

I tried another tack. "It's me, Juliet," I shouted.

His upturned face; the dog's, too. His smile. The rain began again then, this time among it tarot cards: swords and princes mostly. But I saw the Fool card, too, the Lovers and the Magician.

I fled.

Home to Los Angeles. North to Mount Olympus. Back to my Ganymede.

TREBOR HEALEY

Recipient of The James Duggins Lambda Literary Award for Mid-Career Novelists, Trebor Healey also received the Violet Quill award for his first novel, *Through It Came Bright Colors*, and the Publishing Triangle's Ferro-Grumley Award in Fiction for both *A Horse Named Sorrow* and *Through It Came Bright Colors*. In addition, he has penned the speculative fiction novel, *Faun*, and a homoerotic poetry collection, *Sweet Son of Pan*, along with three collections of stories – *A Perfect Scar & Other Stories*, *Eros & Dust* and *Falling*. He co-edited (with Marci Blackman) *Beyond Definition: New Writing from Gay and Lesbian San Francisco*, and co-edited (with Amie Evans) *Queer & Catholic*.

www.treborhealey.com

About ReQueered Tales

In the heady days of the late 1960s, when young people in many western countries were in the streets protesting for a new, more inclusive world, some of us were in libraries, coffee shops, communes, retreats, bedrooms and dens plotting something even more startling: literature – highbrow and pulp – for an explicitly gay audience. Specifically, we were craving to see our gay lives – in the closet, in the open, in bars, in dire straits and in love – reflected in mystery stories, sci-fi and mainstream fiction. Hercule Poirot, that engaging effete Belgian creation of Agatha Christie might have been gay ... Sherlock Holmes, to all intents and purposes, was one woman shy of gay ... but where were the genuine gay sleuths, where the reader need not read between the lines?

Beginning with Victor J Banis's "Man from C.A.M.P." pulps in the mid-60s – riotous romps spoofing the craze for James Bond spies – readers were suddenly being offered George Baxt's Pharoah Love, a black gay New York City detective, and a real turning point in Joseph Hansen's gay California insurance investigator, Dave Brandstetter, whose world weary Raymond Chandleresque adventures sold strongly and have never been out of print.

Over the next three decades, gay storytelling grew strongly in niche and mainstream publishing ventures. Even with the huge public crisis – as AIDS descended on the gay community beginning in the early 1980s – gay fiction flourished. Stonewall Inn, Alyson Publications, and others nurtured authors and readers ... until mainstream success seemed to come to a halt. While Lambda Literary Foundation had started to recognize work in annual awards about 1990, mainstream publishers began to have cold feet. And then, with the rise of e-books in the new millennium which enabled a new self-publishing industry ... there was both an avalanche of new talent coming to market and burying of print authors who did not cross the divide.

The result?

Perhaps forty years of gay fiction – and notably gay and lesbian mystery, detective and suspense fiction – has been teetering on the brink of obscurity. Orphaned works, orphaned authors, many living and some having passed away – with no one to make the case for their creations to be returned to print (and e-print!). General fiction and non-fiction works embracing gay lives, widely celebrated upon original release, also languished as mainstream publishers shifted their focus.

Until now. That is the mission of ReQueered Tales: to keep in circulation this treasure trove of fantastic fiction. In an era of ebooks, everything of value ought to be accessible. For a new generation of readers, these mystery tales, and works of general fiction, are full of insights into the gay world of the 1960s, '70s, '80s and '90s. For those of us who lived through the period, they are a delightful reminder of our youth and reflect some of our own struggles in growing up gay in those heady times.

We are honored, here at ReQueered Tales, to be custodians shepherding back into circulation some of the best gay and lesbian fiction writing and hope to bring many volumes to the public, in modestly priced, accessible editions, worldwide, over the coming years.

So please join us on this adventure of discovery and rediscovery of the rich talents of writers of recent years as the PIs, cops and amateur sleuths battle forces of evil with fierceness, humor and sometimes a pinch of love.

The ReQueered Tales Team

Justene Adamec • Alexander Inglis • Matt Lubbers-Moore

More from ReQueered Tales

Through It Came Bright Colors
Trebor Healey

Neill Cullane is a closeted, conflicted 21-year-old who lives in two worlds: a San Francisco suburb where he's the middle-son of three young men, and, a short drive away in his beat-up VW bug, a seedy portion of the city's downtown. At home, he's the dutiful son of Frank and Grace, and devoted older brother to Peter – who is battling a cruel, disfiguring cancer – but in the city a chance encounter drags him into the orbit of Vince, a troubled, gregarious, very out gay transient. Moth to a flame, Neill is swept up and away by this secret lover, a beautiful junkie/philosopher/thief whose burning desire for truth lights a path Neill is destined to travel. Through Vince, Neill learns about honesty and love and finds the courage to confront his family in the face of tragedy and loss.

Trebor Healey's multi-layered, lyrical prose illuminates a unique, intimate look at a young man's struggle to live openly and honestly, to love and to be loved, free from shame and guilt. It's a compelling family saga of rare emotional, spiritual, and poetic depth.

"I read passages of this novel out loud again and again, absorbing the truth beneath its lyrical language. Trebor Healey understands the beauty and cruelty that spill forth when men dare to express love to one another. He holds up a magnifying glass to the human heart, and his gaze is unblinking." — K. M. Soehnlein

"Trebor Healey delivers coming out as apocalypse – tender, destructive, punk. He tore down a worn-out block of queer lit and built it back up. Sweet, sad, gritty, and real." — Michelle Tea

Winner of the Ferro-Grumley Award for Best Novel in 2003, this new edition includes a foreword by Felice Picano (*Like People in History*).

A Perfect Scar and Other Stories
Trebor Healey

This whimsical, sly, and slightly crazy collection of short stories from award-winning novelist, poet, and songwriter Trebor Healey covers much ground. The range is jaw-dropping: from a Vietnamese gangster with a voracious libido and a small boy troubled by his gay dog to an 1870s hermaphrodite cowboy named Captain Jinx … and then there's the lad who becomes a sex-inspiring satyr, an American Spanish student in Guanajuato seduced by a pair of twins during the Cervantino celebrations, and a housesitting gig that goes terribly awry.

There is humor and insight delivered in lyrical, vibratory phrases, and darker more haunting tales as well, often with a thread of Catholic, as well as Mexican culture, involving young men facing untimely death, reflections on aging, family, duty, sacrifice and sibling rivalry – and the fateful and courageous choices we are forced to make in the name of love.

> "Trebor Healey is all soul … The way he stacks sentences vibrates on the page. There's an impressive, experimental range in this short story collection. Trebor Healey uses multiple narrators to bring voice to a variety of human experiences."
> — Kirk Read, *How I Learned to Snap*

> "Trebor Healey's writing is suffused with the purest emotion, the bravest, funniest tone, and the perfect balance of poetics, daring and charm." — Joy Nicholson, *The Tribes of Palos Verdes*

Originally published in 2007, this new edition includes a foreword by Peter Dubé (*The Headless Man*).

Fidelities: A Book of Stories
Richard Hall

The *Los Angeles Times* says "Richard Hall's prose displays a rare polish, and his accounts of ordinary and exceptional lives unfold in graceful cadences." *Fidelities* is a stunning collection of stories that explores the varieties of gay experience – love stories, both passionate and compassionate; tales of suspense; narratives on the theme of AIDS; even a ghost story. Among the most adept and technically accomplished writers of his generation, Hall's third and last collection of short stories is an eloquent work of immense power.

The author of the novels *The Butterscotch Prince* and *Family Fictions*, Hall's short stories give a sense of having been distilled and polished over time till they glow with depth and wisdom. "Diamonds Are Forever" highlights a gay man and his married sister who are incapable of seeing the shared traits that make it so difficult for them to accept each other; the story's carefully paced wrangling over an heirloom is masterful. "Avery Milbanke Day" features a 70-year-old writer – his seven novels about "the literature of hesitation" long neglected – decides to stay with his old dying lover and nurse him through a final crisis instead of attending a public celebration of his novels and himself. In "Country People" the author presents a gentle, eerie metaphor for the search for a sense of history, reflecting on previous generations of gay men and lesbians.

> "A rich, poignant collection ... The ruminations in *Fidelities* are remarkably palpable, utterly believable. Enlivened by precise flourishes of description, they touch directly on the reader's empathy button, and hold." — *San Francisco Chronicle*

> "Hall's stories evoke comparison with Henry James or Maupassant, Hemingway and Fitzgerald ... A luminous collection ... Hall has found in gay life stories to amuse, entertain, and move." — *Lambda Book Report*

Hall's final publication before his death at age 66 from AIDS-related causes, this 30th year anniversary edition celebrates his art at its peak. This new edition includes a foreword by Alexander Inglis.

Boys Like Us
Peter McGehee

Boys Like Us Trilogy, Book 1 – Peter McGehee's debut novel is a rompish, bed-hopping affair – a modern comedy of manners – in which our twentysomething protagonist, Zero MacNoo performs all the rituals – sexual, familial, and grievous – required of urban gay males in the early 1990s. It is a remarkable comedy about life, love, and friendship in the age of AIDS.

Zero, an Arkansas expat who has swapped out Little Rock for the cool cotemporary tones of Toronto gay life, is perplexed by the curveballs of fate. His best friend has been diagnosed with AIDS; Zero is frantic to organize a circle of support. And when Arkansas also calls, it's to support his mother's second marriage and confrontations with the zany array of crazed Southerners he calls family ensue.

"... a gem of a novel. *Boys Like Us* is funny, sexy, tender, and touching – often in the same sentence." — Larry Duplechan

"*Boys Like Us* is an affable, enjoyable story ... McGehee has the ability, through an ingratiating style and witty observations, to transform Zero's everyday life into something we care about."
— Michael Bronski

"Accomplishes what may seem impossible: a humorous romp in the face of widespread death."
— *Library Journal*

Funny, bittersweet, outrageous, and moving, Zero's adventures make up the first part of *Boys Like Us* trilogy. This new edition is accompanied by introductions from Dr Raymond-Jean Frontain and long-time collaborator Fiji Robinson.

Short Stories 1988-1991
Stan Leventhal

Collected together for the first time in one volume, Short Stories 1988 – 1991, are the twenty-nine stories Stan Leventhal included in *a tiny herd of elephants* and *Candy Holidays.*

The first collection are stories about male relationships and span many literary styles including romance, fantasy, western and erotica. Some are funny, others are serious, but all invariably "playful". There are clear auto-biographical elements, as in much of the author's work. Several stories are about writers and the writing process (as life intrudes); "Schoolmarm" is set in the old west when a substitute school teacher meets his cowboy; "The Crystal Storm" offers us a lonely Warrior King, whose eyes "flash like jewels on fire", as he interrogates a handsome visitor, "unarmed and definitely not hostile". The longer pieces flesh out characters in clandestine meetings with lovers that end in a gift, or a group of tight-knit friends growing into adults at college ... there's even a vampire tale.

> "Stan was a literary activist who always gave to, built and endorsed literature and writers. I can see still see Stan in his apartment window on Christopher Street, next door to the Stonewall Inn, overlooking Sheridan Square as he typed away." — Michele Karlsberg, LGBTQ publicist and friend

The second diverse, entertaining set of tales also cover several genres. In "Candy Holidays", two lovers break up, live apart, and then come back together again, the narrative catching glimpses, of them at Halloween, Christmas, Valentine's Day and Easter. "Razorback" is a dark futuristic tale about surviving in a burnt-out city in which all order has withered and chaos reigns. In "Oasis Motel" a young man on a business trip in Los Angeles finally breaks through the sexual barrier that has contained him all his life. "Seder" is the story of a gay Jewish man's attempt to reconcile his spirituality with his sexuality.

Both collections reflect issues confronting the lives of queer people in America in the late twentieth century. This new omnibus edition features a foreword by Sarah Schulman (*Let the Record Show*), close friend of Leventhal and author of numerous works of fiction and social history.

Slashed to Ribbons in Defense of Love
Felice Picano

Felice Picano's first collection of gay short stories spans the period 1975-1982 as published by the pioneering Gay Presses of New York. Read again forty years later, they are a delicious time-capsule of gay life mostly before AIDS and set in iconic gay meccas such as New York and Fire Island. In "Spinning", we get inside the head of a DJ busy spinning for the customers, tricking in his mind and deftly conjuring up the disco subculture which has since faded away. In "The Interrupted Recital", we eavesdrop into the classical music world where ego clashes lead to disastrous outcomes.

There are marvelous character portraits as in "Teddy", about a handsome Vietnam vet back home for a quick furlough. Or the evocation of Christmas in multiple New York households in "Xmas in the Apple". Longer works such as "Hunter", set in a writer's colony, are pure horror fiction. The longest piece, the novella "And Baby Makes Three", spreads its wings recreating Fire Island of the 1970s and features Picano's trademark surprises and miscues which make the tale memorable long after the last page is turned.

First published to acclaim in 1982, this new edition features a foreword by Eric Andrews-Katz (*The Jesus Injection*).

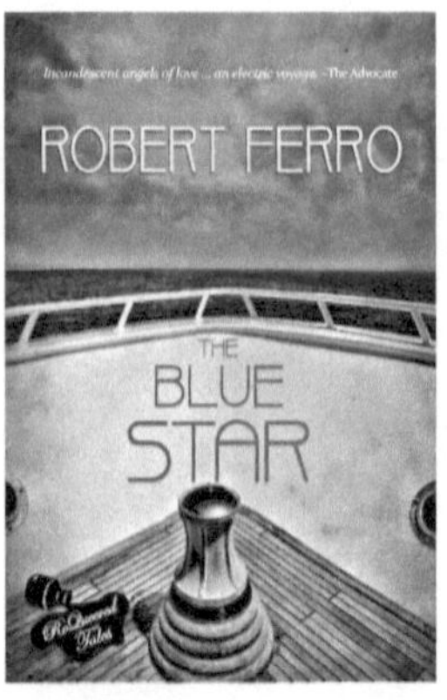

The Blue Star
Robert Ferro

Two heroes, reflective Peter and Byronic Chase, indulge their youthful appetites in Florence. Over the next 20 years their paths diverge and reconverge. Chase marries into the Italian aristocracy and Peter pursues his passion for Lorenzo, a beautiful young Florentine. The past impinges on the present as the story of Chase's ancestor, Orvil Starkweather, is revealed -- the secrets of his life sounding a counterpoint to Chase's. New York City's Central Park and the imposing figure of designer Frederick Law Olmsted provide a mysterious connection to Chase's life. The story of the two men unfolds in Florence and New York exposing the unimagined and startling connection with the past, and taking them finally on a fateful cruise up the Nile aboard the luxury yacht.

> "Incandescent angels of love ... an eclectic voyage. Authentic fiction ... surprising, sad, funny, wise ... communicating gay experience knowingly and sensitively ... a treasure!" — *The Advocate*

> "Enthralling ... euphoric imagination ... we can never forget the bliss we are allowed to share." — Richard Howard

> "A lush chronicle of the heart's education ... Ferro revels in life's ups and downs in a prose rife with pleasures rich as those described." — *Village Voice*

Originally published in 1985, this new edition contains a foreword by Andrew Holleran (*Dancer from the Dance*).

Life Drawing
Michael Grumley

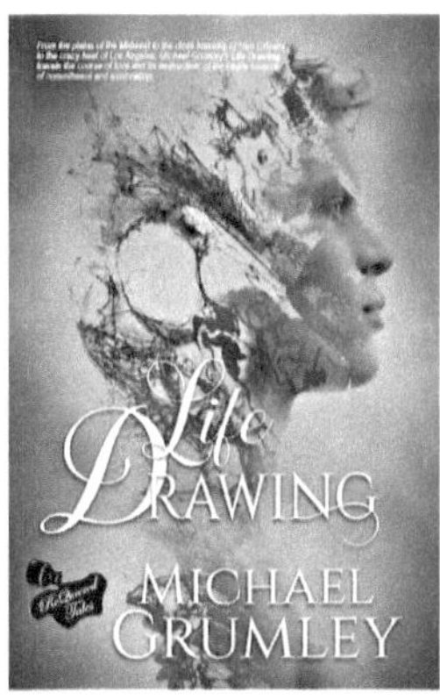

Born in Iowa to the sounds of Bob and Bing Crosby and the Dorsey brothers, Mickey grows up to the comforting images of his living room TV and the reassuring ruts of his parents' life. During the restless summer of his senior year in high school, drifting away from the girlfriend he could never quite love, Mickey spends a night with another boy, and his world will never be the same.

On a barge floating down the Mississippi, he falls in love with James, a black card player from New Orleans, and in time the two of them settle, bristling with sexual intensity, in the French Quarter – until a brief affair destroys James's trust and sends Mickey to the drugs and sordid life of Los Angeles.

> "A simple, classic, engaging, and beautifully written tale of a boy who ran away from home, a man who didn't make it in the movies, an artist who found himself earlier than most and did it all west of the Mississippi, in places which, while very American, few Americans have ever been." — Andrew Holleran

> "*Life Drawing* affirms the rich complexity of passion in the story of a small-town boy's difficult journey to manhood. Michael Grumley's crisp, direct language brings to life the demanding wonder of sexuality and the delicate tightrope of love between black men and white men." — Melvin Dixon

Originally published in 1991, it was Grumley's only novel, completed in the month's leading to his death from AIDS as he was cared for his lover Robert Ferro. This new edition contains the original foreword by Edmund White (*A Saint from Texas*) and afterword by George Stambolian (*Gay Men's Anthologies Men on Men*), close friends of the couple.

Good in Bed
A Life in Queer Sex, Politics, and Religion
Brian Bouldrey

The Strangest Bedfellows Provide The Best Pillow Talk

An adult film legend makes you carbonara while you watch from the couch. A distant uncle alone on his cot gives you immunity. Walt Whitman, reclining in the grass, offers – and rescinds – closure. A week on the ward is a glimpse into sanity. The loveliest things can happen in bed. Novelist and essayist Brian Bouldrey, in this new collection of essays, looks at all the things that happen, and don't happen, in the sack. A lifetime of experience generated these appreciations, thoughts, rants, eulogies, and meditations, all part of a conversational book suitable for any bedroom. From memories of friends we have lost to observations about what we have gained, Bouldrey ranges far over the world of travel, love, culture, art, sex, and books – and brings them straight to your nightstand.

"Brian Bouldrey has traveled further than most – and on foot, survived worse – and lost more, knows the Saints of his religion as only a true devil can, knows the dirtiest words, is suspicious of nostalgia, French men, our pathological need to "relate," Bouldrey's own preference being – and it's the right preference – to remember. *Good In Bed* is brilliant, funny, deeply moving and historic. Bouldrey at his verve-filled best." — Joel Bresland

Good in Bed returns to many of Bouldrey's ongoing preoccupations, not just sex and religion, but travel, too, and personal challenge, and the vicissitudes of friendship and culture. Always deeply felt, often funny, sometimes uplifting, and never dull, Bouldrey's book wants to show us both the striking differences among us, and also, our beautiful sameness. A ReQueered Tales Original Publication.

Something Inside
Conversations with Gay Fiction Writers
Philip Gambone

In the late-20th century, gay literature had earned a place at the British and American literary tables, spawning its own constellation of important writers and winning a dedicated audience. This collection of probing interviews represents an attempt to offer a group portrait of the most important gay fiction writers.

The extraordinary power of the interviews, originally set down from 1987 to 1997, brings to life the passionate intellect of several voices now stilled among them Joseph Hansen, Allen Barnett, John Preston and Paul Monette. Others such as Scott Heim, Brad Gooch, Lev Raphael, Alan Hollinghurst and Michael Lowanthal were just tasting fame, even notoriety and have gone on to richly deserved acclaim. Published near the height of mainstream accolades for gay fiction as a category, Edmund White, David Plante, Andrew Holleran, Michael Cunningham and Christopher Bram had already enjoyed wide readership and two decades of scrutiny and broad readership.

Many of the pieces are accompanied by portraits from Robert Giard who set out, with urgency during the mid-1980s AIDS crisis, to capture gay artists in their prime; these images make a unique and profound contribution to this collection.

> "A rich collective portrait of some of the most important and interesting gay writers of the last three decades."
> — *Montreal Mirror*

Philip Gambone, a wise and insightful questioner, draws out incredible detail, emotion and personality in a context which still makes for compelling reading thirty years on. The author includes a 2022 update welcoming new readers to this indispensable resource.

☙

**If you enjoyed this book,
please help spread the word
by posting a short,
constructive review at
your favorite social media site
or book retailer.**

**We thank you, greatly,
for your support.**

And don't be shy! Contact us!

*For more information about current and future releases,
please contact us:*

E-mail: *requeeredtales@gmail.com*
Facebook (Like us!): www.facebook.com/ReQueeredTales
Twitter: @ReQueered
Instagram: www.instagram.com/requeered
Web: www.ReQueeredTales.com
Blog: www.ReQueeredTales.com/blog
Mailing list (Subscribe for latest news): https://bit.ly/RQTJoin